THE TROJAN HORSE

Sanjukta Nandy is a writer, an architect, and an avid movie buff who lives in Mumbai with her filmmaker husband. She hails from a media family and has authored a bestseller titled *Khantastic*, which delves into the lives of Bollywood's three Khans. With a penchant for fantasy and thrillers, she finds herself drawn to the pace of Sheldon and the intrigue of Christie. She is making her debut in the fiction-thriller genre with *The Trojan Horse*, soon to be dramatized for media audiences.

Rupali Sebastian has been an interior-design and interior-architecture journalist for two decades, and served as an editor for two magazines. She currently freelances with leading design publications such as *Architecture Digest India* and co-curates a platform for Indian spatial design called *India Design World*. She absolutely loves crime fiction, especially the evocativeness of P.D. James. This is her debut in the fiction genre. She resides in Mumbai with her photographer husband and Pablo, who cannot decide whether he is a dog or a hippo.

THE TROJAN HORSE

SANJUKTA NANDY
with **RUPALI SEBASTIAN**

Published by
Rupa Publications India Pvt. Ltd 2025
7/16, Ansari Road, Daryaganj
New Delhi 110002

Sales centres:
Bengaluru Chennai
Hyderabad Jaipur Kathmandu
Kolkata Mumbai Prayagraj

Copyright © Sanjukta Nandy 2025

All rights reserved.
This is a work of fiction. Names, characters, places and incidents are either the product of the author's imagination or are used fictitiously, and any resemblance to any actual person, living or dead, events or locales is entirely coincidental.

No part of this publication may be reproduced, transmitted or stored in a retrieval system, in any form or by any means, electronic, mechanical, photocopying, recording or otherwise, without the prior permission of the publisher.

P-ISBN: 978-93-6156-774-2
E-ISBN: 978-93-6156-273-0

First impression 2025

10 9 8 7 6 5 4 3 2 1

The moral right of the author has been asserted.

Printed in India

This book is sold subject to the condition that it shall not, by way of trade or otherwise, be lent, resold, hired out or otherwise circulated, without the publisher's prior consent, in any form of binding or cover other than that in which it is published.

*For you, Ma and Aai,
because mothers are the heart of creation.
And the family—for supporting and lovingly tolerating
the book-induced chaos.*

Trojan Horse
noun

(in Greek mythology) *A huge hollow wooden horse within which the Greeks concealed themselves to surreptitiously gain entrance into Troy. Used metaphorically to indicate a person or thing intended to undermine or destroy something from within.*

Contents

PART ONE: INTO THE LION'S DEN

Prologue	3
1. The Chatter	5
2. Tipping Point	11
3. Tiger by the Tail	23
4. The Code	30
5. Coward	38
6. The Ghost Who Walks	42
7. Lambs to the Slaughter	52
8. Eka	59
9. The Proposition	65
10. Ghosts of the Past	72
11. The Day of the Dead	82
12. The Turn of the Key	88
13. The Plan	93
14. The Journey to Hell	97

PART TWO: DOUBLE TROUBLE

15. Breaking News	109
16. Litmus Test	116
17. A Regular Day at LalTara	122
18. Chaos Rising	139
19. Paws and Effect	154
20. Suspicion	158
21. Surprise, Surprise!	161
22. Trouble in Paradise	166
23. Raptor	170
24. Contradictions of the Mind	178
25. The Calm before the Storm	185

26. The Storm	192
27. Dead Weight	196
28. *Mehendi Laga ke Rakhna*	200
29. Noose around the Neck	210

PART THREE: BENEATH THE SURFACE

30. The Missing Man	219
31. The Menu	223
32. The Ballad of Baladh	228
33. The Takeover	240
34. Prisha	243
35. The Stalker	248
36. Oblivion	252
37. The Agony and the Agony	254
38. Killing Machines	258
39. The Eye of the Storm	266
40. The Hero	274
41. A Killer Plan	279
42. The Forever Plan	282
43. Stuck in Hell	285
44. The Day After	288
45. Red for Danger	290
46. Unmasked!	293
47. The Unravelling	296
48. The Beginning of the End	298

PART FOUR: ENDGAME

49. The Prep	303
50. Breaking Point	307
51. Two Sisters	318
52. Despatching the Demon	326
Epilogue	331

PART ONE

Into the Lion's Den

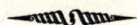

Prologue

Like a powerful panther, Isha's masked assailant attacked her from behind, flinging her against the trunk of an overbearing tree. She slid down the hard wood and collapsed face down on the soft grass and moaned. The dense leaf litter of the jungle muffled her attacker's footsteps, and she sensed rather than heard someone approach, and stop near her. A foot then painfully rammed into her side and flipped her over. Isha was awaiting such an opportunity. She dexterously removed the ketamine pen hidden in her cuff and leapt up to skilfully jab the needle right into her enemy's thigh. She knew the potent anaesthetic would work in seconds.

She heard a gasp of surprise and saw her opponent's hand reach reflexively for the syringe. That was all the time she needed. Isha violently yanked her attacker's leg, knocking down the figure to the ground. By this time, the drug was clearly doing its job. The masked figure got on all fours and tried to sit up. Once. Twice. And then slumped down helplessly, face down, on the forest floor.

Isha extended her hand to gently ease her assailant's arm from under the body and checked for the pulse. *Good! It was still going strong,* she was pleased to note. With a grunt she heaved the inert form on its back and reached under the chin to rip the mask off. As a mass of unkempt curls tumbled out, Isha gasped in disbelief.

When she saw the pear-shaped face, aquiline nose, high cheekbones and full lips, a chill ran down her spine. Isha felt as if she was looking into a mirror. *At her own face.*

1

The Chatter

2025
Raipur

The persistent discomfort induced by a full bladder woke Manish Thakur up into a state of annoyed consciousness. He groaned, got off the bed and squinted at his smartwatch. It was 3:10 a.m. He sighed. *It had not been a good evening,* he thought as he padded towards the bathroom. The poker game on *cardkismet.com* had turned bloody. He had folded, while the Czech guy with aces up his sleeve had laughed all the way to the bank. *Damn! He would have to figure out how to stay afloat until the next paycheck. His meagre government salary would not help much; he was too much in the red.*

The quiet stillness of the room was abruptly broken by a spurt of chatter that repeatedly pinged on his computer system—his Starfleet Bridge, he had dubbed it—a veritable wall of state-of-the-art audio surveillance equipment, specializing in satellite phone interception, that helped him keep tabs on criminals, bureaucrats, politicians, anyone engaging in any suspicious activity. *Ordinarily, a system of this nature would be installed only at the headquarters of the Special Task Force 19 (STF19) in Raipur, but he had replicated it—with official blessings, of course—at home, to be close at hand should 'action' occur during the night. Sure, the 'twin' of this system back at HQ was also monitored around the* clock. But still, his teammates at STF19 had riled him about his obsessive behaviour—'OCD-ke,'[1] they'd called him—but he didn't care. And it was not as if he slept like a baby anyway, with cardkismet.com *for company.*

Another pinging sound abruptly stopped him halfway to the bathroom. *This was the frequency LalTara used for communication.* LalTara was an elusive arms and drugs outfit, operating clandestinely from somewhere within the dense Abujmarh forest in Chhattisgarh. It was also his boss Rakesh Srivastava's bugbear—which is why it was being monitored constantly. Full bladder forgotten, STF19's head of technology now quickly approached the system, eager to catch the exchange even though he knew that the conversation was being automatically recorded. Distant voices filled the room.

—*RED went well? What about the prototype?*
—*It will come with the consignment.*
—*Where? When?* The questions were followed by seemingly endless tapping sounds.
—*Okay. Done.* The conversation continued after the auditory stream subsided.
—*Looking forward. People waiting.*

What Manish had just heard turned him cold. His surveillance team had informed him about Russia developing a Robotic Enemy Destroyer (RED) in Siberia. It was being hailed as THE weapon for remote warfare, a cutting-edge amalgamation of destructive software and hardware that would tip the scale of power in favour of its owner. One year ago, however, there were whispers circulating on the grapevine about a massive technology theft somewhere in

---

[1] OCD-ke: A slang referring to an obsessive-compulsive condition

the erstwhile Eastern Bloc.[2] The heist had been accompanied by some gory news: the scientist who had led the RED project for Russia was found murdered in cold blood. It didn't take them much to figure out that the heist and the murder were somehow connected. Shortly thereafter, all chatter about RED disappeared from the dark web, until a few months ago. And now this cryptic message from LalTara.

Manish called Inspector General (IG) Rakesh Srivastava on his mobile. His boss headed STF19, a unit of covert operations to intercept narcotic and ammunition smuggling. The call was answered after barely two rings. 'Manish, what's wrong?' a sleep-sodden voice enquired.

'Sir, I'm coming to see you. Now.'

'Fine.'

Within two minutes, Manish had downloaded the intercepted audio on his mobile, hopped onto his bike, and was on way to his boss's house. Though it was only a ten-minute bike ride, each minute seemed like a lifetime.

∞

The gate of the small, neat bungalow was already open. A bright lamp lit up the porch, dispelling the darkness of the night. Manish eased his Royal Enfield into the driveway and carefully parked the motorcycle. He shut off the ignition and made his way towards the house. He could see his boss through the window, already waiting for him.

---

[2] Eastern Bloc: A group of eastern European countries that were aligned militarily, politically, economically and culturally with the Soviet Union, approximately from 1945 to 1990. (Source: Encyclopaedia Britannica)

With his tall, lean physique, fifty-five-year-old Rakesh Srivastava could have passed for a much younger man. Manish had always admired him for his equanimity. Mr Cool, they called him fondly at the centre. Perhaps the daily two-hour yoga sessions contributed to his Zen-like calm. Even now, Rakesh greeted him with a gentle smile, his smooth, unlined face at odds with his mostly white, crisply cut hair.

'Isha's sleeping, so let's keep it down, shall we? She returned late from the training exercise yesterday evening,' he said, ushering Manish into a compact, orderly living room. 'Let's go into the kitchen. Coffee is ready.'

Two steaming cups of coffee sat waiting on the kitchen counter. To Manish, their mundane domesticity seemed light years away from the recording on his phone and the message it carried.

'Sir, it's LalTara.'

Rakesh froze for the briefest of moments in the act of picking up his cup. 'What about it?' he asked his junior.

'Something's about to go down. The name "RED" popped up again on the audio unit. The call originated from somewhere beyond Tibet. I've got it on my phone here,' the younger man responded as he extracted his mobile from the pocket of his pyjamas.

'Let's listen to it,' Rakesh said.

Manish located the audio file on his phone and pressed 'play'. Nothing happened.

What the fuck? STF19's technical head thought, furiously jabbing at the red 'play' icon repeatedly. *Why did technology have to be a prick just when you needed it?*

'Bhenchod!' The expletive slipped out of his mouth before he realized it. He bit his tongue. *Under normal* circumstances, he wouldn't have dared to use a cuss word in front of Rakesh sir.

'*Wah! Kya ucch vichar hain,* for this time of the night! Noble thoughts indeed,' a soft female voice exclaimed behind him.

Manish whirled around and saw Isha standing by the refrigerator, a bottle of cold water in her hand. A gentle smile bloomed on her full lips. Her hazel eyes, usually lively, seemed a little tired, but the humour was undimmed. At five feet four inches, she wasn't very tall, but her well-proportioned body created an illusion of height. Dimples crinkled her cheeks.

Manish, as he glanced at her, suddenly realized how dishevelled he must appear: *a t-shirt bearing the stain of yesterday's daal, pyjamas that ought to have been washed last week, the ghost of some stubble on his cheeks hinting at a procrastinated shave. Shit! Shit! Shit!*

Just then, Manish's phone came to life as the audio clip began to play. Silently, the trio listened to the words.

'It's that RED technology we've been hearing about for months, Isha,' Manish said, addressing STF19's youngest captain after the audio clip had played out.

'Months is right, Manish. But what's happening now? Why the urgency?' Isha questioned her colleague.

'The clip indicates that a RED prototype will arrive with a consignment. The tapping is obviously Morse code, specifying a location and date for the drop-off. I think we should intercept this. It's so close to home and right in our region of control. We won't get an opportunity like this.' Manish ran his fingers agitatedly through his thick hair, making him look even more dishevelled.

Engrossed in their conversation, the two colleagues

failed to notice that Rakesh's face had turned white on hearing the audio clip on Manish's phone, especially one particular voice. It was a voice from his past, a voice whose owner had pledged to take Rakesh's blood.

Bishen Rao was back.

2
Tipping Point

1997
Abujmarh

Abujmarh, meaning 'the unknown hills' in the local language of the Gond tribe, is a rugged forest terrain that remains difficult to comprehend. An impenetrable jungle, isolated from the outside world, Abujmarh does not even have a revenue map. Surveys to chart the region, attempted since the British era, have not been successful, not even with the high-end technology available today. A subset of the mythological Dandakaranya (Dandaka Forest)—a stronghold of the *rakshasa*s or demons—it is reputed, since ancient times, to be that dark land where even the rays of the sun would think twice before slipping in. Abujmarh has also been a breeding ground for crime and a sanctuary for ruthless criminals.

∽

The early morning light reluctantly filtering through the trees was tender. The Abujmarh jungle was coming alive with the activity of its inhabitants who took no notice of the two young men sitting on their haunches, their body language tense and alert. The older one was Bishen Rao, numero uno of LalTara, a mercenary organization that dealt in drugs and weapons, and a major source of trouble for India's security agencies. His companion was Prakash Raj, a relatively new addition to the outfit.

Suddenly, a solitary piercing call rose abruptly over the crescendo of birdsong. This was their call to action, given by a lookout posted on a treetop. The two men simultaneously leapt to their feet, swiftly hopped onto a pair of bicycles propped up by the trees, and started cycling along the uneven forest pathway.

As Bishen and his companion pedalled into a clearing, they could see a truck approaching them. While the roads in the jungle were largely unsurfaced and not much better than a pathway, this particular stretch was especially bumpy; it would serve their purpose well.

'Prakash, be ready,' Bishen alerted his partner. Seeing that he hadn't caught his attention, he called out again. 'Prakash, did you hear me?'

'Yes, yes,' the other man said and swore under his breath. He'd have to be alert and very careful; the tiniest slip could prove fatal.

The two men steeled themselves in preparation for what lay ahead. As the truck approached, the driver waved. The men waved back casually. As soon as the vehicle passed them, Bishen and Prakash whipped their bicycles around, and started furiously pedalling behind the vehicle until they were close enough to grip its tailboard. This was the dangerous part: manoeuvring the bicycle with one hand, and holding on to the moving truck with the other. They'd practised this stunt multiple times, but this was the final test.

To minimize the likelihood of being seen by the driver in the side view mirror, they needed to get onto the vehicle from the left side. Prakash managed to gain a firm grip of the tailboard with one hand, and then with a silent prayer, released the handlebar of his cycle, strengthened his hold with both his hands, and heaved himself up onto the back of the truck. He felt, rather than saw, his bicycle teeter wildly before it crashed behind him. Now it was Bishen's turn, but the older man was clearly not doing well. Prakash quickly lent him a helping hand. He caught Bishen's flailing arm so his partner could steady himself, and then pulled him into the back of the vehicle.

They wrapped *gamcha*s[3] around their heads to cover their faces and bided their time until the driver stopped—either to stretch his legs or answer nature's call. Their strategy was clear. Once the driver halted the truck and alighted from the vehicle, they would overpower him, tie him up and leave with the vehicle. However, if the driver did not stop within one hour, they would have to implement Plan B, which was to take over the truck by force and perhaps kill the driver. Prakash had insisted on attempting Plan A first. Fortunately, after forty minutes of driving along bumpy paths, the truck slowed and finally halted. The two stowaways on board heard the driver's door open and the sound of a body jumping down. Then a fart, and the steady tinkle of fluid released from the body. The two men silently alighted from the vehicle. Before Prakash could move, Bishen tugged at his arm, motioning him to stop. He gestured that he would take care of this part of the plan. Prakash nodded.

What ensued next froze Prakash's blood with horror. He watched Bishen bend down to pick up a large stone and heft it. Then, with the agility of a cheetah, Bishen ran up to the urinating man and struck his head hard with the stone. Again and again, till his victim crumpled, gurgling and twitching,

---

[3]Gamcha (Hindi): Coarse cotton towel

and rolled onto his back, wetting himself. Even then, Bishen did not stop. Prakash saw the bloodlust in his partner's eyes, while his face remained calm, composed and cold. The onslaught persisted long after the man went still. Prakash noticed, as if through a haze, that the man's nose had caved in and one of his eyeballs was hanging out of the socket. Spilled brain tissue had created a dreadful halo around his head. The man's lower body was pristinely clean, his penis limp and still dripping urine. Prakash heard a buzzing in his ears. *Not now, not now. Don't faint.* He swallowed the bile that rose to his throat.

'Bishen, why?' Prakash could not help asking.

'Why leave loose ends, *dost*?[4] It's better this way. Come on, hurry up. Put the body in the back. We'll dump him in the ravine.'

Prakash moved like an automaton, consciously numbing his mind to the horrific task ahead.

∞

Three hours later, the truck reached LalTara, a raggedy clutch of tents surrounding a mud patch, in a clearing deep within Abujmarh—historically the home of the demon Dandaka. Bishen always liked to joke: *Dandaka gaya, lekin Bishen abhi bhi zinda hai.*[5] The LalTara campsite was protected by a mined boundary, the exact configuration of which was known only to its key personnel. This negated the need for a physical barrier to segregate the campus from the surrounding jungle.

It was nearly midday and the camp was bustling with activity. At one end, food was being prepared, while

---

[4]Dost (Hindi): Friend

[5]"Dandaka is no more, but Bishen is alive."

soldiers-for-hire exercised at an improvised obstacle course featuring tree trunks and defunct tyres. On the other side, men were engaged in target practice as guns popped and bullets sped towards the target. All activity within the camp, however, ceased—even the mercenaries stopped mid-training—when they saw the truck, with Bishen in the passenger's seat, rumbling to a stop within the camp. Previously, word had spread that the boss was out on a big mission. Clearly, he had returned now with the loot.

Bishen sprang down from the truck. Prakash killed the engine and slowly clambered down behind him, his movements stiff and stilted, as if in pain.

'Let's unwrap the presents,' Bishen roared. 'Get the vegetables down.'

A crackle of energy seemed to ripple through the camp. The boss had accomplished the mission! The sense of jubilation was palpable. Bishen went around to the back of the truck. Several willing hands rushed forward to unload the booty. After the initial cache of potato and onion sacks came the pumpkins, kilos and kilos of them, piled into open crates. Several rolled down from the vehicle while the men were unloading them, fell to the ground, and split open—to reveal small plastic packets of white powder.

'Dope!' someone exclaimed. The cadres of LalTara silently gathered around this scene, awestruck. With this heist, the weapons and drug trafficking outfit had upped its game; it was their biggest haul to date.

Bishen looked around for his partner in crime. He was nowhere to be seen.

'Prakash!' Bishen called out. '*Arre bhai,* where are you?'

'Coming, coming,' Bishen heard his friend's voice and a moment later, he strode into view.

'Where were you?' Bishen thumped Prakash's back. The younger man smiled but Bishen was too full of hubris to notice that it didn't reach his eyes, or that he appeared a little preoccupied.

'You did good out there! For a moment I thought I wasn't going to make it. I'm grateful.'

'*Kya bhai!* You would have done the same for me.'

Bishen smiled and patted the younger man's back once again. But a little voice whispered in his mind—not for the first time, either—*He's too good to be true. Should I rely on him so much?*

Outwardly, however, LalTara's supremo maintained his amiable demeanour. 'Prakash, I'm going to freshen up. You do the same. I need to leave early tomorrow to crack a deal, if you know what I mean,' he grinned at his own pun. 'But we have to talk before I go.'

'Yes, bhai.'

LalTara's commander then triumphantly turned to his small group and bellowed, 'Tonight we celebrate.' Everyone cheered. The mood was infectious.

∽

Bishen entered his tent and sank into his favourite chair with a groan. He did not allow himself too many luxuries, but this recliner, procured at his special request, was an exception. As he relaxed and closed his eyes, he relived the scene of the heist in the morning. He had truly believed—until he was on that truck—that he was going to botch the hijack at the very least, or lose a limb at worst, when he couldn't hold on to the vehicle. *Thank God for Prakash!*

Really? That voice whispered again.

'Send for Kundanlal!' he shouted. 'Immediately,' he

added, although that last word was unnecessary. He chuckled to himself. *In this camp, his word was law, a command to be obeyed with alacrity.*

A minute later, he could hear footsteps approaching. Kundanlal entered the tent.

'You wanted to see me, *Bava*?'[6]

'Prakash. What do you think of him?'

'He's smart. But I've always cautioned you to be careful. We've done a background check on him before. Nothing alarming.' Kundanlal shrugged.

'Even then, spread the word to report anything suspicious.'

'Okay, Bava. I will activate our people once more.'

'See you do that. And also take care of the truck. Salvage whatever is useful and dispose of the rest, part by part, into the ravine.'

Kundanlal nodded deferentially.

'We will have to sell this consignment very carefully,' continued LalTara's head honcho. 'Munnat will be like a raging bull once he realizes he has lost his *maal*.[7] Getting his bodyguard to divulge their plans was a fantastic piece of work, Kundan. We knew everything, the route, the type of vehicle, even the fact that the driver would be alone.'

Kundanlal seemed to grow taller as he received the praise. Such commendation was rarely received, and therefore precious. A faint smile played on his lips as he looked at LalTara's leader.

Bishen had gone silent. He seemed to be recalling his recently concluded daring heist with his equally daring partner. When his rumination ended, he looked at Kundanlal.

---

[6]Bava (Telugu): Brother-in-law
[7]Maal (Hindi): Stuff, material or loot

'Send Prakash in,' he said, dismissing his brother-in-law with a flick of his hand.

Was he looking for things that weren't there? Bishen wondered as he waited. *Prakash had joined the LalTara family about a year ago and had established his credentials. The information he provided about the border security force and police activities had been remarkably accurate. He had also devised an effective plan for the arms consignment pick-up at Narayanpur. All in all, he had proved to be an asset. Yet, why this uneasiness...?*

His musings were interrupted by the entry of their subject. Bishen noted and admired the man's lithe grace. *The chap kept himself in good shape,* he had to admit.

'Come, sit,' Bishen gestured to a chair. 'Today went well, didn't it?'

'It had its moments,' Prakash smiled, taking a seat.

'Modest as usual, huh?'

Bishen reached into a deep drawer near the recliner and took out a bottle and a steel tumbler. Pouring out a generous measure of *mahua*,[8] the local drink, into the tumbler, he handed it to Prakash.

'Cheers,' he toasted, drinking directly from the bottle.

Prakash hesitated and then lifted the tumbler to his lips.

'*Emaindi*?[9] What happened? You seem a little distracted, Prakash.'

Prakash shook his head as if trying to clear mental cobwebs. *Steady, steady,* he cautioned himself. *Don't let revulsion obstruct your purpose. Otherwise you will screw everything up.* 'Nothing, bhai. I just kept thinking about this

---

[8]Mahua: An alcoholic drink produced from the nectar-rich flowers of the mahua tree.
[9]Emaindi (Telugu): What happened?

morning. What if I hadn't been able to give you a helping hand in time?' He tossed back the spirit in a gulp, wincing at its sourness.

'*Arre*, leave it. You did it and that's enough. Now listen. I will be leaving early tomorrow morning to speak to a buyer about the drugs. I won't take them with me. They're staying here until we get a good deal, okay? I should be back the next day.'

Oh! He's leaving the loot behind! 'Yes, bhai.'

There was a rustle outside. 'Anna,'[10] a soft voice called from outside. 'Are you free, brother?'

Bishen beckoned to Prakash to hand over the tumbler to him and hurriedly put it away in the drawer with the bottle. 'Come in, Mitali.'

A young woman entered the tent. Her gentle features and luminous duskiness made the surroundings seem more decrepit. She was Mitali, Bishen's sister. 'Anna, they're waiting for you outside,' she said.

'Yes, of course. Prakash, why the hell are you sitting here like a shy bride, man? Come on, let's go!'

Prakash, who froze on hearing Mitali's voice, gave a start and lumbered to his feet. 'Yes, bhai, let's go.' *Don't look at her, don't look at her*, he commanded himself. He didn't want to, but against his will, his gaze swivelled and settled upon the newcomer. He prayed that Bishen wouldn't notice the emotions playing out on his face.

∞

Prakash moaned, opened his eyes and squinted at the watch. It was 6:30 a.m. His mouth felt parched with the stale sourness

---

[10]Anna (Telugu): Elder brother

of yesterday's indulgence. It almost made him retch. *The fucking things he had to do to keep up the sham. Not for long, though.* This thought aroused the feeling of dread that had retired to a corner of his heart. It uncoiled and bared its fangs again.

He got out of bed, wrapped a blanket around his shoulders, grabbed a towel and stepped outside his quarters. All was quiet in the camp. The strategic lookouts posted at multiple locations around the camp were not in sight. The cool air was refreshing and took the edge off his mild hangover. His eyes darted to the edge of the camp where he observed that Bishen's SUV was missing. He must have left before dawn.

Prakash then noticed the water bucket placed by the entrance to his tent. He bent down and splashed some water on his face. He felt a little better. As he was wiping his face, the entrance flap—two tents away—twitched, and Mitali stepped outside.

'Good morning,' he greeted her.

'Good morning,' she smiled, sauntering closer. 'Quite a party last night.'

'Don't remind me,' he groaned. *Two people making conversation, but not about what they truly want to say.*

'Aren't you going for your run?' Mitali questioned softly.

He stopped wiping his face and stared at her for two seconds, before tearing his eyes away from the only thing that made sense to him in the tangled situation in which he found himself.

'As soon as I put on my shoes,' he replied.

Five minutes later, Prakash jogged out of the camp, waving to Kundanlal who was standing outside his tent, yawning and scratching his balls with the absent-minded air men usually reserve for this activity. This morning jog was an essential part of his exercise regimen, come rain or shine. Consequently, no one had taken any notice of his departure. Except Mitali. Yet, she calmly went about her daily chores, her composure belying her racing thoughts and the churning in her stomach. After about half an hour, she silently slipped out from behind the women's restrooms. No lookouts were posted here for reasons of propriety. She was aware of Prakash's usual jogging route. She knew he would be waiting for her at their usual rendezvous point. They had done this many times in the past year.

∞

Prakash, sitting under a banyan tree, observed that the day was unusually calm. No hint of a breeze. Not a leaf fluttered. It was deathly still. He could sense a storm lurking over the horizon. In this peaceful moment, however, he could hardly have assumed that an event of seismic proportions was about to rock his life, with Mitali at its epicentre. Mitali, who slept with her head on his lap, was oblivious to the impending disaster.

Their friendship, initiated innocuously enough over a shared love of fitness and animals, had blossomed—before either of them realized—into something more meaningful and precious. His heart had melted when she spoke about her dream of having a normal life, away from a peripatetic, crime-centred existence. Or how she hoped to raise and nurture a small family someday. Prakash had thought that finding love against all odds, in the unlikeliest of situations, only happened in Bollywood movies. There seemed to be some truth in the adage that art imitated life. Prakash, however, understood that if Bishen knew the truth, he would be executed. *It was time to make a tough choice.*

He gently lifted Mitali's head and placed it on the makeshift cushion he had improvised with his sweatshirt. Mitali stirred a little, but went back to sleep. She'd had a rough night. Nausea and a general sense of unease had proven to be a potent combination that kept sleep at bay. But Prakash was her salve. With him by her side, this was her little moment of peace. He was her sanctuary. Prakash looked at her and tenderly caressed her cheek. He knew why she had been sluggish lately. The *kukri*[11] she always wore tucked in her waist glimmered. He looked at the knife and hoped she would never have to use this weapon to save herself.

Prakash stood up and looked down softly at Mitali. He felt conflicted, torn. Yet, with the way things stood currently, he had little choice. He had to do what he was meant to. Prakash then turned around, and left without looking back. *This was the tipping point; things would never be the same again.*

Tomorrow would be a catastrophe. But it would be nothing compared to the eruption that would inevitably follow when Bishen realized that Prakash Raj was actually Rakesh Srivastava, a special agent at the Narcotics Control Bureau. And Mitali would bear the brunt of it.

---

[11]Kukri: A knife with a distinct curve in the blade that broadens towards the point. Traditionally used by the Gurkhas.

3
Tiger by the Tail

1997
Abujmarh

It had been two nights since Prakash disappeared from LalTara. Mitali was distraught, and had fallen terribly sick. Bishen was fuming. At his instructions, a doctor was abducted from a nearby town and brought, blindfolded, into the camp.

The medic examined Mitali and administered some tests which confirmed his suspicions. Afraid for his life, he broke the news to Bishen, almost wetting himself in the process. Mitali was pregnant.

∽

Mitali was sobbing in her tent, clinging to Suryamani—Bishen's wife, her sister-in-law—with the desperation of a person about to drown when Bishen walked in, his eyes glinting with anger and a dangerous stillness on his face. Suryamani feared for Mitali, but she understood that Bishen would not approve if she stayed. It was better not to add fuel to the fire that threatened to consume someone she loved like a sister. She scurried out of the tent, where she saw her brother Kundanlal speaking with someone.

Within the tent, Mitali confessed to Bishen that she loved Prakash and trusted him to stand by her in this situation. She was perplexed why he'd left; but she did not believe that he had deserted her.

'Anna, he's not like that...he isn't. He loves me, he said so!' she sobbed.

'You fool! Why isn't he here then? You told him about your situation and he's gone. Gone!' her brother whispered, seething with rage.

'I know he will be back,' Mitali blurted out as her brother continued his tirade.

As the siblings argued, Bishen's hunch grew stronger that there was more to Prakash's disappearance than Mitali's pregnancy.

'Kundanlal,' he summoned his brother-in-law as he finally stormed out of Mitali's tent, leaving her limp with heartache and exhaustion. 'What's the news? Come to my quarters.'

Bishen's second-in-command found his boss seated in the recliner, deep in thought. Judging from his annoyed scowl, however, his favourite chair had failed to comfort him. 'Bava, the news is not good,' Kundanlal reported nervously. He had nothing to do with this mess, but one could never predict where Bishen's anger would be directed. 'Chandu spotted Prakash heading towards the police headquarters in Raipur.'

'Is this confirmed?'

'Chandu and his team haven't failed us yet,' Kundanlal emphasized softly. He was secretly pleased. He had always harboured a deep hatred for Prakash, whose near meteoric rise to LalTara's upper echelons had diverted much of Bishen's goodwill away from him. *Perhaps now the erosion would stop.*

∞

1997
Police headquarters, Raipur

Rakesh sat in front of the superintendent of police Govind Kumar, who quickly concluded a phone call and shook his hand heartily. 'Fantastic show, young man. Honestly, three years ago, when you were sent to me by the Narcotics Control Bureau with your outrageous proposal to trace the narcotic distribution corridor in this region, I was certain it was going to be next to impossible to get positive results from the exercise. Worse, you could be thrown under the bus. I am glad you have proved me wrong.'

'It was my duty, sir.'

'In fact, I thought you were compromised when I received a picture of you with that Rao girl. I realize now, it was an integral component of your game plan.'

Rakesh felt his temples throb at the words 'game plan', but he continued calmly. 'I shall provide you with all the maps and the locations of their hideout, training camp and business dealings. Of course the agency will remain in the loop, sir, but I have one condition.'

Rakesh's masterplan had an unforeseen twist.

∽

Mitali had not slept since Prakash had disappeared from the camp. Her breathing was laboured. Her chest felt constricted with anxiety. She was plagued by doubts about who she had chosen to trust. She also feared that Prakash had abandoned her, and wondered if he really was the traitor that everyone in the camp believed him to be.

She desperately needed some fresh air to clear her head. Mitali was careful not to disturb Suryamani, who slept beside her, as she tiptoed out of the confines of the tent to the rhythm of her sister-in-law's soft snores.

Despite the intense patrolling at LalTara, she managed to sneak out and ventured into the forest, away from the camp. As she neared the forest, she sensed she was being followed. *Why couldn't they leave her in peace for two minutes?* She quickened her pace in the hope of losing her tail, but the crackle of dry leaves drew closer. Before she could turn around to admonish her shadow, she was gripped from behind. She attempted to scream and pull out her kukri, but a hand quickly covered her mouth, muffling her voice. Then, a familiar voice said, 'It's me.' The kukri fell from her hand.

Mitali pivoted and her eyes met his.

'Prakash! You...you bastard! How could you? Why did...?'

Before she could complete the sentence, his lips were on hers, and despite her intention to resist him, she could feel the rage and the angst that had consumed her over the past few days dissolve magically. *She was safe. He was here to take care of her.* She responded to his kiss with fervour, but then he pulled back abruptly. Gently cupping her face in his hands, he asked, 'Do you trust me?'

Mitali looked straight into his eyes and began choking with emotion. He knew the answer. Rakesh gripped her hand firmly and said with some urgency, 'Then run with me. Now.'

As Mitali tried to keep pace with her lover's athletic strides, she noticed fuzzy silhouettes dressed in uniform heading in the opposite direction, towards the camp. Little did she know that the police and the army that worked together with the intelligence agency in Chhattisgarh had been mobilized to raid LalTara. Shortly thereafter, she heard a series of blasts as bombs blew up the camp, followed by incessant rounds of deafening gunfire.

She stumbled as she turned around to face the direction of the camp, but Rakesh's strong arms prevented her from falling. He held her protectively as she buried her face in his chest and wept. When the noise—and what it meant for her family—got too much for her to bear, she placed both her palms over her ears to block the sound off.

'Agent, target Bishen Rao and his family have fled, but we've managed to net the rest. The camp has been destroyed, and some narcotics and ammunition have been seized. We need to evacuate with the asset right now,' one of the uniformed men said to Rakesh with a nod. At that moment, everything started to come together for Mitali. She gathered her thoughts but chose to remain quiet.

Later, seated in the relative safety of an army vehicle, Mitali gave voice to her screaming thoughts with a barrage of questions: 'Who the hell are you? What's your name? Am I just an asset to you?'

Rakesh looked into her eyes and folded her, unresisting, into an embrace. 'My name is Rakesh. Rakesh Srivastava,' he murmured into her ears. 'I'm a special agent with the Narcotics Control Bureau. I know all this must be too much for you to take in right now. I have wished innumerable times that I met you under different circumstances, or that the events unfolded differently. I never wanted to keep secrets from you. But it was dangerous knowledge. I couldn't risk it, not with you. For me, our relationship was the only truth among all the deception and lies. Believe me, Mitali, I love you. I could never leave you behind. I gave the police information about LalTara on the condition that they would let you go free.'

Mitali listened to his words and felt his strong and steady heartbeat, laden with the promise of a better future. She was, however, unable to release the knot of anxiety in her chest. The churning in her stomach served as a reminder of the life growing within her. She was aware that with her actions, she had forever destroyed her ties with her family, for which Bishen would never forgive her. She also knew that one day Bishen would be back to make her pay for the choices she had made.

Rakesh feared the same. But for now, they were safe.

2025
Raipur

'*Baba! Baba!*'

Rakesh snapped back to the present with the sound of his daughter's voice breaking the chain of his thoughts.

Seeing that she had his attention, Isha continued, 'We have to do something, Baba. It's too good an opportunity to pass up. If we can intercept them, we can seize RED and get evidence against LalTara. Two birds with one stone.'

Manish watched as Rakesh considered her words. 'We cannot get the Home Ministry in the loop, as it will take us too long to obtain official sanctions. So, this operation will have to be undertaken without the blessings of higher authorities,' Rakesh pointed out. 'Our jobs will be in jeopardy should things go belly up. But I'm willing to risk it if you are,' he added, looking at the two young people.

'We're in,' they chorused as one.

'Okay. We must move swiftly now. Manish, the ball is in your court. Get cracking on deciphering the code.'

Manish smartly saluted his senior and turned to high-five Isha.

Rakesh looked at both of them. His team was venturing on a dangerous mission. For twenty-seven years, he had been trying to deal a body blow to LalTara, but with little success. A large part of this failure could be attributed to the fact that the arms and drugs dealer had relocated his operations to an unknown location within the dense jungles of Abujmarh. However, the current intel they received could be a gamechanger and flip the status quo.

It was now time to behead the devil and destroy his lair.

4
The Code

2025
STF19 headquarters, Raipur

Manish sat on a chair with his elbows on the table, cradling his head in his palms. In front of him, the table was a veritable wasteland of scribbled sheets. Numbers, alphabets, alphanumeric characters and meaningless doodles vied for space on the paper. Some sheets lay crumpled into tight balls on the floor, indicating solutions tried and abandoned. Manish sighed, grabbed a new piece of paper and started afresh.

The moment he had heard the taps in the audio file, it was abundantly clear to him that this part of the message was in Morse code. To translate the code into alphabets was an easy task, and it was quickly completed. Then he had applied a simple substitution cipher to arrive at a series of numbers. But after that, the techno-fiend had hit a seemingly unscalable wall. 'Come on, come on. It's a location and date for sure. But what the hell do these numbers mean,' he muttered to himself.

Five minutes later, Gopal, the peon, walked in with a bowl of rice *kheer*[12] on a tray.

'Sir, *khana*? Shall I serve lunch?'

---

[12]Kheer: Sweet porridge, dessert

Manish, struggling to break the code, was not interested in food.

'*Haan*, put it down here,' he responded dismissively, moving a sheaf of papers to clear a small space on his table.

'And daal-rice? Should I get it now or...?'

'Later, man, later. You know the order I follow when I eat.'

'Yes sir, we all know it. Your *ulta* lunch that starts with dessert,' the man smiled.

Manish looked up, returned his smile, and then suddenly froze, the rictus stuck on his face as he forgot to reposition his facial muscles. '*Ulta!* Yes!' he exclaimed. 'Gopu, my darling, you are brilliant.' He then began to scribble two new lines of numbers on the sheet, lost in his world of code.

Gopal, used to these antics, shook his head and withdrew quietly. He didn't think his sir would be interested in daal-rice anymore.

∽

2025
Narayanpur

Isha's calls to STF19's head of technology had remained unanswered for two days since their impromptu meeting at her house in the middle of the night. She was aware that Manish puzzling over a technical solution—which at the moment was the date and drop location for the RED consignment—was much like the proverbial dog with a bone. So she had left him in peace.

Now, standing under the scorching sun outside her makeshift office near Narayanpur, she studied the maps of the new road that the state government was building from the west of Orcha, a nearby town, towards Kudmela village, practically in front of her office. Construction activity was going on in full swing. Once the bridge over Kudmela *nala*[13] was complete, the settlement would have access to better habitation, which would be ominous for the drug lords and traffickers. Isha and her team were here primarily to provide protective detail for the Narayanpur-Kudmela road link.

The development work had been going on for many seasons, but LalTara had successfully caused delays and beat their strategic manoeuvres with deviously crafted bomb explosions and kidnappings, and by killing villagers to keep the rampant terror alive.

In the last six years, STF19 had intercepted several contraband movements almost certainly orchestrated by LalTara, but had been unable to glean any valuable information pertaining to their whereabouts, or those of Bishen Rao, the mastermind behind the operations. Isha still broke into a cold sweat as she recalled STF19's last operation here, and the fate of Kamli, a young Adivasi girl she had tried to save—unsuccessfully—from a fatal drug overdose. Flashes of the thirteen-year-old's eyes pleading to be saved from a horrifying death still hounded her. Kamli and many other children like her from Kudmela village were subjected to a process known as body packing or body stuffing, wherein they were forced to ingest packets of drugs. The contraband was retrieved once the carriers had crossed the secure border and passed it out of their system. But sometimes, the bags burst—as in Kamli's case—and the person carrying them died of an overdose. The perpetrators of this heinous racket, however, hid in the shadows of the inaccessible Abujmarh

---

[13]Nala: Canal

forest and networked their market for narcotics, weapons and ammunition.

Isha earnestly hoped that with the audio message intercepted by Manish, they would have an opportunity to get within firing distance of these elusive criminals.

'Madam-ji, madam-ji...'

Her colleague Radu Sinha's insistent voice brought her back to the present.

'*Kya baat hai*, Radu? What's the matter?' she enquired.

'Madam-ji, *thodi baat karni thi*. It's a little personal...'

Just then her mobile pinged. It was Manish. His message was terse: *Sending you a location. Get here as soon as you can.*

All right...but what is it? she messaged back.

I'll explain everything. Just get here.

The mobile pinged again as it received Manish's message with the coordinates for the location.

Dude, Isha quickly typed into her phone as she saw the location, *I can get there in thirty minutes, but it's five hours away from Raipur! Aren't you in Raipur?*

Woman, have you never heard of a chopper? his text quipped.

Just like him to make everything dramatic, Isha fumed. *But if he's requisitioning a helicopter, it must be important. Better to get on with it.*

'*Arre, gaadi bulao*,' she called out to a driver to bring the vehicle out.

'Madam-ji...' Radu continued his bleating insistently.

'*Haan, haan* Radu, *bolo*...' Before Isha could complete her sentence, however, her mobile demanded attention. This time it was Neel Saini, her boyfriend. *Damn!*

'Neel, hi! Can I call you back? This is not a good time.'

'Sure, Ishu. I'll text you. Not to worry.'

She disconnected the call and turned to Radu. 'Get in the car with me. We'll talk on the way.'

Her phone pinged again as she hopped into the rear seat of the all-terrain vehicle (ATV) she had at her disposal to travel through the region, which only had poor roads or none. She motioned Radu to follow suit. Neel had sent her a text message.

Need to see you at the earliest.

What happened? Everything okay? she responded.

'Madam-ji, *baat aisi thi...*' Radu once again tried to claim her attention.

'*Haan?*' she prompted Radu to speak.

Yes, yes, more than okay. Time toh bataa. Neel texted her.

Have some work. She wrote deftly as Radu continued to rant.

'I need some time off, Madam-ji. *Shaadi ke liye bhi chutti ka paroblem tha...* I could not avail any leave during my wedding either.'

'Radu, *pata hai na, kya chal raha hai yahaan*? You understand what's going on?'

I know you're busy, Ishu, but this is important. Neel messaged.

'*Haan* Madam-ji, but you know how it is. Honeymoon *bhi nahin kar sake.*'

Isha's eyebrows went up. Radu blushed.

Neel, if you know I'm busy, then don't push it please. She messaged back.

As soon as she hit the send button, Isha felt remorse. She didn't need to be rude.

Sorry Neel. Sounded like a bitch. Call you when I'm done? :)

'*Aur na*, Madam-ji, *devi ke darshan bhi nahi hue*,' Radu continued to drone on in the background.

No worries, cupcake. Sounds perfect!

'Radu, I understand. *Yeh ek mission pe chalo.* Just this one mission. Once you're back, I'll make sure you get two weeks off. Promise.'

Her favourite rookie's face brightened at the promise of fifteen days off. '*Theek hai,* Madam-ji,' he said, nodding enthusiastically.

Okay, Radu. She typed into her phone and sent the message before realizing her mistake.

Shit! Sorry. Okay Neel.

Heh, heh. Do I need to worry about this Radu?

Neel! Can I call you back later?

Thank God, Manish was flying out in a chopper, Isha thought in the middle of the text exchange. *She would bum a ride back to Raipur with him.*

Okay, okay, jaan. Over and out. Neel ended the conversation.

Isha sighed, and looked up from her phone. She could see figures in the distance. *Ah! Manish and her father!* The vehicle trundled alongside them and stopped.

'Radu, wait in the car for me.' Just as Isha alighted from her vehicle, Rakesh's mobile began to ring stridently. Signalling the other two to give him two minutes, he walked away busy in conversation.

'What's going on, Manish?' Isha turned her attention to her colleague. '*Saale, agar pahaad khodke chuuha nikla na,*[14] I'll bury you in the jungle,' Isha started her usual banter.

'*Yaar,* Isha, you always underestimate me. *Kuch toh* credit *doh!*'

---

[14] An idiom meaning 'making a big fuss over a trifle'

'Okay, okay. Peace. *Bol.* Tell me, what's this about?' Isha demanded.

Manish held up his hand. 'Let's wait for Rakesh sir.'

As they bided their time waiting for their boss to conclude the phone call, Manish struck up a conversation with Isha. As always, the subject was Isha and Neel. He cleared his throat. 'So, have you met Neel lately? How is he doing?'

'Neel is your friend, and you don't know what's he up to, huh? Anyway, I will be meeting him after this rendezvous. I shall convey your backslap.'

Meanwhile, Rakesh finished his conversation and approached his younger colleagues. Manish stood up a little straighter.

'So, Manish? What's the significance of this location?' he asked.

'Sir, I've managed to crack the code. The coordinates lead to this location. It's happening next Sunday.'

'Are you sure, man? There's a lot riding on this,' Isha countered.

'Yes, yes. It was a simple substitution cipher. Once I worked out the key, the rest was easy,' Manish explained, turning away from them to face the landscape. 'Just look at this place.'

The trio stood there and contemplated the scene. A dense tree cover that surrounded a small clearing. Cutting through the insect chatter and birdsong, Isha could hear the continuous trickling sound of water from the nala nearby. If one looked closely and hard enough, a faint outline of a walking trail was visible briefly before it was swiftly engulfed by the dense jungle.

There was something in what Manish was saying,

Isha thought, as she and Rakesh looked at each other and exchanged an unspoken message.
It was time to begin the end.

5

Coward

2025
Raipur

Isha raced to her car in the parking area after being dropped by the helicopter at the STF19 headquarters. She quickly got behind the wheel and sped towards Naya Raipur, the locality where Neel was going to meet her. She'd almost missed calling him before the chopper took flight. Her mind was in turmoil, with LalTara at the core of her chaotic thoughts.

Both she and Baba understood what this new development could signify. If their strategy to intercept the RED drop and possibly find some evidence about the monster heading it succeeded, they could find closure for a lot of loose ends in their lives. Not for their grief, though. That would continue to stalk them; a dull, aching anguish that mostly remained just beyond the horizon, but resurfaced unexpectedly, reminding them of the emptiness at their core, which would go with them to their funeral pyres.

Lost in her thoughts, Isha narrowly missed hitting a cow, leisurely ambling across the road, oblivious to the fast-approaching vehicle in its inimitably bovine stoicism. *Careful, girl!* she gave herself a mental pinch.

And what about Neel? her mind resumed its musing. *She'd shared a lot of her life with him, but never this emptiness about her childhood and family. Not in the way it had happened. It was not a secret; she would tell him sooner or later, but somehow no time seemed right. Perhaps she was a coward. Yes, a coward! She simply couldn't rip off the band-aid to confront that weeping, festering wound. And then there was poor Neel, unaware of this turbulence within her as she orbited around him—much like that cow!*

Would she change this situation today? Would she be able to bare her past to him?

༄

An hour later, navigating the roads of Naya Raipur, Isha wondered what Neel was up to. All around her were tastefully designed residential structures—communities within gated boundaries, which were part of a smart city that would embody Chhattisgarh's new capital. As she neared the location pin on her mobile, Isha noticed that the condominium complexes were being replaced by private villas: some sleek and contemporary, others bearing a more colonial or stately appearance—but all of them well tended and fronted by lush, manicured gardens.

As she drove into a tree-shaded avenue, she spotted Neel's black Honda with its owner leaning against the bonnet, dressed as usual in earthy chinos and a pale linen shirt. *That easy grace! How she loved it!* Most men over six feet tall carried their height like a burden, but not Neel. He had capitalized on it by falling in love with basketball of all sports in a cricket-obsessed nation! As if that wasn't enough, he was passionate about the martial arts—specifically Krav Maga and kickboxing. The outcome? A tall, lean frame, with a head of wavy hair that he tended to keep a tad too long for Isha's comfort. She often teased him about sports being his first love.

'Hey, beautiful,' Neel called out as she parked alongside his car.

'Hey, handsome,' she smiled at him through the car window. 'What are we doing here?' she asked, emerging from the vehicle and giving Neel a quick hug. Isha wasn't inclined towards too much public display of affection.

Neel put his arm across her shoulders and turned her to face a small but beautiful bungalow with a 'For Sale' sign on its gate.

'*Ta daaaaa.* How's this for our new house? Four bedrooms, a study, a lounge, a garden...' Neel rattled off its features like a real estate agent.

'Hey, hey! Slow down! What do you mean our new house?'

'Well, it's not yet, but could be, nah? It can accommodate at least three children and as many dogs,' Neel winked.

'*Yaar*, aren't you putting the cart before the horse? What about your Ma? She'd have a fit if she knew about this!'

'Ma, Ma, Ma. You're such a stuck record, Ishu! I know how to persuade her to accept all of this.'

'Look, Neel. We just seem to be going around in circles. You know I don't ever want to stand between a mother and a son. I understand the pain of being motherless. It's not a curse I would choose to place on anyone, however indirectly. *Woh paap main nahi jhel paoongi.* I cannot commit such a sin.'

'I have a plan,' Neel's voice dropped down to a whisper, as he impersonated the worst possible ham. 'I'm going to London to check out some new printing technology for *Raipur News*. I know for sure that Ma will start getting withdrawal pangs in a few weeks. And then I shall strike.'

'My God, Neel! I can see your father frowning down

from the heavens. He founded the newspaper and ran it with such integrity. And here you are, using it for your personal machinations.'

'All's fair, dear, all's fair. Just leave this to me. I'm flying out tomorrow, and all will be well when I return. You just take care of yourself, okay? I'll ask Manish to keep an eye on you,' he laughed.

Isha sighed. In her current state of mind, she struggled to accept Neel's perspective. In fact, his effervescence only made the situation worse. She couldn't find it in her heart to burst his bubble of joy by sharing with him what was weighing her down. *It was just as well he was leaving for London,* she thought. *She would not have to summon up the courage to discuss her past today. A reprieve for now, at least.*

Coward, her conscience hissed.

6
The Ghost Who Walks

2025
D-day
Near LalTara's meeting point

It was the hour right before sunset. The sharp contours of the trees and the landscape had begun to blur; the reality of the day was softening and dissolving into a mysterious twilight. The sun was already engulfed by a billow of clouds that loomed close to the horizon, dark and pregnant with rain.

A squad of commandos examined their equipment to ensure everything was operational. Manish hovered over them like an anxious mother hen, particularly when they checked each of the various gadgets—machine guns, pistols, night-vision goggles, communication gear and drones—that comprised part of their paraphernalia. Isha and one of the commandos sat in close consultation, poring over a map.

She looked up as an ATV drew close to the camp. Baba! She excused herself, got up and went to greet him.

'Isha! Ready?'

'Yes, sir!' She replied crisply, with confidence.

When he drew close to pat her back, she thought she saw his eyes moisten.

'Baba,' she murmured softly so that no one would hear

a daughter address her father, 'I'm going to give it my all, so we shall succeed.'

'Go over the plan, quickly,' Rakesh ordered, snapping into commander mode.

'We proceed to location, which is about a kilometre away from the actual coordinates. Manish gets the drones out to monitor the drop-off. Team Alpha remains on standby until then. As soon as the consignment is dropped off, we move forward to intercept LalTara, perhaps red-handed with RED, ammunition or narcotics.'

'Go finish your pre-mission checks, Captain Isha,' he instructed after hearing her out. His even-keeled voice belied the storm raging in his heart. *His baby, his only child; was he feeding her to the tiger?*

'Yes, sir. Will do, sir!'

'May the Force be with you.'

'May the Force be with us all,' Isha responded to complete their signature dialogue—a phrase borrowed from a popular space opera series—reserved for their missions to invoke good luck. Both father and daughter were huge fans of this series, and each film represented family time which was both rare and cherished.

While Rakesh strode off to speak with Manish, Isha stood still for a couple of heartbeats. Suddenly, her ears caught a name: Sangha. She turned to see Radu Sinha standing in close confabulation with Ram Yadav and Saud Shaikh, both two years his senior, but sharing that peculiar closeness of brothers-in-arms.

'*Kya chal raha hai, idhar?* What's happening here?' she catechized them sternly.

All three straightened their spines and saluted her smartly.

'Nothing important, Madam-ji,' Radu took the lead.

'Nothing important? Look at yourselves in the mirror. You are scared. *Phat ke haath mein aayi hai sab ki.*'

Radu winced. Sometimes Madam-ji could be so graphic. In this case, though, the phrase had hit the bull's-eye.

'*Ji* Madam-ji...that Sangha...' he steeled himself for the sounding-off that was bound to follow.

'The Sangha chronicles again? Idiots!'

'Madam-ji, listen to the villagers,' Saud piped in. 'There's something supernatural about that name. They are absolutely terrified of Sangha. *Aaj toh jaroor aayega.*' Saud could feel his hands get clammy just uttering the name.

∞

Sangha was the ghost who walked the Abujmarh forests, as if the unforgiving, land-mined terrain was a mere playground. Horror stories about Sangha's cunning plans and smooth operations were the stuff of lore. Common folklore had it that he was the firstborn of LalTara's leader Bishen Rao and the spirit queen of the forest, Rukhchaya. No one had ever seen his face. Some said he was the devil, others believed Sangha was an evil force without a mortal body. No one had ever raised their eyes to see his face and lived to tell the tale. Sangha was a mystery, an enigma that nobody had had the courage to unravel.

Isha controlled her temper with great difficulty. Poker-faced, she ordered her juniors: 'I want all of you to be ready within the next hour. No fuck-ups, please. Make-up *chalu karo...*'

She was alluding to the camouflage face paint they needed to wear to minimize the likelihood of being discovered. She began the task on herself almost mechanically. Her thoughts were far away, shrouded in a scene reprised by her father so many times that all she had to do was close her eyes and witness the horrifying events as they unfolded, second by second. The sound of gunfire, the rain of bullets, the raging flames, her mother's screams, and then the feeling of desolation, hopelessness, frustration and impotent fury at the realization that life as they knew it had changed irrevocably.

∞

2025
The meeting point

It was midnight. Two vehicles had made their way to a spot one kilometre from the nala, near the meeting point coordinates. From one vehicle alighted Team Alpha, comprising eight commandos and Isha as the mission leader. The other van carried Manish's team, who would navigate the drones to capture aerial inputs of the scene once the battle began. Manish himself was stationed at the STF19 HQ and would act as the nerve centre for the entirety of the operations, directing Team Alpha as well as the drone operators. He would also monitor the feeds from their night-vision video equipment, alert them with directions, and warn them about the position of approaching adversaries. Rakesh, too, was monitoring the feed of this covert operation from his home office.

From here on, Team Alpha would continue their journey on foot. It had already started to rain, a continuous and steady drizzle. Aside from the pitter-patter though, the night's stillness had the eerie calm that inevitably precedes a storm. Intruding into this tense silence, a familiar husky voice streamed into Isha's earphones.

'*Aaj ki raat hona hai kya...*'[15] the lyrics of the popular song swirled in from the Bollywood addict Manish's humorous feed.

'*Paana hai kya, khona hai kya*, Don,'[16] Isha responded with an involuntary smile.

'Copy the feed, Roma... Roma,'[17] reverted Manish with an artificial echo, as he busied himself with his gizmos. His calm demeanour, coupled with a razor-sharp instinct, made his team feel safe in every mission.

Isha understood that Manish's light-hearted approach would keep Rakesh in charge of the mission, without his blood pressure skyrocketing beyond the limits of the sphygmomanometer.

Isha and her team checked their audio link with Manish, and then matched the time on their watches with each other.

'Team Alpha. Rain may hamper thermal signatures,' Manish advised.

'Copy that,' all team members acknowledged the warning.

Team Alpha soon started to make their way into the forest towards the nala. They were divided into three groups of three members each, and moved in a pre-planned, tactical V formation to provide cover to each other. Isha and her two group members in team three formed the meeting point of the formation, with teams one and two a little ahead of them. The entire Team Alpha would move as one formation while maintaining distance. They hoped to get the LalTara members into the wedge of the V. Once that was done, in

---

[15]Lyrics of the song 'Aaj ki raat' from the Bollywood film *Don* (2006)
[16]Lyrics of the song 'Aaj ki raat' from the Bollywood film *Don* (2006)
[17]Lyrics and characters from the Bollywood film *Don* (2006)

a pincer movement, the arms of the V would close in on them. The group soon arrived at ground zero and waited, while maintaining radio silence as far as possible.

Suddenly, Ram Yadav from one frontline group spoke up. 'Movement at two o'clock.'

Manish cross-checked on his feed. 'Alpha, movement near Team 1. Team 2 and Team 3, communicate developments.'

Isha scanned the jungle with her thermal goggles. '12 o'clock. Two people,' she responded.

Rakesh, code-named Eagle, cautioned, 'Hold on. Steady. Wait.'

Team 1: 'Bodies increasing.'

Team 2: 'Ditto. 9 o'clock.'

'Team Alpha, proceed to the exact coordinates. Get LalTara into the wedge,' Eagle's calm voice sounded on the feed.

'Copy that,' Team Alpha responded.

'Manish,' Rakesh continued, 'monitor LalTara positions. Relay them.'

'Copy,' Manish replied.

For five minutes, there was no word from Manish. Then, 'LalTara has entered the wedge. About six bodies. Teams 1 and 2, start closing the gap. Team 3, maintain position.'

Another five minutes passed before the radio crackled to life again. 'Team Alpha. Proceed with pincer. Go, go, go.'

The commandos and Isha sprang into action.

Isha took aim and fired. She saw a body drop. One down. She scanned the landscape. A figure suddenly came into view and raised an arm to shoot. She stifled a gasp as a shot rang out and hit her team member in the chest, knocking him over to the ground. Gunfire erupted around her as Isha dashed forward, towards the site of the confrontation, trying to get within firing range.

Closer to the scene, however, she saw a figure standing above her inert colleague. His long hair was bunched into a pony tail. He wasn't short, but the massive bulk of his body made him appear squat and square—like a powerful toad. Waves of animal ferocity seemed to emanate from him. She knew this physique from the surveillance photos taken surreptitiously by their informant. This was Tej, one of LalTara's most feared names. The informant had gulped two glasses of water after he finished narrating the tales of his brutality.

While these thoughts, which mirrored the frenzy of gunfire around her, ran through Isha's head, the much-feared Tej deliberately and brutally planted one foot on his victim's chest and pressed down. As the Team 1 commando struggled to breathe and free himself, the foot that resolutely kept him pinned to the ground was unyielding. Isha looked around to see if any of her colleagues was close at hand to help, but seeing everyone engaged in their own battles, she surged forward, throwing stealth to the wind.

The man heard her approaching. He glanced at her and paused for a single heartbeat. He inclined his head like a dog concentrating on something interesting. Then, turning back to his victim, he whipped out a knife, bent down, held the commando by the hair and slit his throat in one swift movement. Tej then raced deeper into the forest.

Time slowed down, stretched and warped. The flowing waters of the nala added to the sound of static in her head. Isha had no recollection of how she closed the gap to where her fallen team member lay. She quickly whisked off his eyewear. Ram Yadav's eyes stared emptily back at her. The buzz in her ears intensified. She looked up, and to her horror, saw Tej with another hapless victim. Even through the gloomy darkness, Isha knew it was Radu Sinha, who had been deployed to Team 2.

Her colleague was fighting back with all his might, but his assailant proved to be a more formidable opponent. Isha saw the toad stun Radu with a blow to his head and push him into the water. She aimed her gun carefully and fired. *Shit! Missed!* The powerful figure whirled around at the sound of the gunshot, turning to look in her direction before leaping into the nala. *No!* A voice screamed in her head. *Please God! She had to save Radu, she had to! God, please let him be alive!*

Isha dashed to where Tej had been standing moments earlier and peered down into the water. She was unable to see anyone. *No splashing, no movement.* She checked her bearings. *Yes, the bend in the waterway was just a little way ahead. Maybe, if she ran through the forest, she could intercept them ahead of the curve.* Even before that thought could fully form in her mind, she bolted into the thick blackness of the jungle.

'Isha, turn back, turn back!' Manish's voice filled her head via the audio gear. But Isha continued to run.

෴

The rain had intensified. The hiss of the precipitation added another layer of difficulty in their attempts to tune into suspicious sounds. *I have to go old-school, and I have to get to the stream fast,* Isha thought to herself. So intent was she on following Radu that Isha neither realized that her audio gear had gone silent, nor sensed that she was being followed.

So the blow, when it came, caught her absolutely by surprise. *Thank God for the headgear,* Isha thought as she shook her head to clear her vision. She then noticed her adversary: a masked figure, moving with the precision and agility of a jungle cat. This was no ordinary warrior.

Even in that perilous moment fraught with danger, her mind whisked back to the conversation between Radu Sinha, Ram Yadav and Saud Shaikh about Sangha, the terror of Abujmarh. *Was this the ghost who walked the forest?* Whoever her masked assailant was, Isha understood that if she was going to survive this, it would have to be through mind games rather than physical combat. Her opponent knew the terrain better than she did and seemed well trained in warfare.

As Isha lunged forward, her assailant neatly side-stepped her, whirled around and kicked her in the back. Isha stumbled forward, bounced off a tree trunk and tasted the forest floor. She moaned and pretended to be badly hurt. A foot rammed into her side to turn her over. Exactly what Isha was waiting for! With a dexterous move, the STF19 captain sat up and jammed the ketamine pen she had hidden in the cuff of her sleeve into her enemy's thigh. She heard a gasp of surprise and saw her opponent's hand reach reflexively for the syringe. Isha then violently yanked her attacker's leg and toppled the figure over. The potent anaesthetic took effect as the masked figure slumped down, tried to get up on all fours, but failed. Slowly, the figure sank face down onto the forest floor.

Isha extended her hand to gently ease her assailant's arm from under the body and checked for the pulse. *Good! It was still going strong.* With a grunt, she heaved her fallen foe on their back. As she ripped off the mask, she felt her knees go weak. It couldn't be!

The pear-shaped face, the aquiline nose, the high cheekbones, the full lips and the half-open eyes drowned in sleep... Isha felt as if she was looking into a mirror. At her own face.

7

Lambs to the Slaughter

2025
STF19 headquarters, Raipur

Manish could feel his pulse quicken and his legs begin to quiver. The horrific visual feed from the team members filled up his screen. He witnessed Team Alpha combat the LalTara cadre, but he had eyes only for what was happening with Isha.

He saw her, through her visual feed, run towards a fallen colleague, and then saw a short powerful figure overpower another. In the next instant both the attacker and his victim disappeared from view. The visual jerked crazily as Isha ran towards the spot they'd just been in. She stopped, and then started running again, this time towards the tree line.

'Isha,' Manish spoke into his mouthpiece. 'Turn back. Turn back.' But there was no response from her. He examined his equipment to check if he'd lost the connection, but all seemed to be in order. She seemed to be deliberately disregarding his pleas. And then, even her feed stopped transmitting. The link was lost.

'Isha!' Manish yelled in the vain hope that she would somehow hear him.

'No, no, no,' Rakesh's voice screamed out from the speaker. His boss, who'd been plugged into the system, had also witnessed the sequence of events as they transpired.

Manish called out to Rakesh repeatedly on his microphone, but he heard nothing.

In his home office, Rakesh stood frozen, catatonic, alone. In his mind's eye, he could see the disappearing tail lights of a car, and a kukri slick with blood.

∽

1999
Jodhpur

Rakesh had accepted a transfer to Jodhpur to work as an undercover military intelligence profiler. His cover was a desk job in a computer software firm, because he understood that Mitali and their family were safe from Bishen so long as they led a nondescript, invisible existence. Rakesh was aware that their joyful, tranquil life was as delicate as a daydream because somewhere, Bishen would always be plotting and scheming to exact his revenge. Rakesh could not have known that the day would arrive so soon.

It was the fifteenth of August. Another Sunday evening spent happily, viewing a family movie at the cinema hall. Rakesh and Mitali were driving back home in their second-hand Fiat, a Premier Padmini they had recently bought, feeling somewhat anxious and eager to be back with Isha, their baby daughter, a toddler who had been left with a neighbour. Rakesh powered on the music system, and their favourite Bollywood number, *'Kuch na kaho, kuch bhi na kaho... Aur is pal mein... Bas ek main hoon, bas ek tum ho,'*[18] softly filled the car. Mitali gently hummed their song as she

---

[18]Lyrics translation: 'Don't say anything, nothing at all... In this moment, it's just you and me' (song from the film *1942: A Love Story* (1994))

placed her hand on Rakesh's. It was their perfect moment of quiet togetherness.

Once Rakesh pulled into the parking spot behind his house, a small independent one-storey building, he realized that Mitali had fallen asleep, her head resting on his shoulder. He smiled at her indulgently and decided to give her a few more peaceful moments. Drumming his fingers on the steering wheel in tune with the song, he glanced out of the car towards his home when he thought he saw a shadow jump into the ground-floor balcony. His sixth sense triggered, Rakesh carefully rested Mitali's head on the backrest of the car seat, and slid his hand into the glove compartment to reach for the preloaded 9mm semi-automatic gun. Ready for action, he stepped out of the car without switching off the engine to allow the music to play on for Mitali.

When he peered over the veranda, something jumped on the ledge, nearly throwing him off balance. The creature hissed, baring its fangs, and scurried off. Rakesh breathed a sigh of relief when he realized it was just one of the colony felines, scavenging. He consoled himself that his unnatural fear was due to his over-stressed nerves.

Feeling the tension seep out of his body, he turned and headed for the car. However, he had barely taken ten steps towards it when stars suddenly began to explode in front of his eyes as something hard hit his head. He groaned and stumbled to the ground, the gun sliding off his palm. His hands were twisted behind his back in a vice-like grip and secured tightly. A dark cloth was slid over his head, which was throbbing with pain, but it was insignificant compared to the feeling of dread that froze his heart. The grip on his arms was familiar, and he knew who it belonged to. His worst nightmare had just come true. Bishen had found him.

'I trusted you like a brother and you destroyed me,' hissed Rakesh's assailant. Bishen struck his captive mercilessly in the stomach and the chest. Blinded by the dark hood over his head, Rakesh could not fight back. Then he felt a stricture go around his neck. The pressure around his neck increased as his body was dragged a few feet over the ground. Rakesh gagged. He felt his consciousness slipping—but before he could black out, the pressure eased and his windpipe opened up a little. The weakened man coughed and gulped in lungfuls of air. But before he could recover, the torture resumed. Finally, having drained Rakesh of every scrap of energy, Bishen stripped off the black hood from his bruised face.

'I want to see the fear of death in those insolent eyes,' he scoffed, as he peered into Rakesh's face with eyes spitting deadly venom. The noose around his neck tightened again and Rakesh could feel himself being pulleyed up. His feet scrabbled for traction on the ground. He knew Bishen was here to execute him the LalTara way. Rakesh would be hanged to death.

Gasping for breath, Rakesh's world blurred and Bishen's invectives took on a strange underwater quality. He was being hauled up, dangling in mid-air and choking to death. He could only think of Mitali and prayed she would somehow escape when he was no longer alive to shield her from such savagery.

Suddenly, the rope snapped and Rakesh fell, his body plummeting to the ground. The first thing he saw when his vision stopped focusing and refocusing like the damaged eyepiece of a camera was Bishen with his hands upraised.

Then his eyes rested on Mitali. She was pointing Rakesh's semi-automatic at her brother.

'Leave us alone,' she screamed, as she walked over to Rakesh with tears streaming down from her eyes.

Bishen could not believe that his little sister was pointing a gun at him.

Rakesh lumbered up to his feet and stumbled to his wife. Keeping the weapon trained on her brother, Mitali withdrew her trusted kukri from the waist of her sari and cut off her husband's shackles. Freed, Rakesh took the gun from Mitali. Now, he kept it aimed at Bishen.

Bishen stammered, 'I had to come for you, Mitu. To save you. I thought this bastard had you in his clutches because you were pregnant and had no way out. But if you are happy, I shall go away. Just once, let me give you a hug before I bid you farewell forever.'

Mitali looked at her brother uncertainly, with narrowed eyes. *Could she trust him?*

'I have no weapons on me,' said Bishen, beckoning Mitali with outstretched arms.

The confusion on Mitali's face cleared. *How could I have misunderstood him all this time?* she thought. Her past flashed before her eyes. Memories of Bishen as a big brother: *the fun they had by the riverside; the doll he had bought for her from the fair; his warm, protective embrace shielding her from the brutal news of their parents' death. A criminal he may be, but he had never hurt or abused her. Bishen meant what he was saying now.* Before Rakesh could say anything, she ran to her brother who embraced her tightly.

'Mitali, no!' Rakesh yelled, but it was too late. Mitali was now Bishen's hostage, a kukri piercing the softness of her throat. Tiny droplets of blood oozed out as Bishen, threatening to slit it open, signalled Rakesh to surrender.

'Whore,' he hissed into Mitali's ears as he looked at the Fiat parked a few metres from him, and realized what his perfect exit plan would be. Keeping a hawk's eye on Rakesh, he tugged Mitali with the kukri still at her throat. The dagger slashed deeper into her skin, causing her to cry out in pain.

'Whore,' he repeated under his breath as he dragged her to the car.

Rakesh had little choice but to keep pointing the gun at Bishen. With Mitali as his human shield, Bishen knew Rakesh would never risk opening fire. The siblings inched closer to the car, shuffling clumsily like a freakish four-legged beast. When Bishen finally got close to the car and slid into it, Rakesh ran towards him. Bishen hurled Mitali towards Rakesh. As both toppled over, Bishen started the car and reversed with full power, tyres spouting dust.

'Mitali, are you okay?' gasped Rakesh as he struggled for balance and sought to upright them both. But Rakesh knew something was wrong. Mitali wasn't helping herself. As he put his arms around her, the gush of a free-flowing slippery liquid soaked his palms. The kukri was lodged deep into her back.

'My baby...' she whispered. And that was the last time Rakesh heard her speak.

༄

2025
Rakesh's home office

'Sir! Sir! Rakesh sir!' Rakesh heard Manish's voice as if from beyond a hundred cotton shrouds. He gathered himself, took a deep breath, and responded calmly. 'Manish, we must wait and watch. I trust Isha to take care of herself...' he petered off. But deep in his heart, he was terrified.

Would history repeat itself? Would he have to lose Isha too, to Bishen?

8
Eka

2025
Abujmarh

Isha couldn't stop gazing at the face. It became clearer as the rain gradually washed away the mud and the face grease. *How was this possible? Was this a miracle? What would Baba say?* One hundred questions coalesced and formed a paralyzing cocktail of emotions in her mind. She gave herself a shake to return to the present moment. *She had just two more hours before the sedative wore off. Besides, LalTara would be searching for the people it had deployed on this mission. She had to act fast.*

Isha heaved her captive up by the shoulders, and started to drag her along the ground slowly to make her way in the direction, she hoped, she had come from. After twenty minutes of radio silence, her communication set pinged back to life. *Thank God, she was back into civilization.* She set her prisoner down, switched off the revived communication set, and extracted a secondary mobile. With trembling fingers, she punched in Rakesh's number.

'Where are you?' Her father's voice erupted within half a ring.

Isha managed to quell the tremor in her voice and reply calmly, 'Asset. I need immediate extraction.'

Father and daughter had set up a private pre-arranged

protocol for remote communication specifically for this assignment. The probability that something 'personal' would emerge from this raid was immense, which would have to be kept out of the official circuit. Hence, they had agreed that Manish would have to be circumvented, at least for the time being. The asset would be ferried to a safe house north of Narayanpur on the outskirts of the Rowghat mining area. The existence of this safe house was known only to the two of them.

'Location?'

Isha checked her GPS and provided him with the exact coordinates. She was now without the protective cover of Manish's team. Her only hope was her survivor's instinct, and for Rakesh to arrive before LalTara did.

༄

Dawn was breaking as Rakesh accelerated the inconspicuous-looking Matador van. Its exterior appeared like any worn-out vehicle, but from the inside, it was well armoured and equipped with sophisticated technology to carry a high-value asset.

As Rakesh neared the coordinates Isha provided, he was relieved to see his daughter emerge from behind a large boulder that had served her as cover. Isha was carrying the asset on her back, and motioned Rakesh to keep the Matador running. She quickly opened the rear doors, placed the body, clambered inside, and thumped the van's side as a signal for him to drive on.

Inside the van, Isha checked the girl's pulse. Strong and steady. Good! She took a ketamine pen from the SOS first-aid box in the van, and pushed in half a dose, just sufficient to keep her aggression in check. The van maintained a stable pace as it negotiated the deserted and bumpy roads that led towards its destination.

⁂

Rakesh eased the van in front of a decrepit building and stopped. He banged the partition that separated the driver's cabin from the rear of the vehicle. He then heard the vehicle's rear door open, followed by sounds of something being moved, before the door slammed shut. Rakesh carefully manoeuvred his vehicle into the makeshift parking of the safe house, covered it with a camouflage net woven with dry leaves, and headed inside.

The safe house was a partially built bungalow in Rowghat, a mining area four hours away from Raipur. The family that had commissioned the construction had been wiped out in an accident. Some believed the place was cursed; others thought it was haunted. Only four rooms in the entire house could be deemed rooms, the rest of it lay either in shambles or in a state of incompletion. Rakesh had discovered this house and found its isolated location, unfrequented by humans, perfect for their covert missions. The basement, however, was the proverbial cherry on the cake, as it permitted a number of clandestine activities to be conducted in absolute secrecy. A corner of this subterranean room had been designated as the pantry, which was well stocked with packaged food and a variety of beverages.

As Rakesh entered the safe house, Isha walked up to him and gave him a tight hug. Returning her embrace, he could feel her racing heartbeat. Affection welled up inside him. He caressed her head.

'I'm so glad you're safe, beta.'

'You won't believe who I've found, Baba.' She released

him and grasped his hand in hers. 'Come with me,' she urged, and led him downstairs to the basement.

Rakesh saw the captive lying slumped over the table—still groggy from the injection—with both her wrists handcuffed to a chair. The overhead tube light flickered, adding to the palpable tension in the room. Isha gently lifted the lolling head, and cleared away the tangle of curls from the face.

Rakesh felt his world implode. The dam he'd built in his heart burst. Rakesh wept as he had all those years ago, when he had lost his wife.

∞

1999
Jodhpur

Rakesh wailed and howled as he cradled Mitali's lifeless body in his lap. Anguish coursed through his veins, even as a violent anger corroded his innards. He wanted to chase after Bishen and carve out his heart or throttle him. He wanted to turn back the clock to keep Mitali safe. But all he could do was scream in agony. The sound woke up their neighbours and lights began to spring up in the nearby houses. Rakesh heard footsteps running towards him. Someone shouted. He felt someone's arm go around his shoulders. These were mere physical sensations that his body registered as if from a distance. He was far, far away in a hellish place, all alone.

The grief he bore was a heavy one. Not only had Mitali been wrenched away from him in a matter of seconds, but he also lost another piece of his heart: his daughter Eka, who had clamoured to be with her parents when they were leaving. She had been sleeping soundly in a car seat secured to the backseat of the car. She and her twin Isha—who had been left with the neighbour that fateful evening—were the most precious blessings in Rakesh and Mitali's life. Now, with Mitali gone and Eka inadvertently kidnapped, he only had Isha.

The days that followed seemed like an early celluloid film, bereft of sound and colour. Rakesh had poured his angst-filled, red-tinged energy into searching relentlessly for his child, following every clue and speaking to countless people. But no information emerged—about his daughter, Bishen, or the car in which the LalTara chief had inadvertently abducted her. They had just disappeared into a void. Or into the dense jungle that sheltered LalTara's new stronghold, and which also protected the outlaw's secrets. But Rakesh was determined not to give up.

He was very sure that the narcotics trail was key to tracing LalTara and Bishen, and running them aground. So, he pushed all the paperwork needed for a transfer from Jodhpur to Raipur. He then organized some of the best operatives in the state to form a special task force called STF19, which was headquartered in Raipur. The sole objective of the unit was to intercept and eradicate narcotic contraband. But privately, Rakesh hoped, he would discover some answers to LalTara's whereabouts as well. The covert cell reported directly to the state's home ministry.

Over the years, the task force was appreciably successful in its mission. News of their triumphs featured regularly in both state and national dailies. But Rakesh deliberately stayed away from the limelight, as he did not want his association with STF19 to become common knowledge lest Bishen should see the coverage. Later, when Isha grew up and joined the unit, she followed this rule as well.

Meanwhile, through all the successes, the pain persisted.

Had Bishen killed Eka the way he had despatched his sister? The question plagued Rakesh and tormented him endlessly. There were times he teetered on the edge of insanity, when ending it all seemed immensely more appealing. But when he looked into the innocent eyes of the daughter who remained with him, he could not give in to that peaceful darkness. *He had to persevere for Isha and for Eka. He had to look after one daughter and find the other. Just as Mitali would have wished.*

∽

2025
Raipur

Groggy and limp, the girl who lay shackled before Rakesh now was his other daughter Eka.

∽

9

The Proposition

Manish was in panic mode, furiously pacing up and down the signal room at the STF19 communication headquarters. Team Alpha—or what remained of it—had returned with a batch of confiscated arms, but nothing that resembled any sophisticated robotic weapon. Ram Yadav was found dead; Saud Shaikh and three more commandos were critically injured, Radu Sinha and Isha were missing.

Where could they have vanished? Were they safe? Ever since Manish had lost contact with Isha, a tiny worm of unease wriggled in his stomach. *What was the next step? His boss Rakesh Srivastava would know what to do,* he thought. However, when he had called Rakesh's cell phone, it seemed to be continually out of the network coverage area. He had then tried the emergency hotline, which too remained unanswered. Finally, he called Rakesh's residential landline. Vishnu, Rakesh's trusted aide and household helper for decades, answered the phone.

'Rakesh sir wasn't feeling well. He took a tablet and is sleeping now,' Vishnu responded to Manish's query regarding Rakesh's whereabouts.

Rubbish! Manish exclaimed to himself. There was no way in hell Rakesh would take some medication and go to sleep knowing that Isha was incommunicado. *Why was Vishnu lying,* he wondered. Disquiet threatened to invade his brain. *What was happening? But hang on! There was a way to find out.*

Manish returned to his desk and fired up his personal, unofficial laptop. He furiously pounded some keys. The outcome was satisfying. The GPS tracking device installed on Rakesh's car—every department vehicle was equipped with one, in the event it entered a perilous situation—was active! He could see Rakesh's location on his screen, and had a nagging suspicion that Isha would be there too. Both of them were on to something big.

Manish quickly shoved his laptop into his backpack, snatched the keys to his gunmetal grey Royal Enfield Classic and tersely informed his team that he was heading out for some work. Stepping out of the communication HQ, he kickstarted his bike and hit the road, determined to find out what was going on.

༄

Rakesh wrapped both his palms around the cup of lemongrass tea Isha placed before him, drawing strength from its gentle warmth. If he had hoped to find some catharsis in the release of pent-up emotions after all these years, he was mistaken. His mind still roiled with feelings every time his eyes rested upon Isha's prisoner. *How he'd dreamt of this day! To have Eka and Isha by his side. His darling, darling Eka! Feisty and a little hard-headed. How she had managed to get them to take her out on that fateful day! And just when he had resigned himself to never seeing her again, she'd reappeared in his life unexpectedly, and under such shocking circumstances!*

This new-found happiness—the dream of finding his daughter and holding her close against his bosom, like a precious baby bird—however, was now tarnished. For twenty-six years, she had been moulded and shaped by one of India's most dangerous criminals. He had a heartbreaking reality to face. *One daughter battling to ensure the nation's safety, and the other...* Rakesh brushed away the goosebumps on his arms as if getting rid of stinging insects. She would need to be handled carefully. After all, she was one of Bishen's own.

The girl Rakesh knew as Eka was beginning to struggle against her restraints and cough up air. With a gasp, she raised herself off the table and leaned back in the chair, the handcuffs snug against the armrests. She straightened her head, opened her eyes and tried to get them to focus. For some moments, she stared at Rakesh unseeingly, then her gaze sharpened and settled on Isha, who was standing behind her father. Her eyes went wide with shock.

'What the fuck,' the girl exclaimed with a disbelieving gasp.

'Eka,' Rakesh called out.

The girl seemed not to hear him and continued to stare at Isha open-mouthed.

'Eka, listen,' he repeated.

The girl's eyes slid from daughter to father and back.

'What witchery are you guys trying, making people look like me,' she growled. 'And what do you want, old man? My name is Sangha,' she said with a note of pride in her voice as she uttered the word.

Her sister! Rakesh and Mitali's baby Eka was the Sangha! Isha was shocked and surprised.

Amazed by the similarity between the two girls' voices, Rakesh heard Isha sit hard on a chair. 'My God,' she whispered. 'What have they made of you?'

'Made of me? What the hell do you mean?' the prisoner spat out.

'Eka... Sangha,' Rakesh said softly. 'You were named Eka at birth. You are my daughter. Your mother's name is Mitali, and we used to...' he went on to narrate the incidents that had shaped the lives of the Srivastava family in the first two years since the birth of the twins.

∽

What was Rakesh up to? Manish wondered. He'd been riding for more than ninety minutes. Raipur's settlements had given way to sporadic clusters of huts. He'd passed farmlands and rural landscapes, with typical early morning activity—cattle being taken to pasture, women balancing gleaming towers of vessels on their heads. But even these sights had petered off. The GPS signalled him to turn off the main road and onto a dirt track that disappeared into the dense jungle. Finally, as he neared the red pin of his destination, a dilapidated building slid into view. Manish switched off the engine of his motorcycle and coasted to a stop near a line of stones—shaggy with vegetation—the foundation of a compound wall perhaps.

Manish dismounted from his bike. *Was he doing the right thing? Should he call for backup? No. His boss was too crafty to fall into a trap. If he'd sensed something was off, he would have certainly summoned Manish for further investigation.* Reassured by this chain of reasoning underlying the unspoken monologue, Manish carefully approached the derelict structure, taking care to make as little sound as possible. Peering through the broken windows, he could see piles of rubble and splintered beer bottles, but these were old, coated with dust. There was no other sign of any human activity. He cautiously crept along the sides of the building, walking slowly. Suddenly, the hair on his neck stood up, and he sensed he wasn't alone.

'Raise your arms and turn around slowly,' a soft command reached his ears.

Manish was so surprised to hear that familiar voice that, throwing caution to the winds, he whirled around to see Isha standing akimbo, eyebrows raised. 'What the fuck are you doing here?' she asked him brusquely.

∽

Rakesh's piteous, febrile narrative finally concluded. Sangha heard this unveiling of her past poker-faced, without blinking an eye. At this point, Isha, who'd left the room in the middle of Rakesh's foray into the past, returned with Manish, who, the moment his eyes fell upon the prisoner, stood riveted to the spot.

'What the hell!' he exclaimed, and turned to look at Isha, his eyes wide with shock and wonder.

After giving him an earful for his underhandedness in tracking them to the safe house, the 'original' Isha got him up to speed as much as she could about her past and what the raid had unearthed.

While he was still trying to process this information, Manish's mobile pinged and he held up his hand to get their attention. He was looking at an app on his screen. 'We have a problem. I think this...errr...madam has a tracking chip. Isha, check her. Isha, do you hear me?'

Isha, absorbed in her thoughts, returned to the present moment.

'Yes, of course. Sure,' she responded and moved towards her sibling. Sangha hissed and cringed away from her advancing sister, but there was little the prisoner could do as Isha partially unbuttoned her shirt and started examining her shoulders. Moving towards the back, Isha swept aside the cascading curls and spotted a small scar near the nape of the neck. 'Yep, here it is,' she said, showing Manish a barely discernible blemish on the smooth gold of Sangha's skin.

'I've got a jamming software on the laptop which will stop the signal from this chip. Let me figure this out.'

'Why don't we move to the observation room? You can work comfortably from there, Manish,' Isha suggested. 'Baba, you also come. She will be fine here.'

∞

'I have a plan,' Isha said once they were all seated in the observation room, which got its name from the bank of monitors that recorded the visuals of the captive held in the basement.

Isha did not take long to relate the gist of her strategy. There was absolute silence in the room for about a couple of seconds. And then...

'You want to go to LalTara in place of that madam?' Manish exclaimed. 'Are you out of our fucking mind, Isha?' he yelled.

'I'm not out of my fucking mind, Manish,' she replied calmly, 'Four of our men are injured. Yadav is dead. Radu is missing. All this loss... Now just think about it... Bishen doesn't know that Sangha has a twin. I could gather so much information on LalTara from the inside. Then we can destroy them. I could also find out more about RED.'

'He's implanted a tracker in her, for God's sake. He may not trust her. He will also know that we have caught her. You think he's going to roll out a red carpet for her?' he retorted.

'That's precisely it!' Isha countered. 'The tracker means that Sangha's important to him. Because he values her, he won't finish her off in a hurry. Baba...' She looked at her father for support.

'Absolutely not!' Rakesh erupted. 'This is insane. I won't allow it.' *He'd just got his second daughter back. He would not—could not—lose the first one.*

Isha looked at her two companions grimly. She understood the plan was dangerous, possibly suicidal. But what mattered was that it could get them within striking distance of Bishen Rao. And she was not going to give up without an attempt to burn Bishen's Lanka[19] to ashes.

---

[19]Lanka: The flourishing kingdom of Ravana (adversary to Lord Rama) in the Indian epic Ramayana

10
Ghosts of the Past

Sangha realized she was in big trouble. She wasn't afraid, only somewhat uneasy. And shocked to see someone who looked so much like her; to hear her birth name known only to her and Suryamani. Suryamma! The closest being she'd known to a mother. A fleeting tenderness in the aridity of her existence...

❦

2005
Abujmarh

'Sanghu, Sanghukutti...'
Little Sangha, eight years old, was already emotionally scarred. *Why didn't her Appa[20] ever pull her close, pat her back, or even smile at her? He may be Bishen Rao to the rest of the world, why couldn't he just be her Appa?* she wondered wistfully. With no other children in the camp to play with, she had turned to drawing as a pastime and an outlet for self-expression. She'd drawn something once: the birds she saw in the sky, flying so high. But the shame, the embarrassment, the horror of being pushed away when she had run up to Appa to show her creative outpouring still made her cheeks feel warm, and eyes wet.

---
[20] Appa: Father. Also a honorific title—meaning administrator of a region—conferred on the Maratha rulers of Maharashtra and Karnataka

'Sangha, where are you dear?'

Amma's[21] voice pierced the little girl's ruminations. She swallowed the lump of emotion lodged in her throat.

'Yes, Amma, coming!'

'Where were you, child?' Suryamani chided when she saw Sangha. 'I've been calling you for so long! I've made your favourite *rava laddu* today. Come, have some.'

Always quiet and withdrawn, the girl seemed especially grave today. 'What happened, my child? Did you get into a fight?'

Sangha looked at Suryamani, the sun around whom she orbited. The girl wrapped her thin arms around her Amma's comforting softness, and inhaled her familiar fragrance, musky sweat mixed with coconut oil. Before she could stop herself, Sangha felt tears well up in her eyes and soak Amma's cotton sari.

Suryamani felt the girl's sniffles and gently prised her away. 'Come, let's sit and talk.' She took Sangha by her hand and led her to a crudely constructed hut they called home. Making the child sit on a *chatai*, she put a battered tin plate with the newly made sweet and a tumbler of water in front of her, and then took a seat next to her.

'Tell me, Sanghu. What happened?'

The girl whispered, 'Amma, why doesn't Appa like me?'

Suryamani caressed the girl's back gently. 'He's like that. You can't change him. All he understands is power. He has no affection for anyone. But you can get his attention and earn his respect if you are strong and clever. Be more. Be of use to him. Then he won't be able to shove you aside easily.' The woman's heart broke as she spoke these words to the

---

[21]Amma: Mother

child. *A child should not be burdened with such thoughts, not at this age. She should be laughing and playing, secure in the knowledge that she is loved, and has people who would keep her safe.* Suryamani wiped Sangha's eyes. 'Enough, my child. This too shall pass. I'm here for you. Always.'

Little did they know that fate had other plans for them.

⁂

2012
Abujmarh

Go beyond. Rise above yourself. Be more. Be strong and clever. Only then will Rao respect you. Suryamani's words after Sangha's emotional outburst seven years ago became a mantra for the girl, now fifteen years old.

Despite Suryamani's protests that she was too young to begin an intense exercise regime, Sangha had prevailed upon Kundan *Mama*[22] to create a gruelling routine for her. Amma had reluctantly relented, only after obtaining a promise that guns or other weapons would be off limits. *Never mind,* the girl thought to herself. *The time for weapons training would also come.*

Thus far, Sangha had carefully kept her head down before Rao. She had never again made the mistake of calling him 'Appa'. She stayed on the periphery of his existence. A shadowy, nebulous entity. However, just yesterday, when Kundan Mama had exulted in her improved five-kilometre run-time, she had caught Rao looking at her with narrowed eyes.

As she completed her final set of mountain climbers, enjoying the high induced by the adrenaline rush, she could

---
[22]Mama: Mother's brother

hear a raised voice nearby. *Rao was berating Suryamani again. And today, it seemed that he had started quite early in the day! Of late, the LalTara chief appeared to be more short-tempered than usual. And mostly, it was his wife who was at the receiving end.*

Sangha sighed. *She would have to soothe Amma again.* She was aware that her words could only work as a temporary salve. The wound would stay. After all, what solution could she offer Amma? It was not as if they could walk out and lead an independent life. She could visualize the scene. 'Something's not right, Sanghu,' Amma would wail. 'He was never this harsh. He goes away for days on end without telling me. It's all going wrong...'

Amma's grievances were valid. Although Sangha was unaware of the nature of Amma and Rao's marital relations, it was true they had never been this abusive or this public. Of late, Rao had increasingly been staying away from the camp for long spells. The LalTara grapevine hadn't thrown up any information about him. Not that it would; no one could get on Rao's wrong side and live to see another day.

The vituperation next door persisted. However, surprisingly, it was joined by Suryamani's raised voice. Soft, gentle Suryamani, who never had a harsh word for anyone, and who mostly avoided engaging with Rao when he was in one of his moods. *Why is she doing it today,* Sangha wondered, even as the sound of a slap abruptly stopped Suryamani mid-sentence. Sangha was shocked to see her Amma run out of the tent next door. She quickly followed.

Suryamani was stumbling towards the path that led into the forest.

'Amma! Amma! Stop!' Sangha called out to her mother, who seemed not to hear her.

When she caught up with the older woman, Sangha overtook her and blocked her way. They were out of the camp now, and almost at the edge of the forest.

'Amma, what happened? Please tell me.'

Suryamani looked at her daughter, at first unseeingly, and then noticed her worried eyes, trembling lips and creased forehead. She drew a ragged breath.

'Child, it's all over. He has someone else in his life. She will arrive here by this evening.'

∽

When Sangha first set eyes on Marachhiya, she couldn't understand what Rao saw in her. Her nose was too flat, her lips were too wide, and she had large hips. True, her hair was lustrous and thick, but what of it? So was Amma's. But as the days passed, she noticed the men in the camp eyeing the newcomer furtively, admiration dripping from their eyes. Sangha felt compelled to look at Marachhiya again. Imagining herself as a man this time, she saw the glowing skin, taut breasts and a flat stomach. She also observed how the woman dressed to accentuate these traits.

Accompanying the unwanted newcomer were her aunt Phoolma and Tej, Phoolma's son. You could tell they were related; all three had the same dark skin, squashed noses, and a certain slowness about their thick frames. But where Marachhiya's heavyset body oozed sensuality, her relatives' physicality suggested latent strength.

Following this intrusion—Sangha perceived it as no less than that—Amma had moved in with her. Phoolma, too, was directed to share the same cramped quarters, while Tej was placed with the young men. Sangha soon learnt that Phoolma's cheerful maternal demeanour and her personality were poles apart. Innocent conversations between Sangha and her Amma were twisted out of context and presented to Marachhiya—who then passed on warped facts to Bishen. Phoolma also took over Amma's kitchen, severing that last bond between husband and wife. Bishen's domestic life now became the exclusive responsibility of Marachhiya and her aunt.

Sidelined and neglected, Suryamani appeared to be drifting in life. She lost interest in things and stopped caring, even for Sangha. This usually impeccably groomed woman wandered around with unkempt hair and grimy clothes. The two usurpers used her appearance to fuel Bishen's irritation.

Into this explosive, tinder-dry situation came the incendiary news that Marachhiya was with child. When Sangha reflected on the events that unfolded from there on, she realized that this was the definitive moment that destroyed her life as she knew it.

One fateful day, Suryamani disappeared from the camp in the morning. Given her erratic behaviour, people had long stopped bothering about her whereabouts. But Sangha was worried. Ignoring her breakfast and exercise gear, she headed towards the forest clearing which was Suryamani's favourite haunt. But her Amma wasn't there. While Sangha stood in the middle of the clearing, puzzled and unsure of what to do next, she heard a rustle behind her. Turning around, she saw Suryamani step into the clearing, clutching a bunch of leaves in her hand. However, as soon as Suryamani saw Sangha, she quickly hid whatever she held under her saree's *pallu*.

'What are you doing here?' Her voice was dry, lifeless.

'I came looking for you, Amma. What's this?' Sangha replied, pointing to the concealed bundle.

'You don't need to know. Go back. I'll follow in a while.'
'But Amma...'
'Go back, I said,' Suryamani shouted, 'or have you also stopped listening to me?'

That afternoon, just after lunch, there was a commotion in Bishen and Marachhiya's quarters.

Bishen stepped out of the tent and yelled, 'Get the doctor. There's something wrong with Mara.' As someone sped away in the camp vehicle, Sangha hurried towards the couple's quarters.

Marachhiya lay on the floor in a pool of her own vomit. Phoolma cradled her head in her lap. Even as Sangha entered, Marachhiya retched violently, bringing up rancid stomach juices.

'Someone's cast an evil eye on my child,' Phoolma cried. 'My child, my darling, tell me what happened.'

'That juice... Suryamani...' quavered Marachhiya, feebly pointing to a steel tumbler.

Sangha felt a tightness in her stomach. She remembered her Amma holding a bunch of green leaves in her hands.

Bishen strode back into the tent in time to hear Marachhiya's response. He picked up the tumbler and sniffed it.

'What is it? Show it to me,' Phoolma demanded. As she repeated Bishen's action, she went still and then started to tremble vehemently. 'Datura,'[23] she screeched. 'She's given her datura.'

Bishen heard her words but didn't seem to comprehend them. 'What are you saying? Suryamani has poisoned Mara?'

---

[23]Datura: A genus comprising nine species of highly poisonous, vespertine-flowering plants belonging to the nightshade family

'Why don't you ask that bitch?' The old woman screamed.

For Sangha, the rest of the day was a blur. As if in a dream, she saw Bishen rush out of the tent and felt herself following him, jostling for space in the crowd that had gathered at the entrance.

'Rao, sir, please...' her entreaties fell on deaf ears. She heard Kundan Mama instructing her to stay out of the matter, assuring her that he would handle the situation.

But Bishen seemed like a man possessed, beyond all pleading. He strode towards Suryamani and Sangha's quarters, where his wife sat in a corner, rocking back and forth, moaning to herself.

'What did you do?' Bishen shouted. 'What did you do?'

'What had to be done,' his wife retorted. 'What ought to have been done a long time ago.'

Before Sangha could intervene, Bishen had whipped out his gun.

'No! No! Rao, please,' Sangha tried to reach for the gun, for the arm that held the gun, anything that would deflect the aim he had taken.

'If anything happens to the baby...' Bishen thundered.

'The bastard baby...' Suryamani's face twisted in a semblance of a smile.

With that, Bishen snapped, and the sound of gunshot filled the tent. Bishen departed as Suryamani fell, clutching her stomach, where a crimson rose had suddenly bloomed.

Sangha felt her legs turn to rubber. She somehow ran towards her fallen mother and sank down beside her.

'Amma! Amma! Amma!' The one word that meant the world to her. She could not stop repeating it. Suryamani opened her eyes. She wheezed.

'Sanghukutti, my child,' she whispered. 'I'm so, so sorry. I tried to protect you. I failed.'

Her eyes closed, but her chest still rose and fell. Barely.

'Amma! Please, please don't leave me. Please...' Sangha blubbered.

Suryamani's lips moved again. 'I am...not your Amma.'

Sangha moved closer, thinking she'd misheard her mother. She dropped her head closer to Suryamani's.

'Amma, what did you say?'

'I'm not your mother.'

'Amma, why are you saying this? Don't, please don't,' Sangha begged.

'Mitali...her name was Mitali. Rao's sister...your mother. He killed her too. You are her daughter, Eka...but my Sanghu. Remember...bracelet with your name.'

Sangha gasped as though someone had punched her in the solar plexus. 'No, no, no,' she kept chanting hysterically. *Nothing was as it seemed. Her mother wasn't her mother. Rao had killed the woman who had birthed her. Her name was Eka?* Her small world whirled around her in a mad dance. Suddenly, she became aware of Suryamani's feeble movements.

'Hold my hand, don't leave... Sanghu...' Suryamani mumbled. Sangha enclosed the dying woman's hand in hers. She could see her tears mingling with Suryamani's blood. This mixing of bodily fluids wrought a primal connection between the two of them, even if they hadn't been joined by an umbilical cord. A bond that would never go away.

Through blurry eyes, Sangha noticed that Suryamani's gaze was centred on her face. The woman's lips moved and shaped a single word: 'Sangha'. Her eyes closed. And with that, Sangha's world, with her Amma at its centre, plunged into darkness forever.

2025
The Rowghat safe house

Sitting in front of Rakesh and Isha, Sangha felt that the world she knew had started to disintegrate once more. *Was this man really her father? And this imposter who'd stolen her face? Was she really her sister? It had to be. Who else would know her secret? But...*

She hated this feeling of uncertainty. She had to get back in control.

11
The Day of the Dead

2025
One week later
Raipur

The mood was sombre in the large hall. People conversed in hushed tones near a line of garlanded photographs, arranged on an altar-like platform at one end of the room, which were the focus of their attention. A row of chairs arranged parallel to the altar seated groups of people—families of the heroes lost in action. Heart-wrenching sobs, swiftly suppressed, erupted sporadically from them.

Isha stood beside her father in a corner and quietly observed this scene. Outwardly composed, her heart rattled against her ribcage like an enraged animal. Radu Sinha, missing, presumed dead. Ram Yadav, martyred. Saud Shaikh, also martyred. He had died on the operating table. Three more commandos still in the ICU. She didn't know them very well, but they were as real as the others—who she knew and worked with every day. They too had families: parents, wives, children, friends and colleagues.

She wanted to scream. She wanted to shake up her father, make him see how self-centred he was being in the face of all the lives they had lost. They'd barely spoken since their last conversation at the safe house. She was aware that he sensed her anger and anguish. She knew too, that he was devastated by the price they'd paid for the operation. That morning, she'd noticed the tremor in his hands as he tied his shoelaces. *Why, Baba, why don't you see what I see?*

Suddenly there was a flurry of activity near the door. People respectfully moved aside to make room for a newcomer. Binod Rawat walked in, hands folded, face solemn. He was the home minister of Chhattisgarh and her father's close acquaintance. With his short, rotund frame, and his pink, shining visage, he looked like an amiable uncle next door who always brought you treats. Like Santa Claus minus the facial hair, and much more impeccably attired. However, Isha mostly admired his political acumen, foresight, and ability to pour oil over troubled waters. He was even known in political circles as an all-round good guy. Today, his normally cheerful face was clouded with sadness. He signalled his entourage to stay behind as he walked up to the improvised altar. Head bowed and eyes closed, Rawat stood silently in front of the photographs for a minute. He then opened his eyes and looked at each photograph intently, as if to memorize their faces, before he turned and walked away. He nodded in acknowledgement when he spotted Isha, and beckoned to Rakesh.

Isha felt Rakesh's hand on her shoulder. 'I have to speak to Rawat-ji. I'll see you later,' he said before leaving her side.

Grim-faced, Isha nodded, her eyes fixed on the photographs at the end of the hallway.

The crowd surrounding Rawat gently parted as the minister motioned the throng of people to let Rakesh through.

'Whatever happened wasn't good,' the minister's tone was chilly. He confronted Rakesh as soon as he approached. Generally effusive and charming, Rawat obviously didn't feel the necessity for niceties under the present circumstances.

'You made me and my office look like fools, Srivastava, by not keeping us in the loop.'

'Rawat-ji, sir, time was of the essence. We intercepted a critical message for an important shipment delivery within our jurisdiction. To go through the proper channels would have meant...'

'These proper channels, Srivastava, are the ones standing between you and a court-martial,' the home minster interjected through clenched teeth. 'Do you have any idea how many strings I've had to pull to save your hide?' Rakesh was aware that if they were standing anywhere else, Rawat's avatar would have been very different.

'I apologize, sir, I...'

'If this mission must continue, I need to be kept in the loop. Properly. Do you understand?'

'Yes, sir. It will be as you say.'

The minister's stance eased somewhat following Rakesh's apology. Sighing, he clasped Rakesh's hands in his. 'We're in the same team, Srivastava. Never forget that,' he said softly.

⁂

While her father was speaking with the minister, Isha approached the other Team Alpha members attending the event. No words could describe their feelings, and none were exchanged. They stood together as a group, united in grief, affiliated by loss. Just then, there was a hubbub in the row of mourners sitting in front, close to the altar. A young woman seemed to have fainted. Family members and strangers anxiously flocked around her.

'That's Radu's wife Pooja, isn't it?' Isha asked the person standing next to her.

'Yes, Madam-ji,' he whispered in her ear. 'She's in a very bad way. They say she's pregnant.'

Isha clenched her fists. She felt breathless. A series of scenes flashed before her mind's eye. *Radu babbling on about his wife, and how he needed some personal time off; Isha promising that he could take his leave after the mission; the powerful man clobbering Radu in the head and then pushing him into the stream.* Isha felt the bile rise up to her throat. She closed her eyes. Breathe in. Breathe out. Inhale, exhale. When she felt more in control, she opened her eyes and walked ahead towards the ring of people surrounding the young woman who seemed to have revived. Someone cleared a path for her. Isha squatted down next to Pooja—a young girl, actually—and grasped her hand.

Isha's first glimpse of Pooja had been as a shy bride, resplendent in red and bedecked with jewellery, with demurely downcast kohl-rimmed eyes that must have held a thousand dreams. As a soldier's wife, the danger of losing one's spouse is always real. But this was too soon. Too premature. Their lives were just starting. Isha looked at her. Pooja's eyes were red and puffy, her attire askew, and her delicate features engorged with grief.

'Pooja,' she called out gently.

The girl glanced at her with unseeing eyes, and continued to keen. Gradually her sobs subsided, recognition dawned in her eyes. When she realized who was holding her hand, she withdrew it as if scalded. Isha flinched and swallowed a sudden lump in her throat. She felt tears prick her eyes. She stood up, folded her hands in a farewell greeting at the family, and left.

An hour later, father and daughter headed back home in their car. Rakesh hadn't spoken a word; neither had Isha. He looked straight ahead seemingly focused on the road. She felt emotionally drained and rested her head against the window. However, she couldn't close her eyes. Every time she tried, she could vividly see Pooja snatch her hand away from her, a simple gesture of horror speaking a thousand words. That single act caused the anger which had receded to a corner of her mind to surge forward with a roar. Isha sat up straight and turned to her father.

'After this morning, do you still think you can afford to be selfish?' she asked him in an even tone.

She observed her father clench his teeth before releasing his breath slowly. 'Beta, how do you plan to pull this off? It's insane. Eka has grown up before Bishen's eyes. He knows her. It's not a simple question of just switching dolls, my dear.'

'Really, Baba? You think I would propose something like this without considering it carefully? Without conducting any research or understanding the possibilities?' Isha fumed.

'That's not what I...'

'Doppelgangers have been employed in the past; by Napoleon, by Roosevelt, no less. Just look it up, Baba. And here I am, an identical twin!'

'It's easy to say, but quite a different ballgame to execute.'

'So we don't do anything, is it? We shall continue to let Bishen kill people, destroy lives. Just because we're afraid to try. Baba, it makes me culpable in Radu's death. And you too! Think about Radu's unborn child! You're okay to let it grow up without a father, but you are afraid of losing your own daughter?'

Even though he didn't utter a word, Rakesh's grip on the steering wheel of the car tightened. Looking at his white face, Isha immediately felt aghast that she'd spoken to her Baba in that tone.

'Baba, I'm sorry...'

'No, beta, I'm sorry. I understand I have been a selfish coward. I could not bear it if anything happened to you too.' He turned to look into her eyes. 'Promise me you'll come back alive.'

12

The Turn of the Key

2025
The day after the memorial
The Rowghat safe house

Sangha had barely finished her breakfast when Isha walked into the pantry. With a scowl on her face, Sangha stood up to stride towards the door, using the back of her hand to wipe the remnants of an overly sweet tea—the one bright spot in her morning—from her lips. She had the freedom of moving freely within the safe house. *And why wouldn't they allow her that much? The place was high on surveillance, and all the doors were equipped with access control. No dangerous weapons of any sort were allowed to lie around. The only room not being monitored was the bathroom, and its window had thick, immovable bars.*

'Sangha, can we talk?' Isha requested.

Sangha stopped and faced Isha, eyebrows raised.

'Please, let's sit. This may take a while,' replied Isha, offering her a chair.

Sangha stifled a sigh as she took the chair by its back, turned it around and sat down, straddling it, with her arms on the backrest.

Isha pulled up another chair and sat down, facing Sangha. 'Listen, I don't know what your deal with LalTara is, but you can have a better life,' Isha began. 'You have me and Baba. You have a home with us. But until LalTara is destroyed, we can never be at peace. You know that. I have thought of a way to do this. Help me to go to Abujmarh in your place. I have the support of the task force to sort this out once and for all.'

As she spoke, Isha could see a slideshow of emotions run across Sangha's face. Disbelief, surprise, incredulity, and then suddenly, all that was wiped off as Sangha clenched her teeth and her breathing became ragged.

Sangha closed her eyes as her mind whirled with a welter of emotions, red-hot rage ruling the jumble. *This woman, this woman with a perfect life, who had a protective father and everything nice, wanted to emulate her? Take her place! Her! The terror of Abujmarh? How would she fit into her shoes? How could she slip into her skin—she who had experienced years of pain, trauma and rigour? Did she really believe that it would be as easy as everything else that had been handed to her on a silver platter?*

Sangha was about to decline the proposal haughtily when a tiny voice piped into her ear. *Come on*, it said. *Listen to what she's saying. Understand what it means. Consider it! Think! It could be your key to freedom! Swapping roles with Isha meant that this idiot would step into LalTara as her, with a tracking chip inserted in the nape of her neck. Chip! Yes, that's it! Her tracking chip...how could she have forgotten that? They'd have to get it off her, wouldn't they, if this insane plan was to work? And if she was freed of that one thing that fettered her to LalTara...* Sangha's arms stippled with goosebumps at the prospect of freedom.

As it is, conditions at the camp were becoming precarious. Sangha was certain that Bishen was planning something. She had witnessed many sly, secretive glances exchanged between him and Marachhiya. They obviously wouldn't discuss anything openly, but something was definitely brewing. Her mind turned to that evening when her worst fears were confirmed.

⁓

Five months ago
Abujmarh

Sangha had set out for her hour-long run at sunset. She loved her nightly workout routine when her breath dissolved in the silence of the jungle. These times of solitude often tested her courage; a jog into the dense jungle at night was not for the faint-hearted. She had barely started her run when a misstep caused her to twist and sprain her ankle, not badly, but enough to make her turn back. Hobbling back into the camp from the jungle, she crossed Rao's tent. As she approached it, she could hear the sounds of love-making—which quickly reached a crescendo with a climax, and then dropped into pleased laughter and soft mutterings. *The rutting bastard and his whore,* she thought sourly, *discussing sweet nothings, no doubt.* The sound of her name suddenly arrested her limping progress. Normally, she'd never stoop to eavesdropping, but this she could not miss. She crept closer to the room, wincing with every step, yet being careful to be quiet.

'Mara, just be a little patient, will you? And try to be nicer to Sangha. Don't spoil things. We're nearing the end,' Bishen's hoarse voice was laced with tenderness. *An emotion reserved only for that bitch and their daughter Lipi.*

'Rao, I'm counting the days. We have to get our daughter out of here. This isn't the right place to bring up a child. I've told you many times before. Get me and my daughter out of here,' she reiterated.

'You know everything is falling into place. All this takes time,' Bishen explained to her impatiently, in a tone of voice that was sounding increasingly irritated. 'I can't hurry it. People will suspect. The funds have been stowed away for us. The account that we can sacrifice has Sangha's name. Just give it time,' he hissed.

So this was the game! Bishen had indeed opened an offshore account recently, and made her the operating authority. She had unsuspectingly signed on the dotted line and provided her biometrics. Bishen's disappearance along with his family, and the maelstrom that would ensue thereafter, would certainly put her in a compromising position. When things went south, she knew Bishen would offer her as a sacrificial lamb—it was her biometric signature on the account, after all.

༄

2025
The Rowghat safe house

Sangha returned to the present to continue musing along a different track. *What would happen to LalTara post Bishen? There were many who thought they could fill the power vacuum. Many murderous, evil people. Tej, with his lust for young boys and blood; Rambhakt, who worshipped power; Kundan Mama—who had been waiting so long in the wings—would emerge from the shadows. All of them would want the throne, or certainly a piece of the pie. LalTara would be as red as its name if Bishen left. Infighting would follow. Deaths were a certainty. Where would that leave her?*

It wouldn't be a bad deal in this situation, would it, to

let this idiot go to her death? Her inner voice cackled. *This woman has had it easy. So far, anyway.*

Sangha opened her eyes, and spoke for the first time in days: 'So, what's your plan?'

13

The Plan

2025
The Rowghat safe house

Rakesh sat staring down at the table, rubbing the side of his nose. *Damn! He'd have to break this habit somehow. Mitali used to joke about it. You'll never be able to fool me because of your tell, she'd say. The moment you're stressed, or you are lying, you fiddle with your nose. She was right. Whether it was worrying news at work, Bishen Rao-related intel, or mundane household matters, this nose-rubbing was the first sign that gave away the fact that something was bothering him.*

After he had heard Isha's daring plan, and the first wave of alarm had somewhat ebbed, he could see the merit in her scheme. Yet, fear for his daughter's well-being far outweighed his desire for revenge—until Isha's persistent hammering had gradually broken down his resolve. However, even though he maintained an enthused front, the knot of unease in his stomach was still coiled tightly. He didn't want Isha to worry because he was anxious!

When Rakesh looked up, he saw Eka...no, Sangha's grave face across the table. He had spoken to her about Mitali, about her dreams for their daughters. He had replayed those wonderful, joyful days again and again, but never approached the tragedy of losing his wife and daughter that had inked their lives forever. They'd had their fill of that; it was now time for something good, with Eka back in their lives. Slowly, over the days, Rakesh had witnessed the aggression of a hurt animal give way to a wary acceptance of their friendly overtures, a certain relaxation of her usual tautness. Yet, he sensed the way ahead was not easy. His primary concern was that Isha's success in LalTara depended on Eka. Just then, Isha walked in. Rakesh was too late in expunging the worried look from his face.

'Baba, everything will work out fine,' his daughter said, reaching out to hold Rakesh's hand in reassurance. 'I know, Sangha will have my back. Trust her, Baba. She is your daughter. She will do the right thing.'

He peered into Sangha's eyes to search for the truth. They were dark and distant, and he could read nothing. *Could he trust the girl who had been raised by the devil himself?*

'I can help, sir,' Sangha said, pulling up her unruly hair and tying it in an untidy knot.

'You can call him "Baba",' Isha remarked gently to her sibling.

Sangha felt a strange constriction of emotions in her throat. 'Baba,' she uttered softly, hesitatingly, as if tentatively savouring the unfamiliar warmth of that word on her tongue. *Can I get comfortable with this? Should I?* she thought. *No, no...she and father figures didn't mix well.* Unaware of her internal turmoil, Rakesh's heart fluttered with excitement on hearing the word, like a caged bird on the verge of being released. He couldn't take his eyes off her face: with her hair tied up and a new tenderness in her eyes, he could clearly see the differences blurring between his two girls.

Isha pulled up a chair beside Sangha and grasped her hand. 'My life and this mission depend on you, Sangha. Help me become you.' Isha was certain that once she had camouflaged herself in the skin of her sister, learnt to walk, talk and be like her, she would find a way to deceive Bishen and infiltrate LalTara's heart.

Even as they sat there, Manish was busy in the next room, remotely monitoring the development of a software programme that would create a virtual rendition of the terrain of LalTara's jungle domain, thanks to Sangha's inputs. Eyes closed tightly and forehead creased with concentration, she had meticulously described the territory her sister would soon encounter. He had marvelled at her powers of observation and recollection. With this programme, Isha would learn to navigate the real landscape after practising on the digital version. This was as much for her safety as it was to make Sangha's replacement more authentic.

'This information will remain classified, and does not go beyond the walls of this holding room,' Rakesh said sternly. His daughters nodded in unison.

'Now I know it too, so you'll have to kill me,' Manish quipped, walking in. Seeing Isha's deadpan expression, he cleared his throat and became all business suddenly. 'Team, the virtual reality is going super well. We should be ready to test soon.'

Isha fist-pumped hard, glee written all over her face.

'You know,' Manish said, smiling at Isha's enthusiasm, 'we need to name this operation. Ummm, Mission Red Star for LalTara? Or Abujmarh Assignment, or...'

'How about Operation Trojan Horse?' Isha suggested, asking the room at large. Noticing Sangha's raised eyebrows, Isha hastened to explain: 'Just like in the Greek classic, I'll infiltrate the enemy camp impersonating you. And destroy them to win...'

Before Isha's explanation drew to a close, Manish clapped her on the back.

'Super! Operation Trojan Horse it is!'

Isha smiled, and impulsively, pulled her father and sister into a group hug. Sangha squirmed, but Isha clutched her more tightly. Seeing the family huddle, Manish broke out into an ill-timed song: '*Itne bazu itne sar, ginle dushman dhyan se*,'[24] he hummed, breaking into mock applause, and completely diluting an intense emotional moment. Spontaneously, Isha piped in, '*Harega wo har baazi, jab khele hum ji jaan se*,'[25] to complete the song, her spirits back in swing as she pulled Manish too into the huddle.

For Manish, being around Isha made him feel strong and brave. He dearly wished that he had mustered the courage to bare his heart to her before she was whisked off her feet by the handsome and idealistic Neel Saini. He was happy, however, to be a part of a secret in her life in which Neel could not be included.

In the basement of a dilapidated house, remotely tucked away on the outskirts of a town, a secret known only to four people marked the countdown to the launch of Operation Trojan Horse. It was time for the hard work to begin.

---

[24]Lyrics translation: 'So many arms, so many heads, let the enemy count them carefully.' Song from the Hindi film *Main Azaad Hoon* (1989)

[25]Lyrics translation: 'He will lose every battle, when we play with our heart and strength.' Song from the Hindi film *Main Azaad Hoon* (1989)

14

The Journey to Hell

2025
The Rowghat safe house

Rakesh and Manish had planned it all like a complex jigsaw. Only they could see the complete picture. No one else would be cued into the entire plan. Sangha's shared facial characteristics with Isha was an opportunity too good to be lost if they were to bring LalTara to its knees. The operation kicked off with the removal of the tracking chip embedded in Sangha's body nearly a month ago. They'd called in Dr Saurabh Munshi, a discreet neurosurgeon from Delhi, who covertly worked with STF19 and never asked any questions. In a small, sterilized operation theatre, he had carefully removed the chip from Sangha and implanted it in the exact position on Isha's neck.

Manish ensured that the jammer continued to operate without letting out even a whimper of a signal from the tracker. He then strapped a jammer-wristband on Isha to doubly make sure that the tracker would not misbehave. All the data relating to Dr Munshi's moonlighting operation was deleted, following which the good doctor returned to Delhi.

Today would mark another milestone in their mission which would bring them another step closer to transforming one twin into the other. Although Isha had faced the surgeon's knife during the chip insertion with equanimity, what she was to deal with today was another matter altogether. Currently, she was ensconced in the object of her nightmares—the dentist's chair. She closed her eyes and drew a ragged breath. The scene from yesterday evening replayed in her mind. Manish holding up in front of her a plaster impression of Sangha's upper and lower teeth, and a set of dental X-rays like miniature trophies.

'The good news is that your bite and teeth alignment are nearly identical to Sangha. The bad news is that she has a missing molar and you don't,' he had said, smiling a little as Isha winced.

The forty minutes that followed were one of the slowest in her life. Every prick and every bone-juddering pull took on a slow-mo quality, until finally, mercifully, the trusted dentist completed the task and her ordeal came to an end.

She was now back at the safe house, where, with an ice pack pressed tightly over her swollen cheek, Isha studied the briefing note Rakesh had jotted down for her, to undergo the physical transformation into Sangha. Having finished that, she picked up the 3D-printed mask of Sangha's face that Manish had created. Once the swelling on her face subsided, she would put it on to check if her face matched that of her sister, feature for feature. This way, they would be absolutely certain that Isha looked like an exact copy of her twin.

She nudged Manish who sat next to her, pointed to the mask, and gave an enthusiastic thumbs-up.

'What?' he feigned incomprehension.

Isha slapped her forehead. 'Candawk,' she mumbled.

'Huh?' Manish replied. 'Oh! Can't talk? Mouth's still numb, huh? Ah! So, you like the mask!'

Isha nodded enthusiastically.

'Thanks,' her colleague smiled. 'Apart from this mask, Sangha has a subtle scar near the heart, from a knife wound,' Manish said, as he showed Isha the images of a long, almost faded skin scar. 'Tomorrow, our dear old plastic surgeon Dr Joshi will knock you out, and render the final touches with his nimble fingers,' he added.

Isha nodded again. *Easy peasy. Anything, as long as it didn't involve a dentist!*

༄

Three weeks passed, and her training continued. Manish had captured Sangha's movements, posture, ways of sitting, talking and eating on camera, so that Isha could continue to observe and learn to emulate her twin. He would have liked to film Sangha's dreams too, if he could. He was aware how crucial these nuances and minute details were for Isha's survival in enemy territory. The outcome of all the hard work was encouraging. Just like their faces, the differentiating lines between Isha and Sangha's mannerisms and attitudes were dissolving.

It was a typical morning for the core team of Operation Trojan Horse. They were seated around a table in the safe house, planning, evaluating possibilities, and then re-planning.

'Before I left, there was a very strong buzz about the arrival of a consignment that Kundan Mama called RED. It was being spoken of as the biggest deal LalTara had ever done and I remember Bishen mentioning that this deal would change everything for us,' said Sangha, blowing into her cup of jaggery-saturated, caffeine-drenched tea to manoeuvre the thin layer of skin that had formed on the surface of the over-boiled decoction to one side. She sipped at it with a grunt of satisfaction, and put the cup down.

'Isha,' she said, addressing her sister, 'I hope you've done the homework and learnt what I gave you on Rao's people. Who's who, what each one does, and my relationship with them.'

'Yes, I think I've wrapped my head around that. Let's go over it once more, shall we? In fact, let's go through the entire operation.'

Rakesh took the lead and highlighted the strategy. Once Isha, posing as Sangha, was safely entrenched in LalTara, she would gather information on the outfit's illegal activities. The aim was to undermine their trade in whichever way possible. RED was the other high-priority target. Isha would have to ascertain how the Abujmarh outlaws were involved in this deal, and how Rao personally stood to gain from it. She would also confirm Sangha's fears about Rao fleeing the country with his partner and daughter. All the intel that Isha gathered would be conveyed to STF19 via the elaborate communication system Manish had painstakingly configured for this operation.

While the sisters listened to this recapitulation with rapt attention, Manish surreptitiously swapped Sangha's cup with Isha's, containing a lemongrass infusion. Half a minute later, Isha reached for what she thought was her cup and took a sip.

'What the fuck,' she sputtered as a strong, unfamiliar taste flooded her mouth. Immediately, she looked at Manish accusingly. Only he could play pranks like this. 'Manish!'

'Get used to it, madam. This is what Sangha drinks and you will too, from now on. Boss's order,' he grinned.

While Manish and Isha were engaged in this heated banter, they missed seeing Sangha lightly pick up Isha's cup of lemongrass tea and sip it just like her. It seemed Sangha, too, was mapping Isha.

∽

That evening, while Rakesh was sitting in his room and going through the minutiae of the operation, he heard a knock on the half-open door. He looked up to see Sangha standing with her right arm folded behind her back and her right hand holding her left elbow. *This was a stance she'd adopted even as a child,* he mused. *In fact, both he and Mitali had used this behavioural trait to tell the girls apart.* He smiled at the memory. Sangha broke her position to knock again, sharply this time, bringing him back to the present.

'Yes, beta. Come in,' he responded.

His daughter put a sheaf of papers on his table, and laid them out in a matrix, the lines from one sheet flowing onto the next. 'It's ready. What you'd asked me to prepare. Here's the map leading from Abujmarh into the camp and the maze within LalTara,' she said. Rakesh tensed somewhat on hearing Sangha's words. *This meant it would soon be time for Isha to leave.*

Just then, his other daughter walked in. 'Oh great, the terrain maps are ready. Good going, Sangha.'

Rakesh motioned for Sangha to continue.

'Someone not familiar with the terrain would take the jungle route to reach the camp. But there is a shorter, but more dangerous, option,' Sangha continued. Looking at Isha, she asked, 'Do you swim well?'

Before her sister could reply, Rakesh interjected: 'She has never lost the gold medal in marathon swimming and always been the last swimmer to finish a relay.'

'This is the Indravati, not a placid pool,' snapped Sangha,

pointing, with her pencil, to a sinuous form that wound through her hand-drawn sketches. 'The river current is erratic as it flows down the ravine.' She straightened her spine and stood akimbo. 'Most won't even venture into this water, but I have swum through it several times.' She turned to Isha and continued in a challenging tone: 'If you take this route to return, Rao will not have a shadow of a doubt that it's me.'

'Okay then. I am ready,' her sister replied.

Before Rakesh could respond, Manish flung open the door, looked at both the girls, and started clapping exaggeratedly and dramatically.

'Congratulations, you two! You've done it!' he exclaimed.

'What have they done?' Rakesh asked. Receiving no response to his question, he turned to his daughters. He saw Sangha's eyes softening and lips curling up into a smile—just like Isha's. 'Sangha, your smile... You and Isha have the same smile!' he marvelled.

'That's because she is not Sangha. She's Isha,' interjected Manish. 'We knew you had reservations about the next lap of the mission. You weren't confident about the switch. So, we—Isha, Sangha and I—planned this. If we could pass your test, then we wouldn't have to worry about anyone else.'

Rakesh felt a mix of emotions. He was pleased, irritated and sad at the same time. Happy, because they had achieved what they set out to do; annoyed, because he—who had brought up his little girl mostly as a single parent—believed he knew his daughter better than anyone else; and sad, because now there was no turning back! The others saw these emotions play across his face.

'Trust me sir, I have her covered,' Manish tried to reassure Rakesh, hoping it would quieten the storm his boss was obviously experiencing. 'I have set up a satellite connection for her to communicate with us, which will remain masked from LalTara's signal readers. It will remain planted in a hidden location in the forest, as marked by Sangha. It will be shrouded and invisible. Isha only needs to reach that point to connect with us. Any time she needs an extraction, Isha just needs to send a signal from there and we will get her back,' Manish said, sounding confident, but his fingers were crossed behind his back. He knew better than anyone that fieldwork rarely went according to plan.

∞

Finally, the day arrived when Rakesh, Manish, Isha and Sangha stood by the Indravati's turbulent waters, hoping that its current would safely carry Isha to LalTara. While the river's churning, turbid waters mirrored Rakesh's internal upheaval, for Isha, their energy was infectious.

Isha lifted her gaze and looked at her father. Her heart trembled as it perceived the feeling of dread Rakesh was trying so hard to conceal. She gave him a quick hug and a salute. 'I promise I shall see you soon, Baba.'

'See that you do, beta. I'm not a rock. I won't be able to withstand more trauma. I've had enough to last me a lifetime.'

Isha embraced him, listening to their hearts beat as one, just as she had done as a little girl. Tearing herself away from her father, she turned to Manish and Sangha. 'Guys, take care. Sangha, look after Baba.' Briefly, her thoughts flew to Neel. She'd spoken to him a couple of days ago, distracted and fretful because she could not tell him about the mission. The video connection with Neel in London had been poor, sending her pixellated, broken images of the one person she cherished as much as Baba.

The audio quality had been equally bad. It was as if the universe was telling her to stay mum about her plans. Isha was optimistic. *Hopefully, she would be back before he returned; the operation would be closed, and they would be able to continue as if nothing had happened.*

'*Seva Parmo Dharma*,' Isha closed her eyes and whispered this call—'service before self'—from her training days, under her breath. *She would require every ounce of strength from her body and mind on this perilous mission.* She opened her eyes and looked at the trio standing in front of her. Baba and Manish looked worried, but she couldn't decipher the emotion on Sangha's face. 'I shall be back soon,' Isha tried to smile.

She then turned to face the dark, swirling waters that challenged her, breathed deeply, closed her eyes, and took the leap of faith. The sharpness of the cold, stinging water felt almost like a physical blow. For Isha, the river's powerful current presented a more formidable challenge. Sangha had warned her about the Indravati's might, but however Isha may have prepared herself mentally, the reality of it was something else altogether. She felt herself being swept away by the river's vigour. She gritted her teeth and struck out, focusing on her limbs, driving all her energy their way. *One, two. One, two. Yes, that's it! Keep going, keep going.* But after twenty minutes of this gruelling activity, Isha felt her strength ebbing into her watery surroundings.

The going became tough. Indravati started to drag Isha into her dark depths, but each time Isha kicked the waters and surfaced, coughing and spluttering. But not for long. The river tugged harder and Isha went under again. *This couldn't be the end! Baba! Neel! She wanted to see them again, be with them again. There was so much she had to tell Neel.*

About her mother, about where she came from, and what had happened to her. About her twin sister. She wanted to tell Baba how much she loved...

Isha's struggles weakened. Her body went limp, and like a piece of flotsam, she was carried away by the Indravati's relentless waters.

PART TWO

Double Trouble

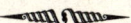

15

Breaking News

2025
LalTara headquarters

LalTara's search for Sangha had been futile. Kundanlal had roped in all their resources and his network of informants. Yet the exercise had not yielded any clues as to her whereabouts. The tracker chip they had installed in Sangha's body was useful insofar as it was live. With it being dead, running her to ground became that much more challenging. It was as if she had disappeared from the face of this earth.

It's been more than a month. Why is Sangha's GPS chip silent? Bishen wondered, not for the first time, as he emptied the full six rounds of his Korth Ranger pistol on the bull's eye of the shootboard, cleanly sieving its centre. Firearm practice was a daily ritual at LalTara. Guns and cartridges were available in abundance, and every soldier in the camp seriously worked to improve their marksmanship, skill and accuracy.

As Bishen left the shooting booth, Tej stepped in. Hot-headed and insolent, the thirty-year-old gave a brief, respectful nod to Bishen, the power of his squat body tempered by obeisance towards his commander. Phoolma's son had risen in the ranks at LalTara owing to his sharp intellect, devious thinking, and a penchant for violence.

Bishen patted the younger man on his shoulder as he stepped away, towards Rambhakt, who stood nearby. Taut as a spring and supple as a tender bamboo stalk, Rambhakt was one more person Bishen relied on to run his day-to-day operations, and he'd proved especially adept at assessing the purity of drugs. Small and wiry, he'd seen his family being wiped out in the skirmishes between the Naxals and the police. His hatred for both drew him to LalTara and eventually, he made his place within its commander's inner circle. Tej, Rambhakt and Kundanlal—who still remained loyal to Bishen—formed the three pillars of support for Bishen.

'Ask Kundanlal to see me, Ram,' LalTara's supremo ordered Rambhakt.

'Yes, Rao, right away.'

Bishen clasped his hands behind his back and gazed into the jungle. He didn't show it, but Sangha's disappearance disturbed him greatly. No, disturb was too mild a word. He was close to panicking, an emotion he had never experienced earlier. Emotions made a man weak. Just the thought of losing Marachhiya and Lipi was unimaginable.

Sangha! That bitch! Alive, she was a thorn in his side, a continual reminder of his sister's betrayal. But dead, she would be an even bigger problem. His plans hinged upon her being alive to serve as a scapegoat. If anything happened to her, he'd have to go back to the drawing board. Undo many actions that had already been taken. This would take time and time was not something he had. Besides, Marachhiya's incessant whining about getting her and her daughter away from the jungle was beginning to create an uncomfortable pressure on him. Not that she was wrong, but some things had to unravel in their own time...

Hearing footsteps, Bishen halted his train of thought and turned around. Kundanlal was approaching.

'Do you think she has been compromised, or is she dead?' Bishen asked the older man as he neared him. There was no need to spell out who 'she' was.

'We have trained her well, Rao. She will not die,' Kundanlal reassured him.

'Well, if she has been taken captive, it will be tough for us. She knows too much. It will be better for us if she's dead. We won't have anything to worry about then,' continued Bishen, his voice devoid of emotion. He knew nothing could be further from the truth for him, personally—but he had to keep up appearances.

Bishen's cold and heartless disposition was nothing new to Kundanlal. It was actually what Kundanlal feared the most, and yet, ironically, it was also the reason he remained shackled to LalTara's commander. The Bishen Kundanlal knew was like a toxic chameleon—what you saw was definitely not what you got. He could change colours in the blink of an eye. Even after all these years, Kundanlal had not been able to figure out who this man truly was.

When his sister Suryamani had died by Bishen's bullet, Kundanlal was shocked and felt an immediate stab of grief—but he hadn't really mourned her. Bishen was too overwhelming a personality for him; whatever Rao did, Kundanlal condoned. Since childhood, he had been too fearful and remained subservient to powerful personalities. Consequently, Marachhiya, Rao's present wife, and their daughter Lipi naturally assumed a superior position in Kundanlal's pecking order. Marachhiya's aunt Phoolma and her son Tej came next in his social hierarchy, and Sangha—although he harboured a distant affection for her—was relegated to an inferior position. He thus viewed Sangha's disappearance with alarm—just like Bishen, who had said that she knew too much—and not with the anguish of an uncle.

As Bishen and Kundanlal strolled through the camp, a small bundle of energy darted towards the former, arms outstretched. Bishen indulgently swept the child off her feet and swung her up in the air, the afternoon sunlight streaming through her curly tresses. Little Lipi embraced her father tightly, her dark skin, just like Bishen's, glimmering in the sunlight, and her kohl-lined eyes shining with happiness. After kissing both her cheeks while making exaggerated smacking noises—just the way Lipi liked it—he gently placed her on the ground. She scurried away to their octagonal two-storey home.

After that bloody massacre led by Rakesh—*that traitorous bastard*—Bishen had strategically reset his camp as a sequence of octangular houses, with large octagonal courtyards separating the work units, interspersed with smaller square courtyards. The entrance to both types of units led from a courtyard. Across from the door was a tiny window in the wall and small netted ventilators that ran high, along the length of the walls not shared with the adjacent unit. This much-deliberated configuration enabled the camp to function as one entity. In the event of an attack, its residents would be able to defend themselves from multiple sides. This layout would also facilitate easier access and free movement within the camp when it was under siege. Units of LalTara's higher echelons were clustered together, flanked by those belonging to the seconds-in-command and the foot soldiers. For the roofing, Bishen had carefully chosen fibreglass camouflage tiles that would render their settlement almost invisible in an aerial survey. For Bishen, these structural strategies and the camp's virtually inaccessible location in an impenetrable jungle meant he was never going to be caught off guard ever again.

Bishen's face, touched by an involuntary tenderness on seeing his daughter, abruptly hardened on her exit. He brushed off the sticky chocolate marks left on his cheek by her chubby hands and headed towards the storage enclosure, with Kundanlal close on his heels.

'Have the mules been delivered?' he crisply asked his chief administrator and accountant.

'This time, the mules are all boys from orphanages. And we've managed to rope in all the deaf and mute ones, just as you wanted,' replied Kundanlal.

'Good! I don't want another Kamli episode. I don't want anyone to blabber. No hearing, no blabbering,' Bishen reiterated his reason for switching to deaf and mute people to carry their narcotic contraband. 'The police have been extra vigilant and I don't want any eyeballs on this consignment.'

'We are being careful,' assured Kundanlal.

'Have you matched the crates with the delivery order? Double check them, but don't open them.'

Kundanlal nodded in the affirmative as he motioned to his runner Gopu to inform Rambhakt to bring the mules over for Bishen's approval. Runners and mules were critical to their organization, and were, therefore, personally vetted by Kundanlal. The former comprised an effective network that ensured the smooth flow of news through LalTara's system and across hierarchies. Furthermore, this manual method of communication kept their coordinates radio safe from the authorities. Mules, on the other hand, were just that—a means for the transportation of goods. Young people were trained—rather, coerced—into carrying contraband. Both systems had been developed by Kundanlal, LalTara's chief administrator.

As he waited for Rambhakt to arrive, Kundanlal pondered why Bishen was being particularly edgy and secretive with this new consignment named RED. *He had supported Bishen to rebuild LalTara piece by piece after Rakesh had destroyed the camp many years ago. LalTara had since reset itself and established a successful narcotic trade haven. Their operations mandated regular dealings with ruthless politicians and bullying narco-mafia groups, but never had Bishen been as nervous and as edgy as he was being with this deal. What was so special about it?* He had discovered by chance that Bishen was focusing his efforts on creating more offshore accounts, and kept these transactions confidential. Although Kundanlal was hurt, offended and suspicious about the secrecy, he knew that staying silent was the best course of action for him.

Bishen, too, was closely observing Kundanlal's immobile posture and expression, and he could sense the thoughts darting through his lonely, frustrated and lethal brother-in-law's mind. Bishen instantly understood that Kundanlal suspected him of formulating an exit strategy. *He would need to be extremely careful. If it ever came to light that money from the RED deal was going to be his ticket to a safe haven on a private Mediterranean island, all hell would break loose in the ranks. He wanted to avoid this possibility at all costs.*

Bishen's cogitations were interrupted by the arrival of Gopu and Rambhakt with a group of twelve teenage boys in tow. Bare-chested and wearing cambric cargoes, they were moderately well built to do heavy work. Most importantly, all of them were deaf-mute—just the way Bishen had instructed. LalTara usually employed young girls to transport the narcotics, but this time Bishen had a different plan up his sleeve.

While Bishen and Kundanlal were inspecting their latest batch of human carriers, Manu, their fastest runner, came in sweating and panting. Between gulping in air and shivering with nervous tension, the lanky, hollow-cheeked boy delivered a piece of news that caused Bishen and Rambhakt to leave their carriers with Kundanlal and sprint towards the ATV. Rambhakt took the wheel and the vehicle roared off in full speed, with Manu hanging out of the window to show them the way.

Sangha's body had been found by the river.

16
Litmus Test

Bishen's mind raced ahead of the ATV. He could not wait to reach the riverside. When they reached their destination, Rambhakt pushed hard on the brakes. The shrill screech of the brakes took the villagers—inquisitively huddled together near the river—by surprise, and they hurriedly dispersed to make way for the ATV. Bishen could see the body of a girl lying by the water's edge, on her stomach. He stepped out of the vehicle and trotted purposefully towards the body. Seeing Bishen, the villagers scattered and fled like a flock of sheep seeing a wolf. He dropped to his knees and turned the body around. It was indeed Sangha. She looked frail, bruised and lifeless.

Bishen checked her pulse and felt a faint fluttering. 'Damn!' he exclaimed. He first inclined her head to one side to let the water drain out, then tilted it back and lifted the chin to follow up with mouth-to-mouth resuscitation. The girl's body jerked. She gasped and spouted out water from her mouth, before starting to breathe laboriously. *The bitch never gives up,* thought Rambhakt as Bishen summoned him to carry Sangha to the car.

Isha drifted back into consciousness. She felt a strong pair of arms scoop her up and stride forward. Though her vision was hazy with exhaustion, she could see a tall, dark figure looming ahead. Willing herself to stay awake, she felt herself being propped up on the seat of a car, between two men. 'Rao,' she heard someone call out. 'We should get her out of here now.' *Rao!* she thought. *The target had hit the mark! She would now have to get back on her feet and begin work.* As her eyelids drooped with fatigue, Isha made a mental note to send a message to her father: *Operation Trojan Horse activated.* She silently said a prayer and hoped she would never again need to jump into the life-threatening, angry and turbulent waters of the Indravati. Ever.

∞

Isha had been slipping in and out of consciousness for days, but when she finally slid out of her slumber, it was dark outside. As she opened her eyes, she became aware of two pairs of eyes staring at her. From the sketches that Sangha had made for her, Isha immediately recognized Marachhiya and little Lipi, who hid behind her mother's back, trying to peek at Isha. The child's kohl-lined eyes were kind and full of questions. Isha could not control the smile that involuntarily appeared on her lips. Lipi was surprised and happy; this was the first time Sangha had smiled at her so tenderly. She shyly waved at Sangha, and immediately, Marachhiya's sharp voice broke the silence, 'Aunt, take Lipi away.' Phoolma stepped out of the shadows and easily sweet-talked Lipi into leaving with her. The little girl skipped out of the room behind Phoolma.

'Nurse, get her back on her feet fast,' grunted Marachhiya, and left abruptly. Isha felt the heat of that hate; the animosity was a good reminder that she was in enemy territory and needed to operate with caution. Her next move would be to quickly reach the coordinates where Manish—with Sangha's help—had carefully drone-dropped the satellite communication system in a 'safe' part of the forest near the LalTara camp. It was her only way to be in touch with base. But before she could leave the camp to access this communication technology, she would have to gain Bishen's trust.

Isha motioned the nurse to come closer. 'Call Rao. I have information for him,' she said, straining her vocal cords. The nurse obediently went away. Propping herself upon the pillows, Isha peered out of her window to spot the North Star. As a child, when she went trekking with her father, they would make a special practice of navigating their way in the wilderness by following the star. Just looking at it now gave her a sense of comfort and security.

∽

There was a fraught silence in the room as Kundanlal and Marachhiya waited for Bishen to respond.

'Her chip may be intact, but keeping her here is dangerous, Rao. If they know about her chip and clone the tracking, they will be here any time,' Marachhiya hissed.

'I have checked the chip, and it is still precisely where we had planted it. She has been here for six days now, and there has been no infiltration or movement anywhere near our borders. Why would the forces hold out for so long?' refuted Kundanlal.

Marachhiya glared at Kundanlal, noting his unusually combative demeanour. 'Why did we not have any signal from her chip for over a month? She must have conspired with the forces. How can we be certain she is not on their side now?' she countered vehemently.

Before either of the men could respond, the nurse came in to inform Bishen that Sangha wished to see him. In the awkward silence that followed Bishen's departure, both Marachhiya and Kundanlal realized that they could debate, argue and fight forever, but Bishen would ultimately rely on his own judgement.

∞

When Bishen strode in, Isha was sitting up, propped up on pillows, sipping a herbal concoction the nurse had given her. When she saw him clearly for the first time, her heart almost leapt out of her mouth. Under normal circumstances, she would have admired the animal force that appeared to ooze out of his frame, giving him a sense of immense power and control. But all Isha could see was her mother's murderer, the destroyer of Baba's happiness, the breaker of her family. Isha could feel the blood draining from her face, a quickening of the pulse, and fervently hoped that the storm in her heart wasn't reflected on her face. She stood up to greet Bishen with an exaggerated grimace of pain, in the hope of camouflaging her feelings.

'How are you feeling?' Bishen asked his niece.

'Okay, all things considered. They jammed my chip so you would not be able to trace my location. They tried to break me, Rao, but I resisted,' Isha spat out, hoping the anger that she was deliberately injecting into her voice appeared genuine. 'It's not just the police force who are pursuing us. They have a special task force dedicated to wipe us out. I know the location of one of their secret safe houses in which they kept me locked up for weeks. They also store their high-end ammunition and weapons there. We should destroy it and let them know that messing with us has consequences.'

Isha delivered her statement in a dry, matter-of-fact, detached tone. Sangha had warned her that the duo shared a relationship bereft of any emotion.

Bishen smiled within. He liked Sangha to be aggressively

unforgiving, just like him. Her captivity and torture had made her angrier, he felt. He was happy that her angst was still sharp-edged.

'Give me the location,' he ordered.

'I don't know the exact coordinates, but I remember hearing the workers' siren from the east of the entrance the day I broke free, when I was being transported someplace else. The security jeep had stopped at a railway signal about a kilometre away from the place where I was imprisoned. That's when I twisted the necks of those pathetic guards and made a run for it. I think it could be somewhere near Rowghat,' recounted the girl.

'How did you make your way back to LalTara after that?' asked Bishen.

Isha swallowed, trying to get rid of the dryness in her throat. Thank God, they had anticipated such questions and prepared a narrative accordingly. 'I hid until dark, and then followed the Dhruv Tara—the North Star—till I reached the Indravati, and then swam upstream.'

Bishen just stared at her with an inscrutable gaze for what seemed like an eternity. Then he grunted and turned away. 'Nurse, give her some more of the Tulsi *kadha*,'[26] he said before leaving the room.

Isha followed and tried to go out with him but was stopped by the guards outside her unit, bearing expensive, magazine-fed assault rifles. *Yes, Sangha did mention that LalTara had changed from the scraggly ragtag of men with locally made guns and pistols that her Baba had seen.*

---

[26] Kadha: An Ayurvedic home remedy made from the leaves of the holy basil

Isha, her heart still racing, turned around and returned to her bed, wondering if she had managed to convince Bishen and pass the litmus test.

17
A Regular Day at LalTara

Isha felt a great deal better the next morning. The throbbing in her head had already subsided to a dull, easy-to-ignore ache. She stepped out in the misty morning. It was just before dawn; the jungle foliage had acquired a velvety mysteriousness in the half-light. She sat on a chair near the door, nodding a good morning to the sentries still stationed by the door. Her eyes scanned the camp, which was yet to wake up to its daily routine. Only around the canteen, which lay diagonally across from her quarters, was there a sign of some movement.

'Akka,'[27] one of the guards called out to her. 'I'll quickly go and get you a cup of tea.' Pointing to his partner, the guard continued, 'He will be here.'

'Both of you go,' Isha replied. 'You also need a break. Don't worry,' she reassured him. 'No one's up. Come back soon. And make mine sweet, will you?'

The pair smiled and hurried towards the canteen.

Isha leaned back in her chair and closed her eyes. *So far, so good,* she thought. *I hope the good run continues. I wonder how Baba is...and Manish. How are they handling Sangha? No, no, Sangha's here, sitting on this chair. You're Sangha. Don't forget that. Never!*

---

[27] Akka: Elder sister

Isha suddenly felt a moist sensation nuzzling her toes. She opened her eyes to see a floppy-eared, brown-and-white puppy, its entire back wiggling with its tail in the hope of a pat. Around its neck was a collar fashioned out of braided rope. Reflexively, she bent down and picked it up, taking pleasure in its warm and innocent affection.

'Hello there,' she cooed at it, tickling its ear while trying to avoid the nip of its sharp teeth. 'What a cutie pie you are.' Dogs! Who could resist them? Not she! Suddenly she stiffened. Not she, but Sangha! Sangha hated dogs!

She quickly put the animal down and shooed it away by stomping her foot. It ran, tail tucked between its legs, towards Bishen's quarters.

Her gaze then casually swept over the camp. *There weren't too many people around, and whoever there was, was going about their business.* She relaxed.

How could she know that her relief was premature? From the shadow of a doorway, a keen pair of eyes had watched this scene unfold with some degree of bewilderment and a great deal of interest.

∽

2025
STF command centre, Raipur

Rakesh rubbed his nose vigorously, once again, going through the strategic plans of Operation Trojan Horse. Ever since Isha left, Rakesh had lived in a state of constant anxiety. Everything seemed to be in limbo. The uncertainty was killing him, which is why he had been reluctant to give this operation his go-ahead. *Was Isha okay? Was she alive?* Just contemplating the unpleasant alternative made him feel ill.

He must have called Manish about four times already that day to enquire if there was any news.

He stared unseeingly at the documents on his table, fiddling with the Mont Blanc pen Isha had gifted him on his fiftieth birthday. It was after 10:00 p.m. The office was silent. The morning shift had ended a long time ago. There was only a skeletal staff that remained to man the critical functions. He chose to keep long hours at work as he couldn't bear to face an Isha-less house.

Suddenly, the door to his office opened with a loud bang, its shutter rebounding on the wall.

'What the...' Rakesh exclaimed but stopped when he saw Manish. His heart sank. 'What happened? Any news?'

In response, Manish silently punched a few keys on his mobile and placed the device on Rakesh's table. A video that played on a loop, showed a huge explosion decimating a building.

'Sir, the safe house is gone.'

Rakesh leaned back in his chair. The strategy to sacrifice their safe house, a mere pawn, to win the trust of the king, had apparently worked. This action was proof that Isha was safe. No! Not safe, she was alive. She had reached LalTara and duly set the plan in motion.

'Feed this to the press, and see that it receives wide coverage,' he rapped out to his junior. Rakesh Srivastava was back in charge! The idea to head back home didn't seem too bad now. Sangha, too, needed to be apprised of this development.

Still, in the office later that night, Rakesh sat pensively. The Rowghat explosion clearly conveyed to him that the mission was on and Isha had reached LalTara. However, he still wanted some sign, a message that Isha was doing okay.

Is she physically safe after battling the Indravati? Fording the river was no mean task.

Just then his satellite phone pinged. The message read: *Roma safe*. Rakesh heaved a sigh of relief.

∞

A few hours ago
LalTara camp

It was evening. Kundanlal had just conveyed to Isha the message from Rao that the plan to blow up the Rowghat house, where she had been imprisoned, was successfully executed. Isha felt relieved that her father and Manish knew by now that she was alive. She was doubly pleased to notice that the security near her quarters was withdrawn. This meant that she had succeeded in gaining Rao's trust. Now, she could implement the next part of the plan.

In the stillness of the night, when the camp was silent with sleep, she sneaked out from the rear window of her quarters and headed out into the forest. She trekked through the dense jungle, while being careful about the landmines planted around LalTara that Sangha had warned her about. It was a new exercise as the terrain was unfamiliar. She was also careful to check that she was not being followed. Despite her caution, however, she was unaware of a silent pair of feet that followed her with astute nimbleness from a safe distance.

Isha was relieved to find the package at the precise location coordinates that Manish had forced her to memorize. She quickly opened it, extracted the satellite phone, switched it on, and entered the PIN to send a short message: *Roma safe*. As soon as she confirmed that the message had been delivered, she deactivated the device and turned to the other gadgets in the package that Manish, her 'Q'—from her favourite James Bond movies, had air-dropped with meticulous planning. Among these was a bullet-shaped pen drive loaded with an algorithm which, when plugged into any computer, could automatically decrypt its password and offer unrestricted access to its contents. Using this device, she could view the files and folders saved on Kundanlal's desktop. She pocketed this pen drive, along with the other useful gadgets, before safely hiding the satellite phone in the bole of the tree. *She could now prepare to initiate her mission of unravelling LalTara's activities; her first target would be Kundanlal's computer.*

During the preparatory days of Operation Trojan Horse, Sangha had cautioned them about Kundanlal's obsessive behaviour with the security of his device. 'He stores all the data on his desktop, which is located in his home unit. Only he has access to the room and his computer password. I have tried to crack the code a few times but...' she had trailed off. 'The room itself is armed with laser beams and thermal sensors. So even if you somehow manoeuvre your body between the beams, the sensors are sure to detect any human presence in the room.'

Manish, as usual, wasn't deterred by this hurdle. 'Leave that to me,' he had said before questioning Sangha about the specifics of Kundanlal's security system.

'After you guys tackle the laser beams and the thermal sensor, you have forty-five seconds to crack the password before the machine goes into auto lock,' Sangha had informed them. 'A heads-up: they have conducted multiple drills to check if anyone can break through, and none of them were successful. They couldn't even get past the beams and the sensor, let alone the computer.'

Even in the middle of the forest, Isha could visualize Manish's gleeful response to this disclosure. He had rubbed his hands in excitement: this was a puzzle worth decoding—and sure enough, in less than two weeks, he'd presented a clever solution, a smart dovetailing of the hi-tech and the low-tech. She smiled at the memory, and also because her heart was lighter now that she had successfully sent a message to her father to apprise him of her progress since making it to the camp alive.

She carefully started to put into action the plan to decode Kundanlal's computer. The first strategic step was to set up the line of attack. This was the easiest. All she needed to do was establish a direct line of sight from the ventilator of her room into Kundanlal's, which was, fortunately for her, right next door. She identified a portion of the ventilator in her room and Kundanlal's, which was not clearly visible from the doorway, that she could tamper with without the unevenness being noticed. Over the past few days, she had been inconspicuously collecting flat stones wide enough for her to stand on. These were casually, yet carefully, placed in the passage between her room and Kundanlal's.

One day, noticing that no one was around and Kundanlal's room was empty, Isha exited her room from the small window to its rear and stacked up the flat stones into a pile. Stepping upon this improvised ladder, she reached the ventilator net of Kundanlal's room, and carefully cut it along the edge of the frame. She secured the cut edges back again with a special glue that Manish had included in the air-dropped package. This adhesive fastened the edges in such a way that they stayed together, yet allowed them to be pulled apart repeatedly—much like Velcro. This way, no one would notice that the ventilator net had been tampered with. She did the same with the ventilator net of her room.

Then came the part Isha referred to as Cry Wolf, a delicate operation that would go on for a couple of days. She bided her time until the day Kundanlal left his room. She then exited her room from the rear, ran to the wall of her neighbour's room, assembled her 'ladder', and opened the ventilator net of his room. That done, she scurried back to her room, and once inside, climbed up on to a chair and took aim. In her hand was Manish's smart invention: a high-tensile catapult with pyrophoric projectiles capable of igniting spontaneously. She carefully aimed one into Kundanlal's room through the ventilator. Once shot, the bullet interrupted the laser beams and combusted in seconds, triggering a temperature rise that set off the thermal sensors. The sound of the ringing alarms was deafening. Putting away her weapon, Isha ran up to the front to join the general hubbub that had ensued.

She saw Kundanlal and Bishen sprinting to Kundanlal's room from the direction of Bishen's office.

'What the hell is going on?' Kundanlal shouted.

'Kundan Mama, the alarms are going off in your room,' Isha yelled out.

'I can hear that,' he growled as he ran up to the door to his room and unlocked it. Stepping inside, he quickly assessed the interior, but everything seemed as he had left it. He hurried to the desktop and clicked the computer mouse. *Nothing.* The machine was still switched off. His eyes skimmed the place frantically, his flared nostrils and sweaty brow betraying his anxiety. Bishen stood at the threshold, arms akimbo.

'What's the problem?' he asked his administrator.

'All seems okay. I don't understand...' he mumbled helplessly.

'Ask Tej to check the systems right away,' Bishen ordered. 'Now.'

That evening, as Isha sat in her room, she could hear the sounds of activity in the adjacent unit. Muffled dialogues, punctuated with exclamations. Nonchalantly, she stepped out and peered through the doorway into Kundanlal's room. Tej sat on the floor cross-legged, next to a disembowelled computer, his hair standing up anyhow.

'Found anything?' she asked dryly, in Sangha's tone of voice.

Tej shrugged his powerful shoulders.

'Hmmm,' she responded, strolling away.

Day One had been successful. She had already closed the flaps of the ventilator in Kundanlal's room. Operation Cry Wolf was in motion!

Her next opportunity came three days later. And then, another one two days later. Isha was careful to keep Cry Wolf random. By the end of eight days, Kundanlal was tearing his hair out in frustration, berating Tej for not being able to figure out the problem. On the morning of the fourth 'false alarm', Bishen and Kundanlal decided to shut down the system temporarily until a solution could be found, or a system engineer could be prevailed upon or abducted to visit the camp.

This was the day Isha was waiting for. The alarm had been switched off and Kundanlal was scheduled to leave the camp for a couple of hours. He needed to visit a cocaine supplier to check on the supplier's distribution chain—a task he trusted no one else with.

Kundanlal firmly believed that drugs were the money tree in LalTara's treasury. Even though Bishen was placing all his bets on the ammunition business, Kundanlal believed it was a dangerous gamble. He was determined to insulate this risk by insisting on the continuation of the narco trade until the weapons trade had proved its lucrativeness.

Isha sat calm and composed in her room, her gaze fixed on the next-door window, waiting for Kundanlal's jeep to drive away. Outside, she could hear him getting ready to leave.

'Manu!' she heard Kundanlal summoning LalTara's number one runner. When the boy got there, more commands followed: 'You are to stay here by the door. If you leave this post even for a second, I'll have your hide.' Kundanlal's orders were strict, but his tone was light-hearted. He liked the boy, who was gentle and sincere.

Isha heard Manu's deferential response and assurances. Like a tigress, crouched still, ready to leap on her prey, all her energy was focused on the mission. She had mentally run through the strategy a million times to nullify the possibility of any error. *She would breach Kundanlal's unit from above, from the roof constructed with camouflage shingles. And then, she would*—her thought was interrupted by the roar of Kundanlal's jeep. *No more revision; it was now time for action.*

Isha stood up and flexed her limbs. She had already layered the soles of her camouflage boots with nano-grip stickers specially procured by Manish. The stickers would give her the extra bounce that she needed. She had also donned gloves layered with a lizard grip sticker, another one of Manish's finds. She allowed herself a quick smile at her colleague's genius and thoughtfulness. She had often wondered how this man-child, with so much grey matter, had never ventured to become a billionaire on foreign shores.

Isha quickly snapped out of the comfort zone of her thoughts. Time was of the essence. She would have to complete her mission before Kundanlal returned. Isha had learnt early in her professional life that field jobs were the embodiment of the proverbial slip between the cup and the lip. She sent out a prayer to the universe, took a deep breath, and after a few light jumps on her toes, leapt towards the ventilator of her room. Isha nearly missed her grip on the wall and slid down, but instantly her nano-grip shoes and gloves helped her stick to the wall like a lizard. Isha let out a sigh of relief as she recalled her training instructions and wriggled forward, mimicking the movement pattern of a house gecko.

Dexterously, she navigated to the ceiling of her unit. Grasping onto the truss of the roof, she pushed at a tile. It creaked a little but lifted up. Good! She gently manoeuvred it, creating an opening, and then the next—until the breach was wide enough to accommodate her slim frame. She hauled herself out of the gap and onto the roof. Exiting from the rear window of her room, scaling the wall of Kundanlal's room to access its roof would have been easier. But chances of someone spotting her were that much higher. Therefore, she had chosen this acrobatic and slightly more tortuous method.

The next couple of steps went well. The leap from the roof of her unit to Kundanlal's was smooth. This was followed by creating an opening in her neighbour's roof, somewhere near the door where the laser switch was located. She worked slowly and quietly. She knew Manu was down below; in fact, she could hear him humming to himself.

Before long, Isha could see the computer sitting below her. *All I have to do,* she told herself, *is jump in, crack the computer password, copy the data, get out through the roof and vault back to my unit. Phew! Easier said than...* Isha brushed aside these thoughts and took a leap of faith downwards. She dropped silently on the floor, near the inner entrance to the room. Standing up, she quickly disarmed the laser switch installed near the door and let out a silent sigh of relief.

Without wasting any time, she headed to the computer, switched it on, inserted Manish's coded pen drive, and pressed the timer on her wrist watch. Illegible codes began running through the screen. Isha's attention was now split between staying alert for movement outside and watching the letters scrolling on the screen. *God! Why can't it be faster?* She fumed as the alphanumerical strings went on and on, while the timer seemed to sprint towards the forty-five-second mark. Isha felt beads of sweat pop up on her brow and upper lip while her throat dried up.

Manish, what junk have you coded! As she gritted her teeth, the wallpaper on the computer screen transformed into a live desktop, complete with all the files and folders. Just as the data started copying into the pen drive, Isha mentally sent a kiss to Manish. *How could she be such an idiot to doubt her very own tech-wiz?*

Isha relaxed...just a little bit. She could hear Manu humming away happily on his assignment. *Thank God, the computer table was placed adjacent to the door and not directly opposite it across the room,* she thought. *If it were so, she would be visible to anyone who walked into the room as soon as they opened the door!*

Abruptly, Manu's humming stopped. Isha went still, her

attention diverted to what was happening outside the door. To her absolute horror, she heard Kundanlal's voice speaking with the young sentry posted outside. *Shit! The man had returned sooner than she anticipated.* Isha's mouth went dry. *It would be mere moments before he entered the room and she was caught red-handed. What was she going to do? A mere closed door stood between the end of her life and that of the mission.* She heard a key being inserted into the lock and being turned fruitlessly. *Kundanlal was struggling to open the door.* She felt her breath quicken and strangely, a peculiar choking sensation within her chest at the same time. Isha clenched her teeth and closed her eyes for a second to pray for a miracle.

And then the door opened with a thud!

∞

A few minutes earlier
Outside Kundanlal's door

Manu was taken by surprise to see Kundanlal return so soon. He alighted from the jeep and walked to the door. 'What happened, Kaka? You are back so soon?' He quickly gathered the paper boats he had crafted while awaiting Kundanlal's return.

Before replying to Manu, Kundanlal scrutinized the lock on the door. LalTara's head administrator trusted no one. Before leaving, he had fastened a fine piece of string to the lock, which would enable him to detect any break-in attempt right away. *Laser and thermal sensors be damned. Nothing beat traditional security methods. The string was intact and everything seemed exactly as he had left it!* He turned to Manu in a good mood. 'Had to return to get something I forgot.

But what have you been doing, you brat? I see you are busier with handicraft than the security of my gate,' Kundanlal added, spying the veritable fleet of paper boats lying near Manu's feet.

'No, Kaka, I have made sure that not even a whiff of wind passes beyond me to get past your door,' the boy bragged.

'Good! I'll put in a word to get you on Rao's personal security detail,' Kundanlal mumbled wryly as he inserted the key into the lock.

'Is there anything you want me to do now, Kaka? Do you need help with anything here, or...?'

'Come back in twenty minutes as I need to leave once again,' Kundanlal said, struggling with the lock. *Saala!* He thought to himself, wiggling the key. *This lock needs oiling.* Finally, the key engaged properly and the door opened with a thud. But before he could step into his unit, he heard his name being called.

'Sir! Kundanlal sir!' Rambhakt shouted, hurrying up to where the older man stood.

Kundanlal scowled as he turned around. 'What is it?' he asked.

Rambhakt stood deferentially in front of him. 'Sir, Muthu called about the distributor chain you'd just gone to check. They're now saying they'll be able to fulfil the entire order. We won't have to negotiate with that bastard Ananta. He's getting too big for his boots anyway.'

Kundanlal heaved a sigh of relief. The matter had been playing on his mind ever since his return. 'Good news, Rambhakt. The payment terms remain the same, I hope.'

'Yes, sir, no change there.'

'Okay, tell them to go ahead. I'll call them in a bit,'

Kundanlal said as he turned around and stepped into the room.

The room was empty.

∽

The loud noise of the door opening had made Isha nearly jump out of her skin. Just as she steadied herself, she heard a voice.

'Sir! Kundanlal sir!' She could hear Rambhakt calling urgently for Kundanlal's attention.

'What is it?' she heard the man reply irritably.

That was all the time Isha needed.

She knew that as soon as this little chat was over, the noose would be around her neck. She had to act fast. So she yanked the pen drive with its half-filled data out of the slot and secured it in her camouflage body suit. She then quickly padded to the wall and jumped. This time, she moved not like a lizard scaling the wall, but rather like a panther on the run. In her hurry to exit the room, however, her hand missed a truss of the roof and she fell back on the wall. Fortunately, the grip of her gloves and boots still held. *Steady, Isha. Slow and steady,* she reminded herself. *Would she have enough time to make it to the top of the roof, replace the shingles and close the opening without being noticed?*

'Okay, tell them to go ahead. I'll call in a bit,' Kundanlal concluded the conversation and stepped into the room.

It was a do-or-die situation! Instantly, she regained her grip on the truss and hoisted herself through the opening, and onto the roof. Just as she pulled up her legs on the roof, she heard the door close noisily. When she silently leaned in to replace the tiles in their place, she saw Kundanlal below, rooted to the spot, his eyes on the blinking computer.

For two heartbeats, she froze, watching the tableau below, unaware of the sweat running down her forehead, the bridge of her nose, and then on to its tip. And then, before she could realize what was happening and wipe it off, a drop of the bodily fluid fell. Time seemed to slow down. Isha watched in horror as it raced towards Kundanlal. *It was over. All this work, washed away by a drop of sweat!* But no, just when all seemed lost, Kundanlal stepped ahead and the drop splattered on the floor behind him, unnoticed. Isha didn't lose any more time. She put the shingles back in their place, praying Kundanlal wouldn't look upwards.

In the room below, alarm bells were ringing in Kundanlal's mind. His computer was blinking and alive. He knew he had shut it down before leaving. *Someone had certainly been in his room! Someone had attempted to gain access to his sacred space! How? Who was it?*

His gaze scanned every part of the room and then turned upwards. *Everything appeared to be as it was supposed to be, except for that glowing monitor. How was this possible?* He even went out of the door to check the veranda and the courtyard outside, but the camp's routine was proceeding normally.

Isha then heard Kundanlal shouting if anyone had been seen loitering near his quarters. She quickly duck-walked to the portion of the roof at the rear and peered over the edge. *No one was around.* She could still hear Kundanlal yelling. Perhaps everyone had headed to Kundanlal's room to find out what the problem was. Whatever the reason, the coast was clear. It took her less than half a minute to clamber down from the roof of Kundanlal's room, run to the rear window of her unit, and jump into the safety of her quarters. She quickly shed her gear and stowed it away safely, after checking to ensure that the pen drive was still in place.

She tousled her hair, rubbed her eyes gently to redden them a bit, and stepped out of her room, yawning.

'What's the shouting all about?' she innocently asked Manu, who stood nearby.

Her strategy had worked. She had successfully hacked into the accountant's computer. Now all she had to do was send the data to Manish. True, she had not completely copied everything off Kundanlal's system. Manish would just have to fill the gaps—something he was rather good at doing. He possessed the contacts and the technology to probe LalTara's secrets and follow its money trail.

Isha was sure this data would point them in the right direction to obtain additional evidence against the elusive and nefarious activities of LalTara.

⁓

That night, Isha sneaked out again after conducting her usual checks to ensure she was not being followed. Her steps were soft, like those of the numerous night creatures all about her. As soon as she reached the communication point, Isha lost no time in uploading the data on Manish's server. That completed, she heaved a sigh of relief. As she was camouflaging the instrument and preparing to place it back in its hiding spot, the hairs on the back of her head prickled. She stopped and pivoted. *Nothing.* Shrugging, she turned back to her task when she heard a small sound. She spun around to find herself facing a figure in black. Quick as lightning, she lunged forward and punched it in the midriff. She heard the whoosh of air being expelled from the body and it crumpled on the forest floor. She switched on her pencil torch and shone the light on the intruder's face.

'What the hell!' she exclaimed when Manu's face sprang up in the beam of light. Gasping for breath, the boy groaned as he struggled to get back on his feet. He stood there for a minute, rubbing his thin, heaving chest with his palms. He licked his dry lips and contemplated her through narrowed eyes.

'Who are you?' he rasped.

Isha went still. *Her cover was blown. What was she going to do now?*

18

Chaos Rising

2025
30 days earlier
Raipur

With the plan to strategically sacrifice their Rowghat safe house as a signal of Isha's entry into LalTara, the members of Team Trojan Horse understood that immediately after Isha's departure, Sangha would have to be moved from the safe house to another location. Rakesh and Isha insisted that the other location had to be the Srivastava household. This way, 'Isha' would not be absent from her home for too long.

While Manish agreed with the logic behind this conclusion, he still thought this move was too personal, too intimate and too close for comfort. *Perhaps it was Rakesh's way of making up for Sangha's difficult childhood,* the tech-junkie reasoned with himself. So, while he accepted the alternative without opposition, he requested Rakesh to give him three days to 'prepare the pen', before Isha left for her mission. In his typically enigmatic manner, Manish was unwilling to disclose what this meant. When Rakesh announced the intended move to Sangha, she, too, was somewhat shocked. A part of her, however, wanted it too. *But for a twist of fate, that's where she should have lived.*

Once this decision was taken, Isha began to tutor Sangha to step into her shoes, just as they had worked on her transformation into Sangha. The lessons covered Isha's favourite food, her go-to pair of pants, and her relationship with Vishnu Kaka, their household help. Sangha listened attentively. Rakesh and Isha were thankful that Neel was away in London. Rakesh didn't think he could handle the complexity of his presence. Both knew it would be easier to pull off the farce without Neel, as Sangha could just lie low under the pretence of having returned from an arduous training schedule.

After Isha's leap of faith into the Indravati River, and just before they exited the safe house, Manish had requested Rakesh for a private word. When both men stepped into the next room, Manish firmly closed the door behind him, opened his backpack and extracted a circular device.

Rakesh looked at it, puzzled. 'This is an anklet tracker. What's the deal?'

'Sangha will need to wear it, sir.'

Rakesh's face went white. 'I... I can't...'

'Don't worry, sir. I'll deal with it,' his young colleague replied, stepping determinedly out of the room.

When Rakesh entered the room again, his heart broke when he saw Sangha's furious, pale face.

∽

As Rakesh eased his car into the compound of his duplex bungalow, the main door flew open and Vishnu stepped out, his normal phlegmatic appearance replaced by quiet excitement. *Isha baby was home! The house hadn't felt normal in days. Now everything would be all right.*

'Vishnu Kaka-a-a-a!' the girl exclaimed, pleasantly surprising Rakesh with the ease with which she seemed to have slipped into Isha's skin.

'Beta, how I've missed you,' said the old family retainer. '*Yeh kaisa kaam hai! Bachhon ko ghar bhi aane nahin deta!*' he muttered, one eye on Rakesh. 'Look at the girl. She doesn't look herself!'

'What do you mean?' Both father and daughter exclaimed in unison.

'*Arre, matlab, dekho toh,* how thin she's become! She doesn't seem like herself at all! *Chalo, chalo.* Come inside.'

'See Kaka, how much Baba makes me work,' Sangha replied, the unfamiliar word, 'Baba', weighing heavily on her tongue.

Rakesh felt a tug at his heart on hearing his long-lost daughter referring to him as 'father'. He sighed.

∽

A sumptuous lunch was spread out on the table to celebrate Isha's return. *Chole-puri,* chicken fry, potato *bhajiya,*[28] *kurkuri bhindi*... Ugh! Bhindi! But Sangha kept a smile plastered on her face. *The chicken curry looked delicious. Perhaps she could drown the bhindi in it and disguise its awful taste.*

'Beta, go freshen up,' her father said. 'In fact, I shall come upstairs with you. Dada, start making the parathas. *Do* minute *mein aate hain.*'

As Vishnu Kaka turned around to return to the kitchen, Rakesh beckoned to Sangha to follow him upstairs.

The STF19 commander opened the door to Isha's room which would now house her twin. The room was neat,

---

[28]Bhajiya: Fritters

almost spartan; no-nonsense like its occupant. Most of the space was taken up by a large, comfortable bed. On the bedside table stood a silver photo-frame with the image of an attractive man: fair, with sexily tousled hair, and a sharp, aquiline nose. The study table in the corner by the window was attached to a floor-standing bookshelf full of tomes arranged in military precision. Rakesh opened the wardrobe to reveal more orderliness.

'Beta, you can take whatever you want from here, but this is what Isha likes the most,' said Rakesh, holding a pair of ecru linen pants and a sleeveless racer-back tee. Sangha nodded. At least the clothes weren't too bad.

'The bathroom's there,' he pointed to a door near the wardrobe.

After ten minutes, father and daughter descended for lunch, with Sangha dressed in Isha's favourite attire. Rakesh marvelled anew at the physical similarity between his two girls.

∞

It had been over two weeks since Sangha started living as Isha in the Srivastava household. Life had settled into a predictable routine. Breakfast with her father, spending the day by herself until dinner with Rakesh, before going to bed.

Today was no different.

Rakesh had left for the command office and Vishnu Kaka had disappeared into the kitchen after fussing over Sangha's breakfast. She was left on her own. At first she watched television, flipping from channel to channel, until she found a programme on martial arts. She was captivated by the power and grace of the movements, which made the completely novel feeling of doing nothing more pleasurable. When that was over, she stepped outdoors for a breath of fresh air.

She took a round of the small garden that surrounded the bungalow, stopping at a lush, flower-laden jasmine shrub.

'Speaking to your mother?' Vishnu Kaka called out from the kitchen window.

'What? Oh yes, yes, speaking to Mom,' Sangha replied, startled and unsure of how to respond.

Back in the house, she wandered into Rakesh's room, something she had not dared to do in all these days. *It was so austere! What was with this father and this daughter? Did they not know how to be exuberant?* On the bedside table, she saw three photographs. One was of a young lady, her hair loose and flying behind her, one hand held in front of her face to shield her eyes from the sun. She was laughing at something the photographer must have said. The other one showed a younger Rakesh with the laughing woman, both dressed in wedding finery. The last frame featured her again, this time seated on a *chattai* in a garden, with two chubby babies playing in the foreground. Sangha's heart constricted. *This was her mother. Her mother! And Rao had killed her.*

She tentatively reached out to touch Mitali's solo photograph and traced the curve of her cheek. She then turned her attention to the one with Mitali and her daughters. Sangha covered it with her hand in such a way that only Mitali and one of the children remained visible. *My mother!* she thought fiercely, staring at the photograph, searching for her own face in that of her mother's, trying to conjure up that lost, happy world.

∽

At lunch, Vishnu Kaka served her more delicious food, thankfully to her liking this time. Rice with sambar, accompanied by fried papadum.

'Baby, you seem to have fallen in love with sambar,' Vishnu Kaka commented, watching her devour her food with relish. 'The last time I made this, I had to exhort you with kheer to persuade you to eat it.'

'I've just missed your food, Kaka. Even if it's sambar,' Sangha grinned, cursing Isha. *Really! Why couldn't Isha like what Sangha liked!*

Vishnu smiled gently. 'Absence makes the heart grow fonder, huh?'

'Yeah, something like that.'

'Then you should definitely go to Sonu's. Her Eva has littered six beautiful pups. Sonu had visited last week, bouncing off the walls as usual, wanting to know when you would return. She wants to show off the little ones.'

'Puppies? Really? How cute! I'll see them in a few days,' Sangha gushed, inwardly squirming at the thought of going near the wriggly mini dogs. *God! How she hated them. Being bitten once would do that to you. First bhindi, then dogs!*

༄

That evening, when Rakesh came home, Sangha could sense his elation. He hummed softly to himself as he stepped into the house and immediately asked Vishnu for his favourite sundowner.

'I've some good news to share,' he told Sangha as he relaxed on the sofa, stroking his glass of whiskey. 'The safe house is gone. The plan is in motion.'

Sangha looked at his smiling face, trying to feel some fraction of that triumph. She couldn't.

That night, as she was getting ready for bed, after surviving the ordeal of eating Vishnu Kaka's bhindi—this time curried—and all the more disgusting for it, Sangha heard a knock at the bedroom door.

'May I come in?' She heard Rakesh's voice on the other side.

'Who can stop you? It's your house,' she quipped.

The door opened. 'Sangha,' he continued, disregarding her rejoinder, 'can you please come to my room? I have something to show you.'

Mystified and intrigued, she followed him to his private domain. Rakesh gently shut the door behind her.

'Sit,' he indicated a bench at the foot of the bed. He turned around, opened his wardrobe and unlocked a steel safe sitting on one of the shelves. Sangha's eyes glinted; she could see several jewellery boxes inside. Rakesh reached inside and retrieved a small, blue velvet pouch.

'Your mother and I made a set of bracelet and chain for both of you when you were born,' he said, sitting next to her. Opening the pouch, he took out a delicate gold chain with a pendant. 'Eka', it spelt out, in beautiful, flowing letters, ending with a trio of three twinkling diamonds. 'You were wearing the bracelet that day,' he reminisced sadly, caressing the piece of jewellery.

'I want you to have this,' Rakesh said, holding out his hand.

Sangha held the offering gently in her palm. Something stirred deep within her, opening her being to an undecipherable swell of emotion. She realized she had stopped breathing.

Sanghu, Suryamani's voice rang in her head. *Your name is Eka. You were wearing a bracelet with that name when you came to me. Remember that name. Never forget.*

'Sir,' Sangha still couldn't bring herself to address him as Baba in private. 'Are you fond of gardening?'

'Me? Oh no. Not me. It was your mother who had the green fingers. Jasmine was her favourite,' he said softly.

They sat quietly for two minutes, each wrapped in their own thoughts. She remembered the fragrant coolness of the jasmine; he went back to the day he and Isha had planted the tiny creeper in Mitali's memory.

'Okay, beta,' Rakesh said, breaking the silence. 'You rest now. I'll see you tomorrow.' She got up, gave him a tiny smile and left.

Back in her room, the warmth kindled by seeing her mother's photograph enveloped Sangha like a protective cocoon as she climbed into her bed. But try as she might, sleep eluded her. The novelty of living in a safe, secure environment, of not having to look over one's shoulder continually, engaging in easy banter with Vishnu Kaka, was starting to fade. While Rakesh's reminiscences of their time together as a family of four still held interest, primarily because she wanted to flesh out the memory of her mother, to really know who she was, Sangha realized that she was getting bored. She felt irritable and even stifled from living a lie. While she was careful to stay in character, the effort was beginning to feel rather jarring. *How was this any different from living in LalTara?* She fumed. She was a prisoner in both cases—the tracker around her ankle was ample evidence of her lack of freedom. *What was she to do?*

Thoughts crowded her mind, buzzing like a horde of angry insects, until she slipped into a fitful slumber, dreaming strange dreams of Rao, her mother and Suryamma.

2025
A few days later
The Srivastava house, Raipur

It was close to 2:00 a.m. when Rakesh's mobile phone rang. He opened his eyes with some effort, as they were gummed together by sleep, and checked the screen. Manish!

'Yes, Manish?'

'Sir, I'm at the centre. The data has been uploaded to the server.'

Rakesh instantly felt his sleep dissolve and disappear. He suddenly felt energized. *This meant that Isha was still safe and on the job.*

'What have you found out?'

'It shows us scans of numerous money trails that lead to a single account which is both receiving and then transferring money.'

Ah! This is the account Sangha had mentioned; the one bearing her name, Rakesh realized.

'What else?' he asked aloud.

'Sir, most of the money is being transferred from this account to a few other entities, some overseas, whose names appear on a fairly regular basis.'

'Damn! These offshore money webs will be difficult to unravel. I don't know how we will trace these beneficiary accounts.'

'Sir, I will ask my external affairs contact. He owes me big time. And he knows people who may be able to assist us with this. I'm confident we shall be able to tie up at least a few loose ends.'

'That's good. You speak to him as soon as you can. I'll see you at the centre tomorrow.'

'Right, sir.'

Rakesh lay back on his bed, staring at the ceiling. *His daughter was doing a fine job. How he missed her!* He hoped to see her soon but realized that for now, things had to run their course. He closed his eyes, and lost in thoughts about Isha, drifted back to sleep.

∞

Rakesh came down late for breakfast, eyes still red with unclaimed sleep, but quietly excited. Sangha was just finishing her breakfast of a double masala omelette with bread.

'The data has started to come in,' Rakesh told her cryptically, aware of Vishnu's presence in the background.

She nodded, matching his cheerful demeanour, albeit outwardly. Inside, she was seething. Last night's angry, confusing thoughts had left her fretful and nauseous. It was as if she was nursing a bad hangover. She barely noticed when Rakesh left for work. As she sat at the breakfast table alone, she began daydreaming about an independent life, without the baggage of a family or a tribe. Rakesh and Isha became inconsequential. Their operation became unimportant.

Could she break away? Yes, it certainly seemed doable. The tracking chip embedded in her by LalTara was off. Yet, she would need to deal with the GPS tracker anklet instead, which was installed by her new captors. That wasn't a big deal, she mulled to herself. *Certainly not as difficult as getting the chip off. She would find a way to tackle it as soon as she broke out. But what would she do when she escaped? She didn't have friends; she wasn't equipped for a job. What would she live on?* And then, the vision of an open safe filled with jewellery boxes floated into view—the ones she had glimpsed when Rakesh gave her the chain.

From then on, Sangha began to observe Rakesh's movements keenly. She followed his routine, noting how he would keep his set of keys in the bedside drawer before his evening shower. She strategized and plotted how she could lead Rakesh and his team on a wild goose chase when they tried to track her whereabouts. Rakesh had already given her a mobile. She would hide it on a public bus while she took a different route. She oiled the door hinges of her bedroom and those of Rakesh's room. Doing the same with the wardrobe proved to be tricky, but she took care of it when Rakesh was in the bath and the wardrobe was unlocked. She also started pilfering money from her father's wallet. Small denominations that he wouldn't notice immediately. *She didn't need too much anyway. That would come from selling the jewellery.*

She waited for the weekend, as Rakesh tended to be freer with his sundowners when he knew he wouldn't have to head to the command centre the following day. She gently nudged him down memory lane, deeper and deeper. The pegs lubricated his tongue and memory. When she knew he had had enough, she made a show of protesting against more drinks and requested Vishnu Kaka to serve dinner. Dinner over, she made sure Rakesh went to bed. Soon, she could hear gentle snores emanating from his bedroom. Sangha gave it another hour just to be safe, and then tiptoed into her father's bedroom. Sneaking up to the bedside table, she opened its drawer and extracted the keys. Taking care that they didn't jingle, she swiftly separated the keys to the wardrobe and those to the safe. She unlocked the wardrobe and opened the door. The safe followed suit. Once she had got the boxes out, she locked the safe and the cupboard before returning the keys to their original location. *If she kept things as they were, perhaps it would buy her more time by delaying Rakesh's discovery of the theft*, she reasoned.

Creeping back into her room, she extracted the jewellery from the boxes, and kicked the containers out of sight under the bed. She then stuffed the loot into a duffle bag she had found in Isha's cupboard. Swiftly and silently, she negotiated the stairs, and stopped to check for signs of movement from Vishnu Kaka's quarters. She knew he'd be dead to the world after his nightly routine of *afeem chillum*,[29] but it would not hurt to be doubly sure. As expected, all was quiet on that front.

She opened the door and stepped outside, excitement coursing through her veins. Nearly there, she thought as she ran towards the gate. But as soon as she neared the compound wall, *wham!* the GPS tracker on her ankle sent a crippling jolt of electricity into her body, activated an ear-piercing alarm and switched on the periphery lights. Sangha's legs crumpled under her. This was unexpected, unforeseen, and even in the midst of all that pain, her last thought before she lost consciousness was that she'd been trumped by Rakesh and that wily Manish. *They'd equipped the sensor with an electrical shock deterrent as an extra precaution and had linked it with the perimeter security system of the house.*

∞

Sangha moaned and opened her eyes. She knew she was in her bedroom, and that it was daylight. The first thing she noticed was the feathery outline of Rakesh's body, silhouetted against the window. She closed her eyes and opened them again. This time her father looked more solid.

---

[29]Afeem chillum: Opium smoked in a hookah pipe

'Sangha, are you okay?'

She moaned in reply.

'Drink this,' he said brusquely, thrusting a glass under her nose. 'It will make you feel better.'

'I'm okay,' she croaked.

'All right, give it an hour. I'll check back on you.'

Sangha struggled to sit up.

Rakesh held up his hand to stop her. 'Your bag with the loot still in it, is right there. You are obviously more concerned about yourself. This operation means nothing to you. So take your bag and get out. Everything else can take a flying fuck.'

She finally managed to sit somewhat upright. 'Have you been caged your entire life?' she rasped. 'I wanted to taste freedom. There's nothing wrong in what I did.'

'Nothing wrong?' thundered Rakesh. 'Nothing wrong? How can you say that? You get out, and how many people will you be able to convince that you are Isha? One chink in what we have so carefully constructed can make it all go to pieces. Everything depends on the success of this mission. Isha's life, your freedom...even our life together as a family.'

'Family is not something you're just born into. It's something you make,' she countered. 'I've known you only a couple of months now. Please don't be under the illusion that I care for you, or even Isha, just because we may share the same blood.'

'You're right, family is something you make. Are you willing to give enough time to us to "make" us a family, Sangha?' Rakesh spat out. 'You seem to have passed judgement already that it's not even worth a shot. What happened with Rao is not something I wished upon you.'

'Is it my fault then?' Sangha screamed hoarsely. 'Did I choose this life? Did I ask for it?'

'What do you think will happen if Rao somehow finds out that Isha is not you?' continued Rakesh, driving his point further. 'He will kill her, no doubt. But what do you think he'll do to you? He will hunt you down. He does that. You know what he did to Mitali, his own sister.'

Sangha went still. *Look at what he did to Suryamani*, the voice in her head continued Rakesh's monologue. The whole gory scene erupted in front of her eyes once again. She squeezed them shut, willing the bloody tableau to go away. *Rakesh was right. There was no other way.*

In all her years at LalTara, she had never thought of resisting Bishen Rao or fleeing from him, because she had nowhere to go and nobody to run to. All she could do was live in self-preservation mode, especially after Suryamani's demise. But now she had the chance to avenge Amma's death, their destroyed lives, even the fact that her real mother was a stranger to her. If she wanted Rao to be dragged to justice's door, she would have to do Rakesh's bidding. She would have to play her part.

Just then, the doorbell rang. Once. Twice.

'Damn!' Rakesh exploded. He had deliberately sent Vishnu to the market as he did not desire an audience for the scene unfolding with Sangha.

He glared at Sangha, then stalked out of the room and ran down the stairs. The bell rang again, stridently.

'*Arre bhai, aa raha hoon. Kyon marre ja rahe ho?*'

Rakesh reached the door and when he forcefully opened it, he felt the blood drain from his face.

Neel Saini stood smiling on the other side.

'Neel!' Rakesh exclaimed.

'Hi Uncle! Is Ishu in? I've been trying to reach her for a while now. Her mobile seems to be switched off. I've got some great news for her.'

Rakesh felt his stomach plummet to his feet. *Why was Neel here? He wasn't supposed to return this early from London!*

The STF19 head honcho stuck a smile on his face. 'Really?' But in his mind he thought, *we're all fucked!*

19

Paws and Effect

2025
Days before Isha's run-in with Manu
LalTara camp

An early riser, Manu headed to the camp mess, eager for his morning cup of tea. He stepped into the shed that functioned as the camp's canteen and greeted the men in charge of the kitchen. He sauntered to a table placed close to a window, taking care to remain in the shadows. The quarters of the powers-that-be were situated just opposite the canteen, separated by a courtyard in between. If Kundanlal happened to wake up early and step outside, he would be able to spot Manu in the canteen shed and then, there was a good chance he would immediately summon Manu to his side. Hot tea was a much better companion than Kundan Kaka, at least to start the day!

As it happened, the door of a 'boss' quarter did open, but it was Sangha's room. Manu absentmindedly saw its occupant step out and stand there, looking around. Then she exchanged a few words with the guards stationed outside her cottage. Having nothing better to do, Manu continued to watch the scene play out in front of him, noting the deference in the guards' body language, even though they were actually posted there to ensure that she stayed indoors through the night. Manu then saw the guards leave. Sangha sat down in the chair on the veranda, leaned back and closed her eyes. A movement at her side distracted Manu, who saw Bullet, Lipi's pet puppy, emerge out of Bishen's room. It waddled around, sniffed the ground intently, peed and continued on its quest to discover new things. It then wandered towards Sangha and sniffed her toes. Manu saw Sangha open her eyes, see the tiny dog and scoop it up delightedly in her arms. A couple of seconds later, she froze. She quickly put the animal down, shooed it away and looked around furtively.

Tea forgotten, Manu sat still, and his mind went into overdrive. *Sangha hated dogs. Actually, she detested all animals. And here she was, nuzzling a puppy she had never liked.* Manu was intrigued. His sixth sense screamed that there was more to the scene than what he'd just witnessed. Obviously he needed to investigate further. *He would have to keep a watch over Sangha.*

That night, Manu watched as the door to Sangha's quarters opened silently. Its occupant emerged, slipping into the darkness. Manu, staying close, matched her quiet steps. When she stopped near a tree, he couldn't quite see what she was doing as her back was turned to him, but it looked as though she was retrieving something from the tree trunk—a package! Holding it with one hand, she seemed to be pressing some buttons.

Manu's heart raced with excitement. It was a satellite phone! He recognized the device from seeing one in Rao Anna's hands. Sangha was involved in something secretive—something traitorous.

Soon she left the spot, but not before returning the phone to its hiding place. Manu tried to find it, but his pitch-dark surroundings made it impossible to pinpoint exactly where she had been standing. Still, his excitement didn't falter. He knew it was only a matter of time before she returned.

He had to uncover more. *Who knew? Maybe this could be his ticket out of this hellhole.*

From the day Manu's father had sold him to LalTara to keep their impoverished family from starving, solace had become a distant memory. His mother's anguished tears as he was torn from her embrace, his sister's desperate wails begging them to let him stay, and the shattering realization that he would never return to school to live a normal life— these moments stripped every shred of happiness from his heart. Robbed of his childhood, he wanted to flee from this dreaded place, run to his mother, every day. He hated the charade of servitude he had to put up to survive here, but he knew he had no way to escape.

So if Sangha was working against LalTara, then the enemy of his enemy might just become his ally. And he might be able to take his flight to freedom.

For several evenings he lurked in the shadows, staying hidden, waiting for his chance. Ten days later, his patience paid off as Sangha's nocturnal routine unfolded once again.

She stopped at the exact point where she had taken out the phone. Holding it with one hand, she reached into her jacket and pulled out something else. Now she appeared to be attaching both the items together.

This time, Manu needed to be closer to see where she was hiding the phone. He quietly exhaled, and moved forward softly, until some dry leaves rustled under his feet. *Damn!* He stopped.

In a split second, the woman spun around and saw Manu—or rather, a dark figure—and punched him in the gut. As he collapsed on the forest floor groaning, she shone a light on his face and exclaimed in surprise. Sensing no immediate danger, Manu struggled to his feet, every breath ragged with pain. He massaged his sore stomach.

'Who are you?' he managed to ask her, surprised at his own confidence.

'You're not Sangha Akka, you're not! You're a spy. No, no, you're a cop! What is this?' he gasped, pointing to her hands.

'You won't understand, Manu,' Isha mumbled, trying to buy time.

'No, you understand. If I open my mouth, you've had it,' he coughed and spluttered.

Damn! Isha thought furiously. *She would need to neutralize this child. Shit! Shit! Shit! What could she do? Could she hold him captive somewhere? No! People would start looking for him, and they knew the jungle better than her. They would easily find him. And what then? He would blab for sure. For fuck's sake!* She balled her fists.

'I won't though,' he continued, staring into her eyes which had suddenly gone still.

'What?' she questioned stupidly, unclenching her hands.

'I won't talk,' he hissed, 'but first, you have to tell me who you are, and then you have to do something for me.'

20

Suspicion

2025
The Srivastava house, Raipur

Rakesh stood rooted to the spot as he faced an ebullient Neel, joyfully requesting to see Isha. The forced smile that had mechanically sprouted on his lips stayed stuck, giving his face a slightly clownish appearance.

'Uncle! Uncle...are you all right?' Neel asked with concern on seeing his girlfriend's father being uncharacteristically apathetic.

Rakesh's eyes refocused on Neel. The older man shook his head, as if to clear the cobwebs in his mind, and then responded, 'Neel, what are you doing here? I am so sorry; I was a little preoccupied with work. Come in, come in.'

What the hell is he doing here? He was going to be in London until we completed this operation, Rakesh thought to himself, acutely aware of Sangha upstairs, only a few rooms away. *Stay where are you are, please, Sangha. Please, please don't come down.*

'Surprised, *haan*? I will tell you all about it, Uncle,' replied the younger man, taking off his shoes and walking in. 'Where's Isha?'

'Uh, yes,' Rakesh cleared his throat, 'actually she's on a covert mission. She'll be back home in a few weeks.'

Neel paused in the act of sitting down on the sofa, and then let himself sink into its depths, shaking his head. 'This job!' he exclaimed.

'Your work in London is complete?' Rakesh rephrased his earlier question.

Neel grinned. 'I don't know if Isha told you why I went there, Uncle. Of course I had work there, but more importantly, Mom was being a little difficult and refusing to understand that I care for Isha. As she was reluctant to accept our relationship, I used a psychological ruse to convince her,' Neel held up his hand to forestall Rakesh's comments. 'There was no other way, Uncle, believe me. With me being away, I knew she would soon start to miss me and that would make her more receptive to what I wanted,' he shrugged. 'And that is exactly how it all played out—a little faster than I'd anticipated. So here I am...!'

'Ah! Here you are...except that here she isn't...' Rakesh joked feebly.

'The story of my love life, Uncle,' Neel quipped impishly.

I have to get him out of here, Rakesh thought furiously.

'Beta, listen, I'm in a bit of a rush. I was just on my way out, otherwise we could have had a nice cup of chai together. Vishnu's out as well,' Rakesh's statements sounded unnatural, even to his own ears.

'Of course, Uncle. No problem,' Neel said, jumping to his feet. Rakesh waited, counting the seconds while the young journalist put on his shoes. When Neel finished, Rakesh patted the younger man's back, accompanying him to the front door. 'Really sorry, Neel. I'll let you know as soon as Ishu's back, all right?'

'Sure, Uncle. See you soon.'

As Neel ran down the steps of the veranda, and walked

up to his car, Rakesh chastised himself. *Why the hell did he say Isha was away on a mission? Neel could easily find out that she—rather, Sangha—was at home. All he needed to do was call Manish and their subterfuge would be blown. Damn! He would have to reach out to Manish before Neel did.*

Rakesh was so preoccupied admonishing himself that he missed the shock on Neel's face. As he started the car and looked towards the house to wave to Rakesh, his gaze was drawn up to the room on the first floor. The window drapes were partially open, and in that gap, he glimpsed a familiar face. *Isha!* She met his eyes and instantly pulled back as if jolted, and quickly drew the curtains.

Why did Rakesh lie, Neel wondered. *And why was Isha hiding?*

21
Surprise, Surprise!

2025
The day after Isha's run-in with Manu
Abujmarh

It was nearly noon. Manu walked briskly ahead of Isha. They'd kept this pace soon after Isha had agreed to help him. They had set out from the camp late in the morning without arousing any suspicion. Isha followed Manu, as he took her deeper into the forest. As they walked, Isha told him she had infiltrated LalTara to gather intel on its operations. Manu told her how he had been bought from his parents and forced to work in LalTara, and how he yearned to escape and taste freedom once more.

Isha was careful to keep the specifics of Operation Trojan Horse from Manu. Most of it was dangerous information which would make the young boy a chink in her armour. But she did confirm his doubts that she was not Sangha but her twin Isha, adding that she was here on a special government mission to take LalTara down. Manu seemed to find whatever she told him exciting—like a movie, he said—and promised to help her in any way he could. However, her queries about where they were heading went unheeded. All he said was: 'This man I know...he's in big, big trouble. You have to help him, please.' He chanted it over and over again, peppering the refrain with 'Tej Anna is away. We have to do this today; we just have to!'

'Manu, I hope wherever we're going is not too far. We cannot be missed back in the camp.'

'Soon now. Very soon,' was his terse reply.

Ten minutes later, they approached the gentle elevation of a hillside where Manu slowed down and finally stopped. He motioned with his hand for Isha to stop too. He then listened intently for anything out of the ordinary. Reassured, he resumed, climbing up slowly, and signalled for Isha to follow.

They ascended the hillside and reached a tiny terrace-like flatness where the side of the hill formed a dense green backdrop. Manu approached this green 'wall' and stood before a thorny tangle of shrubs where he carefully hefted the vegetation aside, little by little, until a small opening was revealed in the stony expanse. This gap was narrow and slightly less than a man's height. Manu paused, breathing heavily after his strenuous exertion, and then, stooping a little, stepped into the breach. 'Come,' he motioned to Isha.

Isha followed, even as the opening constricted a little upon entry. Isha could only see Manu's back as she stepped in. She almost collided into him when he stopped. As he stepped aside to make room for Isha, she discerned a small hall-like cavity. Before her eyes could adjust to the gloom and focus on more details, her nose was assailed by a musky odour, mingled with the smell of urine and faeces. Instinctively, she covered her nose. As her vision grew accustomed to the half-light, she saw a human figure seated on the ground, propped up against a stony wall.

'Hello!' Manu called out gently.

The figure stirred, setting off a rattle of chains. It was a man. His head was covered with thick matted hair, and his face was concealed underneath a scruffy beard and moustache. His clothes were two sizes too large, but reasonably clean. The long sleeves of his shirt were unbuttoned at the cuff and hung limply, exposing thin wrists which were raw and red, chafed by the chains encircling them. His feet were unshod, bruised.

'No, no, no,' the man gibbered.

Something dropped in Isha's stomach on hearing his voice. She rushed towards him, and sank to her knees. The man screamed and shrank back, retreating from her by pressing his back into the stones behind him.

'Please, no, please, please,' he chanted. He squeezed himself tighter, lowering his head into his knees.

Isha ceased her movements. She didn't want to frighten him further. *Was this...? Could it be...?* she thought to herself, as a jumble of horror, hope and amazement settled into the pit of her stomach. 'Radu, is that you?' She whispered to him in a voice that threatened to break down any moment.

'You know him?' Manu asked, surprise and curiosity fighting for dominance in his voice. But Isha signalled him to be silent.

Hearing her voice, the man went still. Slowly, he lifted his head. When Isha looked into his eyes, she had no doubt; this was her favourite rookie, Radu Sinha. Scenes from the past flashed before her eyes. *The young man, shy and blushing, requesting leave to spend time with his new wife. Her refusal to grant it immediately, asking him to complete this mission first. Tej punching him and pushing him into the stream. Her helplessness on witnessing their disappearance into the water. Radu's wife's face, swollen with grief...*

She turned to face Manu. Her face, pale with horror and

rage, glimmered in the semi-darkness. 'What the fuck is all this?' she growled.

'Akka, I only know that Tej Anna brought him here. Tej Anna is very bad. If he had his way, he'd do terrible things to us, dirty things,' his voiced trembled. 'He likes boys; he enjoys hurting boys. But at least I...we—the runners and the boys who carry drugs—are kept safe from him as long as we are useful. However, if we suffer an injury or break a limb, or if we are no longer of use, then we are fed to him. Like meat to a dog...' Manu's voice trailed off with sheer horror.

With a shudder, he resumed his tale. 'I was there when Tej Anna and Rambhakt Anna brought him to the camp. Rambhakt Anna told me what had happened. Tej Anna captured him—Radu, you said his name was? Yes, he captured him the day they were going to pick up a consignment. He overpowered him, beat him up and raped him...and then he brought Radu Anna here.

'This one's endured a lot, Akka. Since he's been captured, Tej Anna has stopped visiting the village, and he doesn't bother us. This man has paid the price for our relief. He's been raped, tormented, beaten and subjected to every kind of brutal torture. I've seen the marks on his chest, his back, his legs, between his legs...'

Isha felt her stomach heave as Manu's narration ground to a halt. Except for the whimpers of the captive, it was eerily silent in the stone prison. She drew in a ragged breath, steeled herself to appear normal. But she couldn't stop the tears welling up in her eyes from spilling.

'Radu, *dekho meri taruf*. Look at me, Radu, I'm Isha. You remember?'

The battered man stared at her. Something shifted in his eyes. The focus sharpened. Recognition dawned.

'Isha madam-ji...' Rusty words emerged from his mouth.

'Yes, yes, Isha. I'm Isha. And I'm going to get you out of here.'

22

Trouble in Paradise

2025
STF19 headquarters, Raipur

Rakesh was aware that he was in a difficult situation with Neel, one that could compromise Isha and the mission. His mind was racing with thoughts on how to resolve this tight spot. Ever since he had managed to ward Neel off from his home without meeting Isha, Rakesh had been mapping out new stories and excuses in his head to convince Neel that he could not meet Isha. However, none seemed plausible enough. He had, of course, tipped Manish off and warned him to be cautious about what he disclosed to Neel. *I will find a way out. I will come up with a foolproof story. I have time to work this out,* he tried to calm his taut nerves as sleep eluded him that night.

The next morning, Rakesh was still somewhat preoccupied as he walked into his office. His angst heightened at the sight of Neel patiently sitting in the waiting area next to his secretary. Neel noticed Rakesh's already grim face turning ashen and then assuming a forced smile. His assistant, meanwhile, chirped in the background with a knowing intonation in her voice. 'Sir, I have already requested the canteen to bring in some special tea and biscuits.' Rakesh grunted politely, and composed himself to invite Neel into his room. He knew that considering Neel's last visit home, and with his journalistic instincts and sharp intelligence, it was not going to be a simple conversation.

As soon as the door closed behind them, Neel erupted like shaken carbonated water without beating about the bush. 'Why didn't you let me meet her?' he demanded.

Rakesh opened his mouth to answer, but Neel was too agitated to hold back. 'I saw her looking at me from the window. She was there in the house. You, you lied to me! Why?'

'Isha did not want to meet you,' Rakesh responded calmly, as he rubbed his nose, his heart pounding against his ribcage. *Isha would have immediately figured out from this gesture that Rakesh was lying. But thankfully, this was Neel.*

It was now Neel's turn to be taken aback. But before he could respond to Rakesh's assertion, there was a respectful knock at the door, followed by the canteen boy bearing a tray loaded with two cups of tea and an assortment of biscuits. A spread for a special guest. Relieved at this interruption, Rakesh frantically scanned various probable solutions to calm Neel down and keep Operation Trojan Horse from being compromised.

As soon as the canteen boy left, Rakesh picked up the teacup and handed it to Neel, acutely aware of Neel's turbulent emotions. On his part, Neel was irritated by Rakesh's cool composure, but he also wanted to tread carefully, not wanting to overstep his equation with Isha's father.

'Sorry, Neel, I lied. I should have told you the truth.' Neel was stumped by this abrupt confession. He had not anticipated this outcome from the meeting.

'I know I should have confided in you but I knew Isha wouldn't want you to worry about her.'

This statement immediately drained Neel of all his pent-up fury, and his eyes softened. Rakesh observed Neel's anxiety and agitation give way to concern, as he ran his fingers through his hair. A gesture that Isha—had she been present—would have promptly recognized as worry.

'She is a soldier, Neel, and a brave one at that,' Rakesh said tactically as Neel frowned, trying to figure out what Rakesh was trying to convey. 'And a soldier does not like to bare her wounds to anyone,' continued Rakesh. 'Isha has been injured in a covert operation. Her face is healing from some scars, and she has lost her voice. She did not want you to see her wounds lest you worry. She was sure her scars would heal by the time you returned from London, but your sudden arrival threw her off guard.'

'How is she now?' asked Neel, his annoyance a thing of the past.

Rakesh smiled; it seemed he had managed to handle the crisis. 'She is mending well, though it might take a while before she's comfortable with the idea of seeing you,' he said, hoping to gain more time.

'Oh! Thank God she is all right. I was so confused. I understand now. But please, Uncle, tell her I won't love her any less, however bad the scars,' he smiled. 'Ishu is such a daring soul. This is so like her to keep me, the civilian, as she calls me, from all things harsh.'

'I am so sorry we had you all worried, Neel.'

'That's all right, Uncle. But it would be nice if I could meet her. It's urgent. I want to convey some good news.'

'Anything I should know?' asked Rakesh. He managed to keep his composure, though he was not inclined to let any such meeting happen.

'Actually, yes. I feel a little awkward saying this, but you know my mother was not pleased with the idea of a soldier wife for me. She needed some time to come around, but it's finally happened and now she wants to meet Isha "officially".' Neel smiled while hooking his fingers into a quote sign. 'And I want this to happen sooner than yesterday!'

'Oh my god! Really!' Rakesh blurted out.

Neel mistook Rakesh's response as a father's exclamation of happiness for his daughter and grinned broadly.

This is getting worse, Rakesh thought, as he managed to keep the smile plastered on his face. *How long could he keep Neel from meeting Isha and how would he stop it? This was going to be impossible.*

23

Raptor

It was impossible for Neel to keep Isha out of his mind. He was curious about her condition. He wanted to know how she was, how she had got hurt, how she was feeling. He wanted to be there for her, but beyond a point Rakesh was a solid wall guarding information, and one who would not share any details about his daughter's well-being. *Rakesh Uncle is a soldier and a tough one at that*, Neel reasoned. *For him, Isha's wounds are nothing but bruises for a cause. Whatever it is, I'm not giving up either. I'm going to find a way to reach her. And who better than Manish to find out more about Isha.* Neel promptly picked up his phone and called his friend.

∞

2025
Manish's house, Raipur

It was early evening. Manish was on edge and restless. Sitting in front of his computer, he was anxiously awaiting Raptor666, his contact at external affairs, to pop up on the dark web chatroom, their usual digital rendezvous point. 'I will give it another thirty minutes, and then I am going to kill him,' he spoke aloud to no one in his room. He was aware he couldn't really do anything, considering that he did not know whether Raptor666 was a man or a woman, their position in the bureaucratic hierarchy, or even the source of their access to information. *Oh, how he hated it when he had no options!*

Manish inhaled and exhaled slowly, trying to calm himself. *No sense in getting so antsy. Acquiring the information he wanted was definitely tricky, but Raptor always delivered.*

When Manish had first received the data from Isha via the satellite phone, it took him over an hour to sift through it until he could start to make sense of it. What became clear was that LalTara's offshore account was overflowing with funds pouring in from a range of overseas sources. These revenues were being routinely funnelled into various obscure businesses abroad. However, curiously small, and seemingly insignificant, amounts were being regularly siphoned off before the rest was being transferred into multiple accounts in a complex, strategic manner—designed to render tracing the transactions an impossible task.

What was undeniable, however, was that money was being laundered. Though every layer of this convoluted financial web would need to be painstakingly unravelled, one trust account in Panama kept surfacing repeatedly in these transactions.

Who were the trustees behind this account? Could they be the shadowy figures at the top, benefiting the most from LalTara's schemes? Manish was convinced that this one Panama account held the key to the entire operation—a lead that could blow everything wide open. Yet, he understood that account details were highly classified information—offshore banks or agencies never let it out easily—and nearly impossible to extract.

Manish, however, was persistent and skilled at data scouting—even Rakesh had remarked on his special talent on several occasions. Although they had never really discussed it, Manish knew Rakesh was aware that Manish traded information for favours and he was capable of pulling this task off.

Deeply immersed in these thoughts, Manish was somewhat startled when his laptop pinged. *Raptor666! Finally!* But before Manish could reach for the keypad of his machine, Raptor's message flashed on the screen: *Need a couple more hours. This is a deeper dive than we thought.*

Manish cursed, but there was nothing he—or for that matter, Raptor666—could do. *If this was going to take time, it was going to take time!* Just as Manish acknowledged Raptor's message and put his computer on sleep mode, his phone rang. He picked it up mechanically, without looking at the caller's name.

'Hey Manish, what's up, bro?' a familiar upbeat voice enquired.

It was Neel. *Shit! Shit! Why the fuck had he not checked who was calling? Rakesh sir had already told him about his friend's unexpected return.*

'*Arre!*' Manish feigned surprise. '*Tu kab aaya* London *se*? I thought you were supposed to be away for a while. Isha had mentioned.'

'*Haan. Kaam jaldi ho gaya, so aa gaya wapas.* What are you doing?'

'Nothing. I was waiting for something, but that's going to take a while. So right now, I'm sitting at home on fuck shit and don't know what to do.'

'Okay, then let's clean the *tatti* together,' replied the cheerful voice. Manish could feel Neel's grin reaching his ears. This was their bro-code and both held it close to their hearts. *But wait, no! Better not to meet. What if he asked about Isha?*

'Hey, Neel, can we do this some other time? I'm really exhausted.'

'*Kya yaar!* I haven't seen you in ages, man. Come on. You'll feel better. *Waise bhi*, I am just five minutes away from you.'

Fuck. No one can stop him now. Manish sighed. '*Theek hai. Chal*, I'll see you in a bit. At my place. Really don't feel like stepping out.'

After all, this was his best pal Neel, who knew him inside out. Almost. The man he loved and tried not to hate at the same time. The man with whom he had to share Isha.

Manish and Neel had been best buddies since college. Later, when Manish joined the Special Task Force and Neel became a journalist, once again life threw them together in their professional capacities. They naturally resumed their friendship, and soon Isha, Manish's colleague, had joined their little gang.

Manish had fallen in love with Isha from the word go but was too shy to tell her. He had invited Neel into the picture in the hope that Neel would become his wingman. But life had other plans.

Isha had felt an instant attraction to the charming Neel, who reciprocated her feelings, sparking an immediate chemistry. Unaware of Manish's secret love, Neel proposed to Isha and the answer was a prompt yes. Manish had no choice but to be happy for them, although he did feel miserable for himself. He then took a step back and dived into *cardkismet.com*, although they continued to be a trio.

In no time after Manish disconnected the call, his doorbell rang and a smiling Neel stood outside his door with a bottle of single malt. It was going to be a boys' night with their fifteen-year-old favourite, Glenfiddich. Manish was aware that this reunion with Neel was going to be laced with a subtle interrogation about Isha. Rakesh had already tipped Manish off that Neel was asking questions.

'What a pig you are,' Neel commented on his friend's messy home. Clothes were strewn around, used crockery lay on the table, crumpled pieces of paper representing discarded thoughts lay on the floor. Neel, however, knew since their time in college that Manish tended to let things slide when he was focused on something.

When Neel poured out a drink for both of them in Manish's cherished Glencairn glasses, he could not help but notice that Manish downed the first drink on the rocks straight into his throat. As a look of pleased relaxation stole over Manish's face, Neel poured him another drink which, too, went down in a couple of quick gulps.

'You are in a whiskey shot mode today!' Neel said, smiling, sure that Manish was walking some stressful tightrope.

'What else to do when I have STF up my butt,' said Manish with a slight slur. The quick shots of single malt on an empty stomach were having an effect.

'I thought you were going to be away longer, Neel, and I was going to have Isha's attention all to myself,' smiled Manish, aware of the truth of his statement, but nevertheless knowing that Neel would take it as a joke.

'Isha is what got me back here *yaar*, but...' Before Neel could finish his sentence, Manish interrupted, '*kisi ke haath na aayegi yeh ladki,*[30] warbling the lyrics of a Bollywood song as he swallowed another shot of whiskey. The alcohol not only set fire to his oesophagus, but also scorched Rakesh's directions to exercise caution around Neel.

'Isha is gone,' Manish declared, clearly forgetting Rakesh's warning. 'Today we are in the same boat. She is gone...'

'Gone?' a confused Neel asked the gently swaying Manish.

'Pooff! On a save-the-country mission,' mumbled Manish, feeling pleased with himself for having cleared the grounds for Isha's absence. Little did Manish know that he had got Neel to wonder why his friend was lying. *Something was certainly amiss,* Neel thought, and determined that he would not rest until he found out what it was. He turned around to ask Manish a few more questions, but the sound of gentle, open-mouthed snores emanating from him arrested all further queries.

He looked at the beatific grin on his friend's face and felt an upswell of affection. A shining trail of saliva drooled from Manish's mouth and rolled down his chin, announcing his state of bliss. Neel took some tissues, wiped Manish's chin, and arranged a few cushions under his head before he left the apartment. His silent exit belied the cacophony of the thoughts hammering inside his mind. Concern for Isha swelled up in his chest; he needed to resolve this mystery around Isha to set his mind at peace.

◦∽◦

Manish woke up on his couch with a cushion under his head and a sheet neatly draped over his body. He could feel Neel's gentle, brotherly touch. He hoped that he had not said

---

[30]Lyrics of a song from the Hindi film *Chaalbaaz* (1989)

anything in his tipsy state that would give away his affection for Isha. Neel had left the bottle of Scotch for him and that was what he was going to focus on. This time, Manish poured out a measured drink, added some ice to it, and drank it in slow dignified sips to honour the hard work that had gone in making the malt.

His mind had cleared after the sleep. As the alcohol gently percolated into his happy place, Manish fired up his laptop and checked for any message from Raptor. Zilch! Okay, so then on to *cardkismet.com*. He felt triumphant, as if today was his day to win.

While he was engrossed in the game, the direct messenger on his game screen beeped green. Manish abandoned the game and clicked on the messenger. It read, *The information you need is here but it is set to disappear at first read.*

'Shit! Shit! Shit!' yelled Manish as he dived for his phone like a mad man. The phone's battery life was low and in the red, but he would have to give it a go. 'Fucker, you cannot outwit Manish, the protector of the realm,' he screamed out loud. He already had a plan and could hear the background score of *Mission Impossible* playing inside his head. He shot out a quick prayer to the god of gizmos that the battery juice on his phone would hold out for a few more minutes.

As the last bit of the message disappeared, the cell phone gave out a frantic beep and died. But Manish had managed to video record every bit of the disappearing message.

'Yes!' The tech whiz shouted triumphantly. When he powered up the cell phone and clicked the video open, his jaw dropped. *Raptor had indeed sent him a list of the members of the board of trustees of the Panama account.*

The list that now sat in front of him had the names of seventeen people from different parts of the world, who were probably the ones benefitting the most from LalTara's nefarious activities.

In the silence of the room, Manish could hear his own heartbeat make uneven thumping sounds.

Because there was one name on the list Manish knew.

24

Contradictions of the Mind

2025
The Srivastava house, Raipur

Sangha's failed attempt to flee had set back her equation with Rakesh. In an unspoken pact, they stowed away the shards of their strained relationship in a quiet place. The uneasiness, however, skulked in the shadowy recesses of their hearts, leaving their communication in a state of hushed stillness. The tracker encircling Sangha's ankle became the symbol of that mistrust. It was the proverbial elephant in the room, casting long, chilly shadows of awkwardness and silence.

Rakesh was instinctively aware that with Neel's arrival, this uncomfortable silence would no longer be tenable. It was time to unearth the buried emotions, to confront the unspoken truths, and unravel the complexities that bound them. He understood what he had to do. Yet, it was a chance he would have to take. He had no other option. He needed 'Isha' with him.

In his own way, Vishnu Kaka sensed trouble between father and daughter and tried to bring them together. He placed Rakesh's morning tea in the porch, as he knew Sangha would be out tending the garden. He then headed out to the market. *Let them not call out 'Vishnu Kaka, Vishnu Kaka' for everything.*

In all these years, Vishnu had never witnessed such awkwardness between the two and it unsettled him. *If they are the only two people in the house, they will eventually have to talk*, Vishnu reasoned and gave himself a pat on the back for coming up with this genius idea. As he walked away with his shopping bag, he hoped his absence would serve as a catalyst to bring the father-daughter duo back to normalcy.

Rakesh watched as Sangha tended the garden she had recently developed a fondness for, oblivious to the mud on her nose and her father's worried, intense gaze. *Until now, the strategy to break down LalTara had been Isha's responsibility. But with Neel back and Isha gone, the entire narrative would have to undergo a drastic change. The confidentiality of Operation Trojan Horse and the fact that 'Sangha' was Isha could not be compromised, as it was critical to the mission. It was also crucial for him personally. He would allow nothing, nothing to breach that secrecy. So what option was left but for the daughter who remained with him to step into her sister's shoes?* Even as he contemplated this scenario, the hairs on the back of Rakesh's neck prickled. *It was awful! A covert mission impersonating someone was one thing...but to take someone's place in actual, everyday life!* Rakesh rubbed his nose. *No! There was no other alternative. For Isha to be safe where she was, for her to have even half a chance of returning home safely, the illusion that she was here, at home, was imperative.*

Sangha, too, would have to play her part in Operation Trojan Horse—and play it to near perfection, enough to fool the one person who knew her every gesture and thought. Would she be able to convince Neel of her identity? And even if she played her part convincingly, how would she handle intimate moments with him? Rakesh resolutely pushed away all these thoughts. *Whatever it took, he—and Sangha—had to make it work.* Rakesh managed to clear the mind fog of racing thoughts and decided to prioritize what needed immediate attention. *It was going to be a challenging journey ahead, but he knew he had to take that first step.*

He strolled into the garden, to the spot where Sangha was working. As she saw Rakesh approach, the girl paused and put down her shears.

'We have to talk,' Rakesh said in a calm and matter-of-fact way.

'What about? Neel's return?' responded Sangha perceptively.

Her father nodded. 'The success of Operation Trojan Horse now depends on what happens here as well. Isha has to be here, as Neel has already seen you and has become extremely suspicious.'

Sangha looked at him, and then wordlessly picked up the shears and resumed pruning.

Keeping his irritation and exasperation in check, Rakesh went on with presenting his case.

'We cannot afford to take any chances with this mission. Everything has to appear normal.' Rakesh controlled his voice, which had risen a little with emotion.

Sangha continued to do what she was doing.

'You understand,' her father stated, 'that by the success of this mission, I mean the end of LalTara and of Bishen Rao. If we don't do this right, and if Rao gets even half a whiff of the switch, none of us is safe. He'll come after us, he'll pursue us, and we won't even know he's close by. Do you want to spend your life continually looking over your shoulder?'

The clicking of the shears ceased. Sangha looked up into her father's eyes.

'What do you have in mind?' she asked.

∽

Rakesh's first task to project Sangha as Isha was the most challenging. Opening Isha's phone and delving into her private chats and photos with Neel made him most uncomfortable. Isha had always shared her passwords with her dad for emergencies and Rakesh reasoned that this indeed qualified as an emergency. He mustered up the courage to proceed.

Sangha proved to be a quick learner and her rapid progress made Rakesh proud. She had always been jealous of Isha for being the luckier twin. So, while she had trained Isha to take her place at LalTara, she had closely observed Isha's actions, often role-playing as Isha in front of the mirror. Today, it seemed as if destiny had orchestrated her chance to be Isha. Initially, Rakesh was doubtful about Sangha's ability to portray her twin convincingly, but as time passed, he began to feel more confident.

After an intense and gruelling session, Sangha felt a vibration on her ankle. Glancing down, her heart skipped a beat; the anklet tracker had unfastened and lay loose on the floor. Looking up, she locked eyes with Rakesh. He held the tracker remote in his hand, his finger hovering over the unlock button. Sangha's logical brain acknowledged that Rakesh couldn't have kept the device on her in Neel's presence. Even so, the trust he showed in her, not waiting until the end to unfetter her, ignited a rush of emotions.

Wordlessly, she nodded her thanks.

∽

The arduous, emotionally taxing process of transforming one daughter into another was taking its toll on Rakesh. He wished he could share the burden with someone. *But with whom? Manish was busy investigating the money trail and Rakesh was loath to disturb him. There was Binod Rawat, of course.* Rakesh wished he could confide in his mentor and share all the information about LalTara. A few times he had reached for the phone to confide in Rawat, but then had stopped short, compelled by the pact he held as sacrosanct—that word of this mission must not go beyond the core team.

It was Friday, the day Rakesh was scheduled to meet and share information with Rawat. After the failure of Rakesh's last mission to stop LalTara, the home minister had been quite annoyed. 'How can I have your back when you don't trust me, Rakesh?' he had expressed his barely restrained anger. Now, as Rakesh sat in the minister's study waiting for the man, he felt his guilt sharpen as he thought about that exchange.

Binod Rawat's arrival interrupted Rakesh's chain of miserable thoughts. The STF19 commander stood up respectfully. Rawat walked in, and shook hands with his visitor. 'How are you, Rakesh?' he asked cordially, gesturing for him to take a seat. 'Ready for our usual pow-wow?' he smiled. Rawat was a large-hearted host and a caring mentor. He graciously kept a bottle of Rakesh's favourite Scotch in his collection for their meetings. As always, their first drink together was a toast to their camaraderie. How many times and in how many different ways had Rawat said to Rakesh: 'Though you are way younger than me, you are first my friend.'

The second drink always marked the transition to work.

So Rakesh was prepared when, raising a toast for the second drink, Rawat asked eagerly, 'Make me proud, my best officer! What do you have for me today?'

'Manish has acquired some classified information on LalTara. I'm awaiting further details from him,' Rakesh replied.

'Bravo! Can we take them down soon, Rakesh?' Rawat enquired earnestly.

'Fingers crossed, sir,' Rakesh said, aware that the information imparted was heavily filtered. Yet, he was pleased to see Rawat happy. Genuine moments of joy had been rare since the day of the LalTara ammunition intercept.

'Now, work mode off,' said Rawat, and Rakesh felt his mind lighten. He was grateful the minister didn't enquire further about the details.

'I heard that Neel is back. So when is he tying the knot with Isha?' Rawat asked casually.

The mention of Neel and Isha tightened the knot of anxiety in Rakesh's stomach that had just begun to loosen. He dreaded Neel and his mother's visit home, while praying that Sangha would pass the litmus test. He was anxious about the impending encounter.

∽

2025
Manish's house, Raipur

After reading the name in Raptor's message, Manish sat frozen for a while, his mind refusing to process the information. As reality began to sink in, uncertainty flooded his thoughts. *Should I escalate this? How would they handle it?* His mind raced, considering the broader implications. *What did this mean for him personally?*

Unable to sit still, he got up and began pacing the room, his footsteps mirroring the chaos in his head. Then abruptly, he stopped, his decision made. He picked up the phone and dialled a number.

'I would like to meet him for a few minutes,' he insisted over the phone, his voice tinged with irritation. 'Tell him it's about LalTara.'

The voice over the mobile kept him on hold for a few minutes and then returned to give him a time and the location where he should reach. It was an old warehouse, half an hour away from the city.

Manish disconnected, then patiently uploaded the data to a safe, third-party Google Drive. He smiled because he knew the owner of the Google Drive would not be able to access the data for some time. Then he reformatted his computer's hard disk to make it squeaky clean, after which he picked up his satchel and left.

He understood it was blackmail, but the money was going to be his ticket to financial freedom.

He could not have imagined that he was venturing into a rattrap.

25

The Calm before the Storm

2025
Abujmarh

Leaving Radu alone in that cave was one of the hardest decisions Isha had ever had to take. She had tried to pick the lock and even smash it, but the chains proved stronger and foiled her attempts. Almost weeping in frustration and anger, Isha had reassured Radu over and over again that she would return to release him. Each time, the battered, broken man had wept and beseeched her not to go. Eventually, hardening her heart and squeezing his hand one final time, she had left him. Stepping out in the open, she took a deep breath as if to cleanse her soul of the darkness she'd just witnessed, but it still lingered.

'Akka, we have to hurry back,' Manu urged her, noticing her hesitation at the mouth of the cave. Isha started to mechanically climb down after him, her mind preoccupied with formulating a plan for Radu's release.

'Manu, listen. When does Tej return?'

'Two days, Akka. He should be here the day after, sometime in the late evening. He keeps the keys to Radu's shackles with him.'

'Okay. I'm going to keep Radu company as much as possible in these two days. Who gets him food and a change of clothes?'

'I do.'

'Great. Get him more food. Let's try to get some strength back into him. Meanwhile, we have to figure out a way to free Radu.'

∞

Two days passed uneventfully. No one seemed to notice Isha's prolonged absences. On the second day, in the late evening, Tej's car came roaring into the camp. Soon, his loud voice shattered the relatively peaceful atmosphere. Phoolma emerged from her room, all smiles that her son had returned. 'Shall I serve you dinner, beta?' she asked her son.

'No, Ma, I've eaten on the way. I'm not very hungry. But I could do with some snacks and a drink,' he smiled.

'All right. Don't overdo the drinks, though. You need to rest.' After imparting this motherly advice, Phoolma withdrew for the night.

'Hey you!' Tej called out to one of the men. 'Send some snacks and a bottle of water.' This order was passed on to Manu, who was deliberately loitering nearby so he could be called for a chore.

He went into the kitchen and piled a dish with piping hot bhajiyas that had already been prepared on Phoolma's orders, in anticipation of Tej's arrival. He also grabbed a bottle of water and a glass. Manu's heart hammered against his ribs as he thought of what he had to do, but he forged ahead. Nervously, he entered Tej's room. 'Anna, snacks and water,' he announced.

Tej, lounging on the charpoy,[31] motioned him to keep

---

[31]Charpoy: A bed consisting of a frame strung with light rope or coir weaving

the tray on the table, where a bottle of whiskey already stood. 'Mix,' he ordered Manu.

Pretending to clear some space on the table for the tray, Manu turned his back to Tej. He poured out a generous dose of liquor into the glass. Then with trembling hands, he extracted a small bottle from the pocket of his pants. This was a concoction made from passionfruit and it was incredibly effective for reducing anxiety. In large doses, it could knock you out. Manu quickly added a generous quantity and topped the glass with water. He took the drink with the plate of fritters to Tej.

Tej took the glass and swallowed deeply, grunting in satisfaction. Crunching on a fritter, he looked at Manu. 'Want to keep me company?' he asked him mischievously.

'Anna... I'll w-wait outside if you need anything,' the boy stammered, slinking out of the room.

Twenty minutes after serving two more drinks, Manu peeped nervously into the room. Tej lay on the bed, snoring gently. Manu drew back, stood in the doorway and coughed thrice.

Standing in the shadows of her quarters, Isha heard this pre-arranged signal. She looked around cautiously to make sure no one was nearby, before running softly into Tej's room. 'Get away from here,' she whispered to Manu, and then stepped inside. She closed the door gently and contemplated the sleeping figure. The man lay on his back, his mouth slightly open. His clasped hands rested on his stomach, which rose and fell with every breath. Isha crept up to him and circled the bed, looking for the keys. Nothing on his belt. They must be in his pocket then.

She squatted down on her haunches and gently touched his pockets, trying to feel an outline of something resembling a key. Yes, there was something on the right side. Angling her neck and crouching further down, she tried to peer down the pocket, hoping to catch a glimpse of something metallic. No luck. Clenching her teeth, she slipped two fingers inside it. Just then, Tej groaned and turned on his right side. He was now face to face with Isha, his sour, whiskey-laden breath wafting unpleasantly up her nose. She could see each pore on his oily skin and the puffiness of his eyelids, which were mercifully closed. Worse, her right hand was caught under his body, the strings of the charpoy biting painfully into her skin.

Fuck, fuck, fuck, she exclaimed silently. All she could do was sink down below Tej's eye level and go down on the elbow of her free arm. She froze in that position, one hand trapped under Tej and chafing from the coir of the charpoy, and her elbow stuck at an awkward angle. However, her fingers could still move and she continued probing. *Yes! She could feel the shape of something key-like. If only she could get it out quietly and run.*

In his slumber, Tej grunted and gasped before he stirred. *Turn, turn,* she prayed. No such luck! Then she heard the high-pitched whine of a mosquito's wings. It approached and receded and then went silent. Disturbed, perhaps from the mosquito's bite, the sleeping man turned on his back again, freeing Isha's trapped hand. Sending a silent prayer to the universe, Isha maintained her position, and waited for Tej to resume his snoring.

Once she was satisfied he had slipped into deep sleep, she lightly pulled the hardness at her fingertips little by little, until a tiny metallic sliver emerged from the depths of the fabric. She paused, clenched her teeth, and continued. The keys, finally! She extracted them, trying to make as little sound as possible. Once they were completely out, she enveloped them tightly within her fist, rose to her haunches and then to her feet. She walked stealthily to the door, shut it softly behind her, and fled.

∞

Manu and Isha entered Radu's prison and released him quickly. They massaged his hands and feet, helping him stand. He staggered like a drunken man and almost fell, managing to maintain his balance at the last moment.

'Good,' Isha encouraged him. 'Radu, you'll be all right now.'

The plan was to take Radu to the main crossroad, and set him on the road that would eventually lead him to a settlement where sympathetic villagers, who were tired of LalTara's atrocities—especially Tej lusting after their young men, and them being used as drug mules—would be willing to help him. Isha wrote two numbers on a piece of paper and gave it to Radu to keep safely. Once he reached a friendly village, they could help Radu establish contact with Rakesh Srivastava. Isha and Manu would then hurry back to the camp and return Tej's keys.

'Come on, Radu Anna,' Manu said, holding out his hand for the newly released prisoner. The gaunt man smiled and put his arm around his young rescuer's shoulder. Isha patted Radu on the back and cautioned both to be careful. She gave him a bag of food and water for sustenance until he reached a sanctuary.

'Go ahead,' she told them. 'I'll follow soon.'

They had deliberately chosen a staggered exit so that Isha could follow the duo without being noticed, and have the advantage of surprise just in case they were accosted. She waited for the sound of their descent to die down. Now she could start her journey behind Manu and Radu. Carefully, she picked her way through shrubs and loose stones. *Earlier, she had Manu with her on these trips; now she was alone. She had to be careful; she couldn't risk a fall.* Her STF19 training helped, but the terrain was furiously unforgiving. The going was slow, but finally she reached the base of the hill.

'Manu,' she called out softly.

'Here,' came the equally hushed response.

Isha moved towards the direction of the voice and found the two young men crouched in the shrubbery.

'*Chalo, jaldi karo,*' she urged them to be quick. 'We have to return the keys too. No time to lose.' Saying this, she put her hand in her pocket, anticipating the hardness of steel. *Nothing!* Frantically, she checked her other pocket. *Empty!* She slapped her forehead. *In the urgency and excitement of freeing Radu, she had forgotten the damned keys in the cave.*

'What happened, Akka,' Manu asked, worry dripping from every word. 'I forgot to bring the keys,' Isha whispered, embarrassed and angry.

'*Ab kya karenge*? What shall we do now?' Manu asked, alarmed.

'Don't worry. Change of plan. You drop Radu to the junction. I'll go and fetch the keys. We meet at the clearing on the way to LalTara. You know which one I mean, right?'

Manu nodded and gulped. 'Akka...' he started tremulously.

'Don't worry, Manu. It's just a little hiccup. Everything will be all right. You can do this,' she said encouragingly, patting him on his back. 'Radu, you take care, and remember to make the call.'

Both nodded and turned to walk away. Their frail figures were soon swallowed up in the darkness.

Isha sighed and headed up the hill. It's always harder going up, they say, and this was eminently true for Isha's tedious ascent to Radu's erstwhile prison.

༄

One hour had passed since Tej had consumed the passionfruit-infused whiskey and slipped into a deep slumber. He grunted and shifted in his sleep. Turning on one side, however, he got too close to the edge of the bed and tumbled down. With a cuss, he sat up and rubbed his arm.
'Bhenchod!'
He lumbered to his feet and stretched his back. *Now that he was up, he may just as well take a leak.* He exited his quarters and headed to the rear of the room. He couldn't be bothered to use the toilet. He would simply conduct his business at the back. A stream of fluid disappeared into the shrubs. *Aah!* Relief! He finished and wiped his hands on his trousers. Suddenly, he stopped mid-action. *Something was missing! The keys! Where were the keys? Must have fallen in the room.* But then, when he couldn't find them in the room, the alarm bells went off stridently in his head.

༄

26

The Storm

Isha ascended the hill and made her way to the cave. Even without its occupant, the cave still wore a menacing and depressing air. A quick sweep of torchlight picked up a glint near the stone walls. Isha swooped over the keys, picked them up, and looked at her watch. *Damn, all in all, she would lose a precious half hour due to her carelessness.*

Cursing herself, she started down the slope of the hill, willing herself to maintain a slow, steady and silent pace. She wanted to reach the meeting place before Manu did; otherwise he would worry needlessly. Soon, she could discern the land getting flatter, which meant that the descent was almost done. Just this last patch of dense vegetation and she would reach relatively open ground.

Suddenly she stopped. Something had flickered in her peripheral vision. *Was it torchlight?* She stood still for a minute. *Nothing. Must be a visual nerve firing,* she decided before she resumed her descent. She broke free of the last tangle of shrub and reached the base. She looked about, but there was no sign of Manu. *She would have to take cover and wait.* But just as she was about to look for an appropriate place, the shadow of a tree to her right appeared to break free and separate.

And before she could react, a blow to her head sent her reeling into unconsciousness.

The darkness that overcame Isha was not a still, peaceful blackness. It whirled madly at first, and then seemed to settle into a gentle rocking accompanied by a soft sound. Isha couldn't decide which was more annoying. *Perhaps if she opened her eyes, both the sound and the movement would stop.* She tried, but at first her eyelids refused to part. Then, they slowly opened. The world was still black, but now there were degrees of blackness. She could make out silhouettes, branches, leaves overhead, a form, a human form. *No, two: one standing, one prone on the ground.* She willed her brain to start functioning. The standing person turned his head and looked at Isha directly. *Tej!* He walked towards her, gun directly pointed at her face.

'You look so much like her. I wonder how they did this,' he looked genuinely awe-struck. 'Who are you?' he questioned.

Isha remained silent.

'Hmm. We're playing silent movies today, are we? No worries. They'll turn into talkies very soon. That chit of a boy also tried that tack with me,' Tej continued, inclining his head in the direction of the other person. Isha's eyes mechanically followed Tej's movement and rested upon Manu. He lay on his side, hands obviously shackled behind his back, whimpering.

'But he squawked in the end. He even informed me where he took my toy. But there's not much he could tell me about you,' Tej said.

Isha turned to look at Manu for confirmation. He looked at Isha and shook his head. He mouthed a word: *Sorry!* She closed her eyes. Her head hurt. *Was this the end of her and Operation Trojan Horse?*

She heard Tej's footsteps approach her, closer and closer, and suddenly he was on her, straddling her stomach.

She whimpered. He held both her hands securely in one of his and easily raised and pinned her arms above her head; with the other, he fondled her breast. 'Rao is going to be so happy, when I bring him this news. But first, let's play a little, shall we?' he smirked. Sitting atop her, he put his hand behind him to grope between her legs. 'You have no idea how long I've wanted to do this. If not Sangha, her look-alike will do.' Then he leaned close to her. She felt his wet tongue lick her lobes and probe her ear. She cringed and moved her head away. He held her face, his fingers digging into both her cheeks. 'Want to play rough?' he smiled.

'Please, don't do this,' Isha pleaded, opening her eyes and willing them to well up.

Tej's grin widened. *This was good. This begging and pleading; it was good foreplay.* His face drew closer to hers. As his eyes devoured her mouth, Tej's grip on Isha's face loosened. This was the opportunity Isha needed. Drawing strength from her core, Isha closed the gap between their faces and bit him hard on his chin. The suddenness of this attack surprised him, causing him to relinquish the grip on her hands that were pinned above her head. Quick as lightning, Isha twisted her leg and reached for the blade concealed in her boot without letting go of Tej's chin. Once, twice, thrice, the deadly steel rose and fell, burying itself deep into his back. Tej reached for her throat but Isha was prepared. Now, it was frontal assault. She gripped the handle of the knife tighter and drove the weapon into his stomach, and then the chest. Tej's cries became weaker and weaker, until he slumped over her. She could feel his blood wetting her shirt. She hefted his body away from hers, gasped for air, and sat up. She wiped the blade on Tej's trousers and returned it to its hiding place. Then she staggered to her feet, the adrenaline sending tremors through her body. She ran to Manu, who was bound with his own shirt. She unknotted it and helped him stand up.

'You okay?'

He nodded. 'I couldn't fight him, Akka,' he sobbed. 'He was too strong...'

'Never mind. It's okay now. You are safe. You managed to drop Radu?'

'Yes Akka, but what are we going to do with him?'

They both looked at Tej's body. This was a twist they hadn't anticipated.

27

Dead Weight

Manu grunted. 'Chutiya, he weighs as much as a baby elephant. Akka, can we stop for a bit?'

They had been dragging Tej's body away from the hill where Radu was held captive. When Tej was missed, this would be the first place LalTara would despatch people to. The longer it took for Tej's body to be discovered, the better it was for Manu and Isha to formulate their alibis, because an in-house investigation would surely follow.

'No, Manu,' Isha responded, panting with exertion herself. 'We don't have much time. Burying him would have been the best thing to do, but time *nahi hai*. So our only option is to hide the body. We'd better hurry, because I have to get rid of my bloody shirt as well.'

Manu nodded as he wiped the sweat from his forehead. 'Just a little bit more to go,' he gasped. They struggled on, until they reached a thicket surrounding a hollow. Manu had suggested this spot as a good place to dump the body.

'Akka, give me your torch. Many animals like this location for its security. Let me check first. We've had enough surprises for one night.'

Manu approached the thick underbrush, making as much noise as possible, pounding the ground with a piece of wood he had picked up from the forest floor. *If there was a wild animal in the hollow, he wanted to give it enough time to slink away or make its displeasure known.* He got nothing. *Good!*

Then, spotting a thin spot in the tangle of bushes leading into the hollow, Manu unbuttoned his shirt and hung it on a shrub to mark the place before walking back towards Isha.

'Akka, all clear,' he said. 'There's a space through which we can push him in.'

The two heaved Tej's body to the spot and then manoeuvred to push it through the thicket, until it was completely covered by the shrub and no longer visible on the outside. Then they stood looking at each other. For Isha, the sense of unreality that had beset her since Tej's attack on her and the subsequent unfolding of events, had receded while they were occupied with disposing of the body. It now returned, more intense than ever.

Trying to get a grip on reality, she removed her bloodied shirt and used a clean portion to wipe her face. She then looked at Manu piercingly.

'Manu, now is the only time we have to discuss this incident. When we return to LalTara, we shall never speak about this again. Never.'

Manu nodded dumbly.

Isha patted his back. There was nothing more to say. 'Some wild animals will hopefully make a meal of... of...' she felt ill at the thought. Finally, all she could say was, 'Let's go.' It seemed like the longest night of her life.

∞

Isha and Manu managed to reach their respective rooms without exciting any suspicion. The first thing Isha did was grab a towel and some fresh clothes before heading to the washroom block, greeting the guards that stood outside her room on the way. She bathed, washed her clothes, including the bloodied shirt she had wrapped in her towel, and hung them out to dry. To all appearances, Sangha had just started another day at the camp.

She headed to the cafeteria, casually nodding to Manu, who, similarly refreshed, was hanging around the mess.

'What's up, Manu?'

'Good morning, Sanghakka!'

Isha nodded to him, smiled and patted his back. They looked at each other, silently drawing strength to face the inevitable storm which would certainly be unleashed. After a quick breakfast, which tasted like sawdust in her mouth, Isha went to oversee some repairs to the firing range. Three hours passed as she worked. When Rambhakt passed through the range, he saw Isha guiding the workers and turned and headed in her direction.

'Sangha, have you seen Tej?' he asked.

'Tej? No. Wasn't he supposed to have come in last night?'

'He did, but the night guard saw him leave again. He went towards the jungle on foot.'

Isha pulled at her earlobes, remembering with distaste Tej's tongue darting all over them. 'Oh, that's strange. I've been up early and I haven't seen him around.'

'His mother's going mental,' Rambhakt told her conspiratorially. 'I think she'll soon send out a search party. All of her famous fucking spy network that keeps her informed about every fart in this place,' he spat in disgust.

'So things are obviously in good hands,' Isha responded nonchalantly. 'Anyway, let me know if you need any help,' she said, walking away.

She went to her room, closed the door, and slumped against it. 'Fuck,' she swore softly.

∽

2025
A few hundred kilometres away

Manish's plan to blackmail the person mentioned in Raptor's message had backfired disastrously, plunging him into a nightmare of pain and punishment. What was meant to be a calculated move had crumbled, leaving him trapped in a dark and isolated warehouse, where his captor and his coterie held him, subjecting him to relentless torture.

His tormentor spared no effort in extracting information. Hours of brutal beatings were followed by days of abandonment in a crumbling room, with the rough floor soaked with his own blood and sweat. The corridor outside was always under watch—he could hear voices, footsteps, the murmur of unseen guards. After what felt like lifetimes, someone would enter and demand the same answers over and over again.

During one excruciating session, on the edge of delirium, Manish had mumbled something about following the money trail on Rakesh's orders. But even in his most broken state, he did not utter a single word about Operation Trojan Horse.

The agony was overwhelming, his strength was ebbing away, and his thoughts were slipping into darkness. Yet, with the last remnants of his will, he clung to a single thought: *I have to escape. I cannot fail Isha.*

28

Mehendi Laga ke Rakhna

2025
Raipur

The day of Sangha's litmus test dawned. While respecting Rakesh's wishes to let Isha get over her mission-related trauma in peace, Neel had insisted—and succeeded in this endeavour—on a telephonic chat with his girlfriend. The conversation had initially been filled with Neel's affectionate concern for 'Isha', and then—with Neel apparently reassured—turned into a request for a meeting between the two families. Sangha tried her best to discourage this plan, stating that she was in no mental state to handle something as important as this. But Neel had gently persisted, and finally won.

Neel and his mother Kaveri Saini were expected to come to their house that evening. When Rakesh glanced at Sangha across the breakfast table, he knew that she, too, had passed a restless night. *Her face appeared drawn, and the skin below her eyes looked smudged, as if she'd rubbed her kohl-lined eyes through the dark hours.* He gave a mental shrug. *They could attribute her appearance to anxiety about meeting her soon-to-be mother-in-law. The fuck-up was that this wasn't the first time Kaveri would be meeting 'Isha'. As her son's girlfriend, she had often visited their home. Sangha would need to be very careful in her presence.*

Rakesh had briefed Sangha over and over again, about how and where Isha had met Kaveri and how they had interacted. He even managed to find an old video which partially captured them together in one of the get-togethers they had attended. He nevertheless wondered whether this information would be sufficient for Sangha to get under Isha's skin.

Sangha could sense what her father was going through, what he was thinking. One didn't have to be a rocket scientist to figure out that the imminent meet-and-greet weighed heavily on his mind. She felt slightly nauseous herself. However, the image of Neel's upturned face looking at her kept popping up in her mind's eye and sent her heart racing. She'd never felt this way about any man before.

'Are you all right?' Rakesh's question interrupted Sangha's reverie. 'Today's a big day,' he continued. 'You're feeling fine, right?' He didn't want to say anything more revealing in the presence of the house help. Even at that early hour, the house was full of activity. A team of three was busy cleaning the garden, while Vishnu Kaka presided over the two women who'd come to assist him in the kitchen.

Sangha swallowed her tea and nodded. 'Don't worry. I'm okay. Everything will work out fine.' She seemed to understand exactly what Rakesh was hinting at. *She's a clever girl*, he thought. *My girl*.

Father and daughter spent the rest of the day mostly busy with the preparations, but also horribly anxious. It was soon evening. Sangha was in her room—rather, Isha's room—ready and waiting. When Rakesh entered the room, he stood at the threshold, pleasantly surprised at the sight. Sangha, standing by the mirror, was wearing a pale peach salwar-kameez; the soft fabric, sprinkled with a constellation of delicate sequinned stars, complemented her bright eyes. Her ears and throat were adorned with small pearls and her thick curls had been disciplined into a messy bun. Rakesh felt an upswell of emotion that threatened to spill out through his eyes. He blinked, cleared his throat, and said, 'Beta, you look lovely.'

Sangha had blushed under her father's appreciative gaze, her hand self-consciously reaching up to tuck a stray curl behind her ear. Hearing his words, she froze in the act. *Not that he had never called her beta—child—before, but today was different. It seemed like a call from the deepest part of a father's heart.* Before she could stop herself, she stepped forward and hugged him. Rakesh seemed taken aback. She could sense his momentary hesitation at her sudden outburst of emotion, before his arms enveloped her protectively, and father and daughter stood embracing each other for a couple of heartbeats. Rakesh then stepped back gently. 'I don't want to spoil your dress,' he said in a choked voice. 'I will pray for such a day to truly come into your life.'

That broke the spell for Sangha. It quickly dawned on her that this was not her special day. *It was Isha's. And she, most definitely, was not Isha.* Sangha nodded to the man in front of her, her emotions already reined in. 'Pray that this one goes well,' she replied matter-of-factly. The sound of an approaching car pierced the mantle of coolness that abruptly seemed to shroud the room.

'They're here,' Rakesh exclaimed anxiously, turning away from Sangha as he hurried out to receive the guests.

By the time Sangha collected her thoughts and stepped downstairs to the living room, Neel, his mother and a few relatives were already seated around the coffee table. But Sangha had eyes only for Neel. The attraction she had felt for him at that first fleeting sight was cemented by this encounter. Neel quickly stood up when he saw her standing at the door, and despite the anxious churning in her stomach, Sangha could not help but admire his lean physique honed by basketball, Krav Maga and kickboxing.

Neel walked towards Sangha, and gently took her hand. She suddenly felt shy. 'Isha,' he said, and Sangha drew in a sharp breath. 'You're looking gorgeous! I don't know why you and Uncle were so reluctant about a meeting. You'll always be beautiful to me, no matter what. You know that, don't you?'

'Y-yes,' Sangha managed to stammer.

'And I'm sorry if I've been a cad and insisted on this, even though you weren't feeling up to it. But I thought there's nothing like striking when the iron is hot...'

Sangha summoned up a weak smile.

He looked into her eyes. 'That's great then,' he whispered, putting an arm around her shoulder. 'Come, say hello to Mom. I'll also introduce you to the rest of my family.'

Walking into the room with Neel by her side, and looking at the circle of interested, smiling faces—two ladies, a young girl and a boy—Sangha felt the whole situation take on a dream-like, surreal dimension. As if from behind a gossamer veil, she saw Neel's mother, elegant and sophisticated.

'Hello Aunty-ji,' Sangha stammered, smiling at Kaveri. She bent down to touch her feet.

'*Jeeti raho*,' Neel's mother spouted the mandatory blessing.

'These are my aunts, Shivangi and Nisha, and my cousins, Suhana and Aseem,' Neel said making the introductions. 'Guys, this is Captain Isha Srivastava, and this is her father, Commander Rakesh Srivastava. They both work with the Government of India.'

Sangha mustered up a smile, folded her hands in a namaste, while her father greeted everyone.

'Come, Isha,' Kaveri said, patting the seat next to her.

Sangha complied.

'Neel talks so much about her, you know,' she told her relatives, and then, turning to Sangha, said, 'I'm proud of you, my dear. I like it when girls make bold life choices.' Sangha heard Rakesh cough beside her and reach for a glass of water. She felt a strange urge to giggle. *What a lying bitch you are, my dear,* she thought. *My father has told me all about what you think of Isha.* Outwardly, she smiled. 'It's elders like you who encourage us and shape who we are, Aunty-ji. My father also thinks exactly like you,' she said.

The older woman's eyes sharpened and her nostrils twitched, as if there was something foul-smelling under her nose. She couldn't figure out whether the girl in front of her was being genuine or cheeky. Her hand strayed to the large diamond and emerald pendant that nestled in the folds of her elegant pastel green *chikankari* sari. *The mighty family jewels are being aired to impress,* Sangha thought cynically.

'Neel tells me you have returned from a particularly sensitive mission?' Kaveri continued, making small talk.

'Yes, Aunty-ji,' concurred Sangha, tensing up a little.

'Secret mission and all, huh? How thrilling!' Aseem piped in.

'Do you do stunts like in those kick-ass thrillers?' Suhana asked excitedly.

'Well...' Sangha began uncertainly, when Rakesh intervened. 'There's a reason these missions are secret, Suhana,' he quipped. 'If we tell you what goes on in there, they won't remain secret, will they?'

Everyone tittered. The atmosphere relaxed a little.

But Suhana, the movie buff, would not let go of her favourite topic. 'Who's your favourite hero, Isha?'

Sangha was stumped. This was not something Rakesh had covered in their sessions transforming her into Isha. 'Ummm...' she looked at Neel and smiled. 'Neel. Of course it's Neel, my one and only hero...' she completed her response. Even to her own ears, it sounded lame.

Neel grinned and blushed. He wasn't accustomed to such romantic statements from Isha. *What has come over her,* he wondered.

'Oh, come on, don't be such a diplomat,' urged Suhana, while Neel's family looked on indulgently. Rakesh's face, however, had whitened. 'Beta, how can you forget your favourite Khan,' he said, frantically attempting to give her a hint. Khan? thought Sangha furiously. Sure, but which one? There are three!

'Salman...' she stammered. 'Salman Khan.'

Neel laughed. 'Ishu, since when have you changed sides? Shah Rukh was the only man for you earlier.'

'Yes, of course. But now I like both. Of late, I like Salman too...' Sangha slapped a quick smile on her face.

Just then, Shah Rukh's popular song *'mehendi laga ke rakhna'* erupted from Aseem's phone. 'Bro, that's your cue,' he addressed Neel, looking at his elder cousin pointedly.

Neel grinned nervously. He took a deep breath and dropped down on one knee in front of Sangha.

'Isha Srivastava, will you marry me?' He whipped out a crimson rose and offered it to Sangha.

The girl stood frozen, rooted to the spot. She heard a gasp behind her. *That can only be Rakesh,* she thought. *What was she to do? Flee back to her room? Would that resolve the situation or lead to more complications?* Her brain went catatonic and as if in a dream, she saw a hand—*was it hers?*—reach out for the rose and heard the whispered words, 'Yes, I will,' as if from a great distance. *Was it her voice?*

Neel's clan enthusiastically broke out into spontaneous clapping. 'So this is what you were planning all week,' exclaimed Neel's aunt, Nisha. 'The amount of whispering that was going on in the house,' she shook her head indulgently.

Neel stood up now. The smile that had spread wide across his face as he popped the question had faltered a little. Isha's peculiar, subdued, somewhat scared reaction was not the response he had expected. *Maybe it's all those medicines,* he reasoned to himself. *But even Rakesh—he wasn't looking all that happy either.*

'Sir, is everything all right? You don't seem to be too pleased...' he asked the older man.

'*Arre na, na,* Neel. It was just somewhat sudden, that's all. We thought this was going to be just the first meeting between families and we would take things slow...'

Kaveri stood up. 'Ah, slow-show *nahi*. No, no, Rakesh-ji. *Chat mangni, pat byaah.* Let's fix up a date for an early engagement. I don't think there are any auspicious dates in the upcoming month. I consulted our Pandit-ji before coming here. However, I shall visit him again and we can figure something out soon.'

Rakesh could only nod his head.

༄

The party dispersed after partaking of Vishnu Kaka's excellent culinary fare. However, Neel lingered and decided to stay back for some more time, much to Kaveri's displeasure and the amusement of his aunts and cousins.

Mehendi Laga ke Rakhna » 207

As Rakesh retired reluctantly and tensely retreated into his room, Neel requested Sangha to take a walk with him in the garden. As they strolled away from the house and towards the fragrant jasmine shrub, he gently took Sangha's hand and stopped. He placed both his hands on her shoulders and turned her towards him. 'Ishu, tell me the truth. Is something bothering you? Are you happy? Are you having any second thoughts?'

Sangha was terrified. She was unsure whether to buy some time by saying 'yes', or say 'no, everything is fine'. Something compelled her to opt for the latter. *Was it because despite being terrified, this heady physical proximity to Neel was even more exhilarating?* She couldn't say.

Neel looked relieved. 'Look, I know you've been through a lot. I can see it on your face. Perhaps the theatrics we planned were a bit too...dramatic? I want you to tell me if ever there's a problem, won't you?'

He cupped her face in his hands while speaking to her, and there was nowhere she could look but into his eyes. She was lost. 'Yes,' she whispered, 'I will.'

He smiled, leaned into her and kissed her gently on the lips. 'I love you, Ishu,' he breathed into her ears.

Sangha's eyes were closed. *She didn't want to open them. Ever.*

∽

Anxiously, Rakesh watched from his bedroom window as Neel and Sangha strolled in the garden, turned a corner and vanished from view. He sighed and scanned the road in front of their house. It had become a habit, possibly a response to the hazards of his profession. Isha always ribbed him about never being truly at ease. *Everything seemed normal outside—*

except for a black Kia with tinted windows. It was not one of the regular cars that he had seen parked there. Maybe his neighbours were having guests over.

Claiming a headache, Sangha retired to her bedroom immediately after Neel left. Rakesh let her be as even he didn't have the energy to take part in an intense discussion. Yet, both Rakesh and Sangha were aware that there was a lot to review and deliberate on. After a bowl of soup, Rakesh fired up his laptop. His eyes were mechanically reading about global events headlined on his favourite website, but his mind was preoccupied with events that had unfolded earlier in the day. *What would Sangha do? What would they do? The marriage proposal and an early engagement were totally unanticipated developments! Dealing with Neel was one thing, but now they had his mother and family to contend with, and possibly even a wedding.* He closed his laptop, and sauntered to the window, as if the fresh air would help him to find a way out of the present complication. He watched the quiet street with unseeing eyes and scratched his nose. At first nothing registered, but then he frowned. *Something was not right.*

His eyes scanned the street once again. There, partially hidden by some bushes, was a black car. He whipped out his mobile, opened the camera icon and zoomed in on the screen. *A black Kia—surely the same black Kia!* It had moved from where it was parked previously, but he had no doubt it was the same car. He couldn't see clearly through the tinted glass, but could make out two heads in the dim, reflected light of a street lamp. They appeared to be angled in his direction. He attempted to take a photograph of the car's number plate, but it was too much in the shadows.

Half a minute passed in what he could only think was a face-off. Then the engine whirred to life and the vehicle drove into the night without turning on its lights.

29

Noose around the Neck

2025
Abujmarh

Isha paced back and forth, her mind whirling with thoughts, yet too restless to do anything. To keep herself centred, she got her firearm out, dismantled it and began to clean it. That done, she started her indoor exercise regime: planks, pull-ups, push-ups and squats. However, despite her best efforts, Tej's spectre continued to haunt her. Feeling too keyed up, Isha left her room once again. It was nearly dusk. The shadows had lengthened, the air had cooled slightly. Suddenly, a heart-rending wail emanated from Bishen's quarters.

Mechanically, Isha's feet veered in the direction of the hubbub. Just as she approached the boss's room, the door opened with a slam, and Phoolma emerged, dishevelled, mouth agape, and screaming like a banshee. Marachhiya rushed out after her, trying to hold her. Isha approached the knot of men who stood at Bishen's door and sought Rambhakt out.

'What's the matter?'

'They've found Tej in the forest. He's been brutally assaulted, but he's alive, although just barely,' he updated her in hushed tones.

Isha felt her legs go weak. Her hand moved reflexively to cover her mouth. Since the time Manu and she had returned from the jungle, Isha had worried if she would be able to fool everyone with her feigned horror-stricken reaction to Tej's death.

Clearly, she had wasted her time. There was nothing fake about the shock on her face.

∽

Isha observed Tej being brought back to camp on a stretcher. It seemed like a horrible dream. In the blur that feathered her vision at the edges, she could see Manu's pale and terrified face. She dared not look at him.

Information about what could have happened to Tej continued to trickle in. Tej's imprisoned lover was nowhere to be found but the keys to his shackles had been found abandoned in the bushes on the path coming towards the camp. This was the scene of the crime, declared Phoolma's spies, who were expert trackers as well. Tej had been dragged from here and dumped in the bushes where he had been found, they said. Thank God, they had spotted a pack of hyenas near the bushes and had gone there to investigate.

Tej was rushed to the 'hospital'. Many years ago, Bishen had ordered a reasonably advanced medical station to be set up in the camp, once LalTara's fiscal health had reached a certain threshold with its expansion into the arms and ammunition trade. The drugs and solar-powered medical appliances for this contraband unit were easily procured from the black market, through Bishen's network of contacts. The station was manned by doctors, immune to danger and lured by the fat payouts LalTara provided for their medical attention. The availability of this infrastructure had saved countless lives in LalTara.

Tej was brought to this medical centre and placed in an 'ICU', cordoned off by plastic curtains. The physicians swung into action on a war footing, hooking his battered body to life support systems and pumping it with life-saving drugs to stop the internal bleeding and manage his blood pressure.

Time passed. An intensive investigation into everyone's whereabouts led by Phoolma's spies failed to uncover anything suspicious. Phoolma sat by her son's bedside, lips moving in silent prayer. With her unwavering gaze focused on his face, it seemed as if she was endeavouring to pour her life energy into his inert body through her eyes. As if she was willing him to live. Phoolma remained deaf to the doctor's entreaties that she should not enter the sterile environment, lest she caused a secondary infection in the patient.

Isha started to visit the hospital to find out how Tej was doing. Not everything was going well. While Tej's blood pressure continued to hold and his body's dependency on drugs was reducing, the man continued to remain in a comatose state.

On one such visit during the afternoon, Isha found Bishen, and Marachhiya too, in the room, engaged in a close discussion with the doctor. Seeing Isha step in, Bishen beckoned to her to come nearer.

'...we're doing our best,' Isha caught the tail end of a patent medical statement issued by the doctors, usually when the patient's health was critical, or not responding positively.

'It's impossible to predict when or even whether he will ever wake up,' the doctor continued, hesitating, as though fearing Bishen's reaction. 'And even if he does, we don't know what his physical and mental state will be. It's possible that he may remain in a vegetative state. You may have to take a decision...'

Bishen's eyebrows rose. 'Decision?'

'Sir, don't force me to say it, but it seems like the writing is pretty much up on the wall.'

'What do you mean?' Phoolma let out a cry. Engrossed in their discussion, the group hadn't realized she had left her son's bedside to listen to the doctor's assessment.

Marachhiya rubbed her aunt's back. 'Please, Aunty, the doctor is simply giving his opinion. We're not...'

'Fuck his opinion! How can you even think something like this. I refuse to permit it, I won't!' she screamed, oblivious to the fact that her injured son lay nearby and this sort of commotion was vitiating the atmosphere.

'Look, Aunty,' Bishen started to reason with Phoolma.

'No, *you* look, Rao. If you touch him, if any one of you touches him, you'll be sorry,' she shouted, spittle spraying out from her enraged mouth. She rushed to her son and started sobbing. 'Bastards, murderers...' her rant continued.

Bishen turned back to the doctor and rubbed his forehead in frustration.

'Another week?'

'We can try. But going by the past days...'

'Tej! Tej! My son. Marachhiya, did you see? Did you see? It's a miracle!' Phoolma's exultant cries interrupted their conversation. The rest of the group moved as one towards Tej's bed.

'I saw his toe twitch,' the old woman declared jubilantly. 'Tej is going to come back, he's not dead.' Phoolma crouched by Tej's bedside, clutching his hand, her head buried into his bedclothes. Her shoulders shook violently. 'My son, my son,' her muffled voice reached them.

Marachhiya caressed her back, and then, bending down, hugged her. 'Yes, it's all right, it's all right.'

Isha, positioned behind everyone, viewed this tableau as if from a great distance. *The doctor and Bishen standing at the foot of the bed; the two women by the patient's side.* Her gaze shifted to Tej's prone figure. But for the gentle rise and fall of his chest, he lay motionless. *Had Phoolma really seen his toe move?* she wondered.

∞

That night, Bishen summoned Isha to his quarters. He was alone, sitting in his chair. One more chair stood empty in front of him.

'Sit,' he said, pointing to it. As she perched warily on the seat, he continued, 'Someone definitely unlocked the shackles of the man Tej had imprisoned. That same person also assaulted Tej, someone who has an ulterior motive.'

Isha stared at Bishen blankly as he continued. 'This man...or woman, whoever it is, is a traitor. And...' he paused, '...I don't believe in letting traitors get away easily,' he continued. His tone was soft, but there was an undercurrent of something dangerous in his voice.

Isha's heart stood still for a moment and then started hammering so hard that she thought her ribcage would crack open. *What was he saying? What did they find out? Is it Manu?* Isha willed herself not to gulp.

'I don't know what Phoolma saw; whether Tej actually moved or not. But we're not pulling the plug,' he continued, shifting his gaze to the ceiling. 'I believe Tej will come back to us one day, and when he does, we shall find out who let the government flunkey escape and who attacked him. I've instructed the doctor to leave no stone unturned to resuscitate

Tej, and bring him back to consciousness. Additionally, Kundan will ensure that Tej's security is tightened.'

Bishen trained his eyes back on Isha. 'I feel this traitor might try to kill Tej again. So I'm giving you a job. Find him and get him to me.'

Isha knew Bishen was more than capable of finding the culprit himself. So this was a test to see how she would react. If she played her cards properly, she could still get away with it. *But Tej? Tej was another matter altogether. If he regained consciousness, she would be well and truly screwed.*

Isha could feel a noose tightening imperceptibly but definitively around her neck.

PART THREE

Beneath the Surface

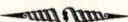

30

The Missing Man

2025
Raipur

Sangha felt slightly foolish when she finally admitted it to herself. *She was in love.* That's why she could only see Neel's deep, intense eyes, shining like the brightest stars in the galaxy. That's why all she wanted to do was touch him, embrace him, talk to him...

From the first time she'd set eyes on Neel, until the wholly unexpected marriage proposal episode in Rakesh's living room, her attraction to him had only grown stronger. Often, she was lost in her own fantasies. *What if Isha did not make it back? Could she step into her shoes and pull it off in the foreseeable future? What would a life with Neel be like? And why did life always have to be so complicated for her?*

Sangha's mind raced with thoughts. She was sure Neel must be worried about her mixed reaction to the proposal and would probably want to call her. However, Rakesh had declared her to be still convalescing and hadn't even handed Isha's phone to her. *So how could Neel get in touch with her?*

Downstairs, sitting at the table for breakfast, Rakesh was pushing the upma around in his plate. He was tired and irritable. As if this damned engagement wasn't enough, Manish had vanished, gone AWOL. It's not as if this hadn't occurred before. Manish often disappeared when he needed to figure out complicated clues during an investigation, and only emerged after he had unravelled a few knots. Rakesh had reprimanded him about this annoying habit—but obviously, the idiot did not pay heed to his boss. *Bhenchod! Everything had to happen all at once!*

Suddenly Isha's phone rang. It was Neel again. Neel had already made a series of calls since the morning, but Rakesh had somehow managed to keep him at bay. However, each time, Rakesh had sensed the increasing impatience in the young man's voice. *Better pick up the call, else the boy would land up at home!* Reluctantly, Rakesh answered the phone.

'Sir, how is Isha now? And when can I speak to her? Is she upset about the proposal? Is something wrong?' Neel typically embarked on his barrage of questions.

'No, beta,' Rakesh replied reassuringly. 'I've told you, it's just the painkillers and the meds. Not to worry, she will see the doctor soon.'

'Let me take her to the doctor. I would like to speak to him too,' Neel insisted.

Realizing that Neel and Sangha's meeting was inevitable, Rakesh fabricated one more lie. 'The course of the medicine concludes this weekend, Neel, so there is no need to see the doctor right away,' he responded, trying not to sound too harsh.

'That sounds great, Uncle,' Neel's relief was palpable even through the phone.

Rakesh sighed. He had navigated another challenging situation. But his relief was short-lived.

'Mom is planning to arrange a small get-together next week. With Isha on the mend, shall I tell her to go ahead then?'

'Neel, I don't think that's...'

'Sorry, Uncle, but you know how Mom gets when she's set on something,' Neel cut in. 'Isha's been through a lot, and I don't want to rush her. So why don't you speak with Mom and discuss the details? I shall see you both soon,' Neel added before the line went dead, leaving a stunned Rakesh holding a silent phone to his ear.

'Fuck! Fuck! FUCK!' Rakesh exploded, throwing Isha's phone on the table, where it skidded and came to rest next to his. Just when he had begun to believe he had a grip on one situation, another scenario had spiralled into new and dangerous directions.

Feeling irritable and worried, he picked up his phone and re-dialled the number that appeared so many times in his outgoing call log. Again, the phone went unanswered. *Manish, how the hell can you be so damn irresponsible when you know what's at stake?* Rakesh fumed. *He had left countless messages for the boy. This unresponsiveness was highly unusual.*

Manish hadn't come to the office for a couple of days. Rakesh had even despatched someone to his house, but it was locked. The building security personnel's words troubled him even more: 'Sir, he left in a terrible hurry a few days ago. And he looked quite anxious.'

'Where are you, Manish?' Rakesh muttered to himself. *Something was definitely off. What could be worrying Manish? And why hadn't Manish called him to share any findings?* A fog of unease engulfed Rakesh. *The tech-savvy young man had always found a way to be in touch with him, even when he was missing in action for others.*

Feeling helpless, Rakesh could only hope that this time too, Manish's silence would not be an exception.

Cold and lonely, Manish sat crouched in the corner of the warehouse. He knew he had very little time. His persecutor was losing patience and it was only a matter of time before he drew his last breath.

Manish's only chance of escape was to gather strength, somehow untie himself and jump out of the second floor of the warehouse. He was frail with torture and had accepted that the chances of him making it out of here were slim.

It was a toss-up between his resolve to survive and giving up forever.

31

The Menu

Rakesh's phone rang stridently early on Monday morning, just as he was trying to scan through the intel and piece together Manish's whereabouts. Rakesh clicked his tongue irritably. He did not need any interruption. His frown deepened when he saw the name flashing on the mobile screen. *Kaveri Saini!*

This woman could not be ignored. She would just keep calling back. Rakesh had no option but to answer his phone. He cleared his throat and wished what he thought was a cheerful good morning.

'Rakesh-ji!' she tittered. 'Hope you've been well, and Isha too. Neel mentioned that she's completed the prescribed course of medications. So now that she is well, we must forge ahead with the engagement.'

'What's the rush? We can give Isha some time to recover,' Rakesh protested feebly, well aware that it would be no use. 'She's just finding her feet, so to speak. Can we not wait for a couple of weeks?'

'A couple of weeks!' a shriek emanated from his earpiece. 'No, no, Rakesh-ji. The girl is ready, the boy is ready, I'm ready. So why wait?' Kaveri remarked, conveniently forgetting the girl's father. Obviously his opinion did not count in this instance.

Rakesh let out a sigh. *It was a lost battle.* 'What date are you considering, Kaveri-ji?'

'Let's meet at our place for lunch on Friday to finalize the engagement date,' she replied cheerfully before hanging up.

Rakesh restrained himself from smashing the phone against the wall, out of sheer frustration at the breakneck speed with which Kaveri-ji was moving ahead with his daughter's engagement. *What on earth would they have to deal with next? Was he going too far with this? Wouldn't it be better to tell Neel everything? No! He would go berserk. He would surely go out looking for Isha and with his journalistic doggedness, would probably succeed in unearthing some information. The tremors of an upheaval of this sort could then reach Bishen, the spider, who constantly monitored his evil web. So, no, no, no. It was better to go along with Kaveri-ji's wild scheme. They could not jeopardize the mission and put Isha in danger.*

So, Friday it was. Anxious about another social meeting with the Sainis and their relatives, and weighed down by Manish's continued disappearance, Rakesh appeared far from the happy father of the would-be bride. For her part, Sangha shone radiantly with an inner glow. Her feelings about Neel had progressed with the consolidation of their relationship into a formal bond. If she had previously thought about him in a detached manner or admired him from a distance, her musings now took a proprietorial air. The unease about Isha's return was deliberately shoved aside. Her heart raced when she daydreamed about Neel, his lips, or when she fantasized about his fingers and how they would feel on her sensitive skin. Her breath quickened as her thoughts strayed deeper into the realm of sensuous carnality. She wondered if Isha and Neel had ever been intimate, and if so, how would this play out when they were together?

∽

Father and daughter reached the Saini residence on the designated day, having barely exchanged a word on their way there, each one lost in their own thoughts. They alighted from the car and stopped short. A gaggle of aunts, sisters and grandmothers formed a chattering wall in front of them. Beyond this cordon of femininity, the duo could spy the male members already busy with drinks. *If this was a get-together to plan the engagement, what would the engagement look like? And the wedding!* Rakesh rubbed his nose.

They were excitedly escorted through the gate into the garden, where Neel stood in a corner. Sangha and his eyes sought each other out and stayed connected. He smiled.

'Hey, Ishu! Hi, uncle,' he said, stepping forward to touch Rakesh's feet and seek his blessings. The older man patted Neel's back, amazed at his own sanguinity in this farcical situation.

'Uncle, any news of Manish?' Neel continued, a shadow crossing his happy face. 'I've been trying to get in touch with him to tell him about Isha and me, and all the developments, but the fu...umm...idiot is just not answering his phone. So annoying!'

'Don't worry, son, all is well,' Rakesh tried to allay the young man's fears, feeling the weight of the lie on his tongue. He rubbed his nose and mumbled, 'I'm sure he'll turn up, and...'

Before Rakesh could finish his sentence, Kaveri Saini erupted on the scene. 'Rakesh-ji, welcome, welcome. *Arre*, Neel beta, please get him a drink. And ask Naina to bring some snacks.' She waved her hand vaguely in the direction of a table groaning under the weight of plates heaped with food. Tandoori chicken, a couple of paneer preparations, *tikkis, tikkas...* Neel's mother had obviously pulled out all the stops for this celebration.

Rakesh felt his bile rise. *Under normal circumstances, this should have been Isha's day; these moments should have been her milestone moments. She would have been so happy that Neel's mother had finally relented and blessed this relationship.* Rakesh was aware that the prospect of causing any resentment between a mother and son had disturbed her greatly. Rakesh's thoughts were interrupted by the arrival of snacks and of Neel, who handed Rakesh a glass of whiskey before hurrying off to join Sangha.

'What's what?' Sangha asked Neel coyly, looking at the culinary delights on offer.

'Mutton, potato, paneer, chicken, mixed veggies,' he rattled off, pointing to each starter by turn. 'And my favourite...mushrooms!'

Sangha smiled as her hands fluttered delicately over the plates. 'Hmmm...' she made a show of picking out her selection. 'What shall I have? I think I'll have...' Her hand reached out for the mushroom preparation and before anyone could react, she'd popped the piece into her mouth. 'Umm...' she said, savouring its flavour, 'this is delicious.'

Beside her, Neel and Rakesh's faces went ashen. Neel was horrified as he knew Isha was severely allergic to mushrooms, and Rakesh because he realized his daughter had made a dangerous mistake.

'Isha, you can't eat this. You'll be in trouble,' Neel exclaimed, snatching the plate away from Sangha. Immediately, Sangha understood she had made a mistake. For a fraction of a second, she stared deep into Neel's eyes, and then clutched her throat and gagged.

'Isha, Isha, are you okay?' Neel called out to her frantically. He turned to Rakesh, who stood by helplessly, not understanding Sangha's game. 'Call her doctor, Uncle!'

Shit! Rakesh thought. *The game would be over if they actually had to call the doctor. Any medical practitioner would quickly realize the girl wasn't experiencing any allergy-related distress.*

Next to him, he heard his daughter's choking gasps turn into laughter. He looked at her.

'What the hell, Ishu!', Neel yelled.

'Don't worry, Neel. I'm already on anti-allergens because of all the meds.'

'Not funny, Isha. Seriously not funny.'

Sangha reached out and gently held Neel's arm. 'I'm sorry,' she apologized, smiling contritely.

Rakesh slowly let out his breath, but Neel continued to look at the girl with narrowed eyes.

Strange, he thought. *Isha never ever messed with mushroom preparations, anti-allergens or no anti-allergens. Why would she take such a risk?*

32

The Ballad of Baladh

2025
Abujmarh

For a while now, Kundanlal had not been sleeping the sleep of the damned to which he was so accustomed. Ever since the break-in in his quarters, he knew the traitor was within, mingling with them in the camp. At the time, his suspicions were nebulous, a general feeling of unease not converging on a specific person. However, since the vicious attack on Tej, who was severely battered and lying in a vegetative state, he could link the timing of both these violations to only a single thing: Sangha's return. *The bitch had definitely sold herself to the government fuckers.*

Convinced of Sangha's duplicity, Kundanlal decided to have her in his sights. He invented excuses for keeping her close around him. If she was planning more mischief, it wouldn't happen on his watch. As much as he itched to voice his feelings to Rao, Kundanlal thought it would be wiser to first gather some hard evidence of the girl's deceit. Kundanlal had also noticed that she was now spending more time with Manu. He'd have to speak to the boy. Perhaps that could provide him some proof.

That morning, when the runner came with the usual 'business' reports, Kundanlal motioned him to wait.

'How's everything in the camp, Manu?'

Manu frowned, unsure of what kind of response was expected from him. *What could he tell Kundanlal that he didn't already know?*

'Anna, everything is okay...' his voice trailed off.

'Sangha and you seem to be getting along fine,' Kundanlal asked, alert to the boy's body language. One nervous gesture and he would be caught.

'Oh that!' Manu shrugged. 'Anna, I don't want to stay a runner all my life. She's teaching me how to fight and also giving me tips on gun training. I want to become like Rambhakt Anna, and strong like Tej Anna. Poor Tej Anna...' he sighed.

'What has she taught you till now?' asked Kundanlal, sticking firmly to the topic under discussion.

'Only activities to build strength and endurance. She makes me run in the jungle. I don't like that that much, but what to do! She's so strict,' the boy complained.

'Does she talk about when she was caught?'

'Ummm...not much. Only that I should become strong like her, enough to face those *sarkari* chutiyas the way she did.'

'She says that, does she?' Kundanlal seemed lost in his thoughts. Manu stood by the door, unsure of whether to leave or stay. Abruptly, the older man emerged from his reverie. 'Manu, you will now tell me everything she says, do you hear?'

'Y-y-yes, Anna.'

'Okay, get going. And not a word about this conversation to anyone.'

How Manu managed to get away from Kundanlal's room nonchalantly, only he knew. His insides felt like jelly. *Thank God, Isha had discussed with him how to explain their long* absences away from the camp beforehand. Anyway, now he would have to avoid her that day, just in case Kundanlal was watching him as well. That crafty devil!

The following morning, Manu sauntered towards Isha's cabin, saluting the guards who stood nearby. Isha sat on the veranda, nursing a cup of sweet chai.

'Good morning, Akka!'

'Morning, Manu.'

'I completed fifty push-ups yesterday,' the boy said, flexing his skinny biceps.

Isha looked into his eyes and then smiled. *This was a phrase they had decided to use when Manu had something urgent to share with her.*

'Good show! Soon, you'll become Mr Universe! What say, guys?' She asked the guards nearby, who were listening to their conversation innocently. As they guffawed, she turned back to Manu.

'Now the next goal is sixty. Come in, let's do it now.'

'Now?' Manu asked, seemingly reluctantly.

'Yes, lazybones, now,' Isha replied, stepping inside her cabin, and gesturing Manu to follow. Soon, the counts of one, two, three...began to emerge from within. Manu, apparently, was working out hard.

Inside, Manu was recounting his encounter with Kundanlal the previous morning. 'What are we going to do, Akka? There's Tej Anna also...' his words trailed off worriedly.

'I'll think of something, Manu,' Isha replied, her confident tone belying the fear and the growing feeling of dread in her heart. 'I tried to access Tej to...but the security was too tight,' she continued. 'I almost got caught. Anyway, the doctors have largely ruled out his recovery. Kundan

Mama is a bigger threat at this point.' It seemed to the boy that Isha was talking to herself, figuring out things aloud.

Isha closed her eyes and ceased talking. Manu let the silence shroud the room, afraid of interrupting her thoughts. He then saw her jaw tighten before she opened her eyes.

'Come on,' Isha said, nodding towards the door, 'that's enough of training for today.' She ushered the boy out of the room, patting his back. 'Keep it up. We'll make a man out of you,' she winked at him. 'See you later.'

As she turned away to return indoors, Isha's mind was made up. She knew how she would tackle Kundanlal. It was time to play the ace she had been hiding up her sleeve.

∞

Bishen was sitting in his quarters a week later with a bottle of vintage Glenfiddich by his side, already down by three pegs. The sky outside had darkened, the treetops had melded into the firmament, black on black. He had sent Marachhiya and Lipi to Phoolma's quarters as there was an important task to be completed. He'd tried hard, but the energy surging in his body refused to be tamed. *Damn!* He hated it when he got like this. A cool mind—and a cool body—were always better. Anyway, this could not last long. It had to end.

There was a movement outside the door. One of his men, no doubt.

'Yes?' He called out.

'Anna, Kundanlal has returned.'

'Ah, okay. Ask him to see me when he's free.'

'Yes, Anna.'

Bishen made a fourth drink for himself and as he emptied it down his throat in a single gulp, Kundanlal entered the room. Bishen gestured him to a chair.

'Sit!'

Kundanlal did as he was told, wiping the sweat on his face with the sleeve of his shirt.

'Did the trip go as planned? Did Aslam understand our point of view?'

'It was a bit touch-and-go at first, to be honest. They weren't very happy with the rates. But with the cost of paying for silence and continued loyalty...'

'Ah! Loyalty. Now that has to be bought, doesn't it! It's Lakshmi[32] who rules. But what do you expect in Kaliyuga?'[33]

'I agree. That's what I wanted to speak to you about,' Kundanlal answered.

Bishen raised his eyebrows, waiting for Kundanlal to continue.

'It's Sangha. I suspect there is something wrong. From the time she has come back, things have not been going well.'

'You mean she has been compromised?' Bishen looked straight at Kundanlal.

'Perhaps,' the other man replied a tad uncertainly.

Bishen kept quiet. The silence stretched on. After a while, Bishen leaned forward to open the table drawer and take out one more glass. He then made a peg each for Kundanlal and himself. He handed the glass to his administrator and walked with his glass to the window, where he looked out at the dark sky.

'I remember a story my mother used to tell me,' he said softly, speaking almost to himself. 'There was a king called

---

[32]Lakshmi: Hindu goddess of wealth and good fortune
[33]Kaliyuga: A cycle of Time, an age of darkness, full of conflict and sin, ruled by the goddess Kali

Baladh. He ruled with an iron fist. He had a son, Dharma, who was the apple of his eye. As the child grew up, he witnessed the adulation his father received from the people. A worm of envy infected his thoughts. He desired to be the one to receive the respect, praise, admiration and love.'

Bishen paused and sipped his drink. 'Dharma had a friend, Vivek,' he continued, smacking his lips. 'He used to share everything with him. Dharma confided his plan of usurping the throne to Vivek, who was shocked and horrified. He tried to dissuade Dharma from going down that road, but to no avail. With no other alternative left, Vivek went to Baladh and told him the evil intentions his son harboured towards him.' Bishen turned away from the window, put his drink on a nearby table, and started pacing up and down behind the chair on which Kundanlal sat.

'Baladh was justifiably angry and aghast, and confronted his son with this information. But Dharma proved to be too clever: he deflected the situation with a counter-narrative about how Vivek had come to him, Dharma, urging him that the kingdom needed new leadership. He obviously wanted to drive a wedge between father and son.

'Baladh was a father, after all. His son had never disobeyed him in any way. So he chose to believe him.'

Kundanlal heard Bishen stop his movements, and move closer to the chair. He felt Bishen's hand on his shoulder. LalTara's supremo went on with his tale.

'Baladh ordered Vivek to be imprisoned and executed. Vivek protested in vain, maintaining his innocence till the end. His last words were "O King, before the next two full moons are over, death will come for you." His words proved prophetic. Soon after this, Dharma poisoned his father and took over the kingdom.'

The hand on Kundanlal's shoulder suddenly retracted, and before the seated man could realize what was happening, he felt a stricture go around his throat. He gasped and reflexively let go of his glass. He clawed at the constriction, wriggling to turn around. But the man behind the chair proved to be too strong. The pressure persisted relentlessly. Kundanlal's feet scrabbled on the floor for purchase. With his oxygen supply cut off, his vision blurred. His hands moved from the object that was strangling him to the arms of the strangler. He tried to claw at the hands that were suffocating him, but they seemed to be made of iron. The scratching weakened and eventually stopped.

Bishen held the stranglehold for one more minute, his face dripping with sweat. In his eyes, bloodlust and rage battled for supremacy. He bared his teeth and rasped, 'I am not Baladh. No one stabs me in the back and gets away with it.'

※

Six days before Kundanlal's murder

Isha knew Kundanlal was dangerous. As an adversary, he had Bishen's ear and too much clout in the camp. He would have to be removed. The information she had been holding on to had to be leveraged.

※

Ten days before Kundanlal's murder

Returning from one of her nightly excursions to check if Manish or Rakesh had tried to contact her, Isha had seen a figure skulking in the shadows. Intrigued, she followed the figure. In the weak illumination of a faraway lamp, she finally realized it was Rambhakt. As this piqued her interest even more, she stole after him to one of the warehouses where the drugs were stored. Rambhakt furtively opened the locked door; he must have previously taken an imprint of the key to make a duplicate, as only Kundanlal retained the possession of all the critical keys. Rambhakt emerged from the warehouse after ten minutes, secured the door and vanished into the darkness.

Isha decided to investigate this curious behaviour. The next day, as soon as the warehouse opened, she went in with the men under the pretext of helping them with the stock. Her intent was to look for any indication of disruption. Sure enough, on one table, she spied a faint dusting of white powder. The packets, while appearing to be undisturbed, had clearly been tampered with.

Later that evening, Isha retrieved the tiny camera Manish had thoughtfully included in the equipment package that STF19 had dropped for her in the forest. The next day, she installed it at a strategic location in the warehouse. It would take pictures every three seconds and store up to three days' worth of images. Hopefully, it would capture something interesting.

She bided her time, patiently sitting in the darkness by the warehouse. On the third day, her efforts were rewarded. Rambhakt stole up to the warehouse, unlocked the door and disappeared inside for ten minutes. After he left, Isha crept back to her quarters and passed a restless night waiting for daybreak.

The following day, as soon as she got the chance, she retrieved the camera and went through the footage. *Bingo! The photos clearly showed Rambhakt carefully unsealing a packet, extracting some amount of white powder from it, replacing it with a similar-looking product, and resealing the packet. Now she had him in her grasp!*

∽

Four days before Kundanlal's murder

With this ace that she had up her sleeve, she could win this hand. Any hand, for that matter. She casually strolled over to where the men hung out and sought Rambhakt out.

'*Arre* listen, Rambhakt, I need your help with something. Can you please come with me?'

The man got up and started walking with her. She took him to the firing range where no one was practising. It was empty. She went up to the table stocked with guns, picked one up, and remarked, 'I can't seem to get the hang of this firearm. I always miss bull's eye. Wait, let me show you.'

She aimed the gun purposely off target but made a show of trying to meticulously align it with the red circle in the distance before firing it. As expected, it didn't hit the mark. Isha sighed, as if exasperated.

'Come, see how much the damn thing is off.'

Both walked towards the target and when they drew closer, Isha stopped. Rambhakt halted too, as he turned to look at her with his eyebrows raised.

'What happened?'

In response, Isha got the camera out of her pocket, turned it on and showed Rambhakt the photographs.

'Explain.'

The man's face turned ashen. He gulped, 'Sangha...'

'Explain. Now.'

'I needed the money. Hulgi...my girlfriend. She's high maintenance. I thought if I take just a little bit...'

Hulgi? Ah, that sultry siren she'd seen with Rambhakt. With her slinky clothes and flashy gold jewellery, she certainly seemed to give the impression that she would stick around only so long as the gifts were coming her way!

'You've done this for a woman? Are you out of your mind? Do you know what Rao will do to you?'

Rambhakt winced. Isha thought she could almost see tears welling up in his eyes.

'It was just a little bit. Please, Sangha, don't rat me out.'

Isha drew in a deep breath and made a show of thinking.

'You'll have to do something for me. No questions asked. Otherwise...' she stopped meaningfully.

'What do you want me to do?'

'Get me some of the coke. Not a little bit like you pilfer. Much, much more.'

∽

Two days before Kundanlal's murder

Under the pretence of training her to handle the problematic gun, Rambhakt handed over the packets to Isha. With the pilfered drugs in her possession, her plan moved one step further. It would all have to be timed well. Kundanlal was to leave for a couple of days to meet one of their distributors. Her scheme would have to be rolled out the day he left.

After Kundanlal's departure, she accessed his room once again the way she had earlier, hoping this was the last time she would have to do it. It was getting to be quite stressful. She planted the objects she had with her, working quickly and efficiently. Then she extracted a screwdriver and a pair of pliers from her pocket and got to work. She first disabled the electricity and exposed the wires of a switch. Having uncovered their metallic innards, she expertly joined the negative and positive wires. She then installed a timer on the electric mains. *The timer would count down to one minute and the electrical supply would be restored. However, due to the joined wires, a short circuit would occur.* Task accomplished, she quickly exited the room.

Her strategy worked. Soon, black smoke started to billow out of Kundanlal's room. Frantic shouts erupted, spreading in the camp with a swiftness Isha appreciated. Bishen stepped out, and seeing the sooty air, ran towards its source. Isha joined the hubbub. She had to be around when they entered the room. Supervised by Bishen, the men were getting ready with water. Two of them were trying to break open the door.

'Stop!' Isha commanded. 'Don't put the water on the fire. First check the cause of the problem.'

Bishen looked at her and nodded.

The door gave way at the hinges and thick smoke belched out. Putting towels and scarves on their faces, Bishen, Isha and a couple of men entered the room. The switchboard was spluttering and sparking.

'Switch off the supply,' Bishen roared. 'Go now!'

Starved of power, the spluttering soon died down and the smoke thinned out.

'We need to check for any damage,' Isha spoke, addressing the group in general.

Several heads nodded but looked in Bishen's direction for the final go-ahead.

He waved his hand in approval, supervising the men as they pulled out the furniture and files.

Anytime now, Isha thought to herself, taking care to work elsewhere in the room so that she wouldn't be too close when they discovered the things she had strategically planted.

As one armload of documents was tossed into the centre of the room—untouched by the fire—a couple of packets spilled out of the files, spewing white powder. All activity came to a standstill, as one by one, the men saw their leader staring at the torn packets. There was silence in the room, until a low growl rumbled in Bishen's throat.

'Go!'

As the men filed out, Isha stuttered. 'Rao...'

'You stay. See if you find anything else.'

Isha's heart jumped with excitement. This was a godsend opportunity.

'Yes, Rao,' she deferred softly.

Isha started systematically from one end, going down on her fours, probing the undersides of the furniture until she came upon—as she knew she would—the other items she'd left behind.

'Rao, there's something here.' She wiggled under the table and pried loose the two things taped underneath. She emerged and looked at the objects in her hand, seemingly puzzled with a frown on her face.

'I don't understand... what are these...?'

'Tej's satellite phone and keys,' Bishen whispered. *There was no way these could have been in Kundan's possession unless he was the one responsible for the attack on Tej.* 'Kundan has made a pact with the devil.'

33

The Takeover

2025
Abujmarh

Bishen Rao's ruthlessness and brutality were well known. People who got in the way of his ambitions, people who snitched on him, or even those who could be used as examples...he had despatched all of them, and more, to Yamraj, the Lord of Death himself. Others who heard the news usually received the information with a shrug and a certain nonchalance. Things happened, particularly when Rao was around. But Kundanlal's death was different. It seemed as though one leg of the throne had been hacked off by the king himself while he was sitting on it. *What happened? Was it true that Kundanlal was a traitor? Had he challenged Rao's supremacy?* Questions buzzed around the camp, hither and thither, like bees disturbed by smoke.

Isha played her role perfectly. Horror-stricken at first, curious later. She noticed Bishen glance in her direction more than once, his eyes narrowed, as if assessing her intentions. Each time Bishen looked, her heart raced and her pulse quickened. *What had transpired in that room before Kundanlal died? Had that moron Rambhakt spilled the beans before Rao?*

It was three days after they'd buried Kundanlal's remains in the jungle that she received the summons. She consciously slowed her breathing as she made her way to Bishen's quarters. *Don't panic, don't get fazed*, she told herself. *Remember what Sangha said. Bishen has a habit of throwing statements at you just to gauge your reaction.* She knocked on his door.

'Come in,' Bishen called out gruffly.

Isha stepped in and saw Bishen standing with his back to her, facing the window.

'Sangha, did you really think I wouldn't know?' came the question laced with an accusation.

Recalling Sangha's words, Isha replied calmly, 'Know what, Rao?'

Bishen turned on his heels.

'Kundan told me before I silenced him forever. He said you were the traitor.'

'He did, did he? That's a laugh!' Isha bared her gums. 'You sure it wasn't a ploy for misdirection?'

Bishen didn't say anything but continued to stare at her.

Don't fall for this, Isha's mind whispered. *He has nothing on you.* But her insides seemed to be slowly turning liquid.

She decided to hold Bishen's gaze to give herself time to frame her response and ease the trembling in her innards. *Screw you, Bishen.*

She shrugged her shoulders.

'You think I'm a fool? To cross to the other side and think you won't find out? What would you like me to do to prove you wrong?'

Bishen saw the fire in her eyes, a fire he believed he had ignited with his accusations. He relaxed. His face softened a little.

'Sit, Sangha,' he said, motioning her to a chair. He remained standing. 'I'm a hard man and I have little space for emotions in my life. But I realize I have been harsh with you, for which Kundan was somewhat responsible. He was too insecure, too ambitious. He knew, as I did, that you possess that strength that runs in our blood.'

Bishen stopped as he approached his table, and picked up a bunch of keys. 'So this is what we're going to do,' he continued. 'You are now going to take over Kundan's responsibilities. Here are the keys to the data room. It's now under your care. See that you don't fuck up.'

Isha could hardly believe her ears. This was fantastic and completely unexpected. Now she could *officially* monitor everything happening in the camp and also investigate LalTara's role in the RED affair.

She stood up, her face mirroring her elation and incredulity. 'Thank you, thank you, Rao. I won't let you down. I won't give you a chance to regret this decision!' she exulted. *Oh man! What a liar I am!*

34

Prisha

2025
Raipur

Following her perilous slip with the mushrooms at the Saini residence, Sangha had sat down with Rakesh to review Isha's preferences, dislikes and medical history once more. She could not risk another incident that made Neel suspicious. She had gone out with Neel on a couple of quick coffee dates since that get-together, but had been careful to tread on neutral ground. When Neel had suggested an evening out with friends on the previous date, Sangha tried her best to talk him out of it, but he insisted. He wanted to celebrate their relationship, which would soon be formalized into marriage. She had to acquiesce.

When Sangha shared this development with Rakesh, he groaned. Isha's friends were unfamiliar territory for him. In fact, he had identified this information gap right in the beginning, while coaching Sangha to be Isha. His daughter actually did not have too many friends of her own, and had adopted Neel's social circle by default. While this group was not known to Rakesh, he was certain that Isha had been drawn to a soft-spoken financial analyst named Anvesha. From what Isha had shared with him, Anvesha's sensitive and empathetic nature resonated with her. Rakesh admitted to Sangha that apart from Anvesha, he wasn't familiar with other members of this group. All he could do was show Sangha the videos and photos saved on Isha's phone, besides material from other avenues, such as social media accounts, as they tried to glean some information about these personalities.

Armed with this insubstantial information, Sangha would have to play Isha before an audience who, most probably, had shared much more with the STF19 captain. But what was the alternative? So when Rakesh saw her off that evening, he shook her hand as if wishing her well on an important mission.

※

'The couple of the season is here!'
'*Aaiye, padhariye...*'
'Isha dear, how are you...?'

The clamour that erupted as Sangha and Neel stepped into the party hall they'd reserved for the evening drowned out the peppy beats emanating from unseen speakers.

Rahul, Shreya, Thomas, Vinita, Rujuta, Myra, Aryan, Anvesha... Sangha mentally ticked off the names against the faces, her relief at being able to do so manifesting as a warm smile on her face. Many hugs and air-kisses later, the friends settled down with drinks, catching up on Neel's proposal, Isha's health, and generally ribbing the couple about their upcoming engagement and nuptials.

Anvesha sat next to Sangha, chatting about her work. Just then, Myra, drink in hand, planted herself between the two girls.

'*Oye, bata tu,* tell me, have you started shopping for the big day?'

'Shopping? Not really. *Kyun*?' Sangha asked noncommittally.

'*Arre*, I know this woman, she designs really sexy lingerie. We'll go to her.'

'*Chhod* Myra,' Rujuta, standing nearby, piped in. 'You know Isha and her thing with bra-panties. Just give her some boxers; she'll be happy.'

Giggles erupted from around Sangha. She looked around. All the girls were gathered around her, smiling, their eyes twinkling. She could even see Neel trying to cover his smile with a glass.

Try as she might, Sangha could not wipe out the blankness from her face.

'*Bhool gayi*?' Rujuta persisted. 'You've forgotten the Bhopal road trip?'

Shit! Sangha thought. *What Bhopal trip?* She licked her dry lips.

Seeing her reaction, Rujuta became more animated. '*Yeh lo!*' she exclaimed.

'Madam has got fish memory. *Arre bhai*, don't you remember? You'd only packed Neel's underclothes because he was joining us midway and had forgotten to pack any for yourself! *Kya tu bhi!*'

'Ohhh that! Heh, heh! I remember, but what's so funny about it,' Sangha stammered. 'It could happen to anyone...' She looked at Neel. He was staring at her with a deadpan expression. She stood up and went up to him, putting her arm around his waist. 'That was so embarrassing. I was desperately trying to get them off the topic,' she whispered to him, 'but they just wouldn't take the bloody hint!' She heard him expel his breath slowly.

Just then, the door opened and a slim figure slipped in. Sangha saw Anvesha get up and wave. Sangha could now see it was a girl, dressed in a boyish checked shirt and jeans. Her hair was styled in a crisp and smart crew-cut.

'Come,' Neel whispered to Sangha as he strode towards the newcomer who was now standing with Anvesha.

'Hi!' the girl called out cheerfully.

'Hey, bro!' Neel gave her a friendly backslap in response.

Sangha smiled, her mind frantically flipping through the faces she'd studied. *Yes, the girl looked familiar, but wasn't one of the core gang. Fuck! Who was she? Wait, wait, it was on the tip of her tongue. This is Priti, no Priya. No, no. Her name rhymed with Isha's.* That's how she had remembered it. *Prisha! Yes, Prisha.*

She observed Anvesha, Neel and the girl looking at her expectantly, as if waiting for her to say something.

Sangha cleared her throat. 'Hi, Prisha!' she said cheerfully and somewhat triumphantly, with a hint of satisfaction.

'Hey Isha! How are you? Are you okay now?'

'Yes, yes. As good as new,' Sangha smiled. To change the topic, she turned to Anvesha: 'So, Anvesha, how's Rick?' From what Sangha and Rakesh had gathered from their social media sources, Anvesha had a husband, Rick, who lived in London. *At least there would be no fuck-up here,* Sangha thought to herself.

'Rick?' Anvesha cocked her head like a dog. 'He's fine.' She smiled politely, a tad uneasy.

'When is he coming to India?' Sangha continued.

Anvesha's smile disappeared from her face. She peered intently at Sangha before turning to Neel, eyebrows raised.

'Isha, that's enough.' Neel was speaking to Sangha as if she were a small child. 'Let's change the topic. Can't you see Prisha is here?'

'Yeah, yeah, of course. I just asked her about Rick, Neel.'

Neel's hand gripped Sangha's arm firmly. He looked

around. Everyone seemed to be occupied, dancing, conversing and drinking. With an apologetic smile towards Anvesha and Prisha, he drew Sangha aside.

'Isha, what's wrong with you? This is not funny,' Neel whispered fiercely in Sangha's ear. 'Rick is a closed chapter. Anvesha is still hurting because of the ugly divorce. Remember, Prisha and she came out a year back, but only to us? They knew we would understand. Please don't mock them.'

The room went silent for Sangha. The music and laughter receded into the background. All she could hear was the hammering of her own heart. *Rick was Anvesha's ex. Anvesha and Prisha were a couple. Shit. Shit. Shit. Okay. Maybe she could still salvage this situation.*

'I wasn't making fun of them,' she whispered. 'I was just being discreet because I thought Myra was listening in.'

Neel stepped back, astonished. He knew Isha was not speaking the truth. *No one was listening in. Nobody. Why was Isha behaving weirdly? It couldn't be the medications, as Rakesh had told him that Isha was off the tablets and was in good health now. Something seemed terribly wrong. But what?*

35

The Stalker

It was late in the evening when Rakesh switched off the table lamp on his office desk, locked his room, and took the stairs. He climbed down slowly. He didn't believe in elevators. There was something about enclosed spaces that set his teeth on edge. Exiting the STF19 headquarters, he nodded to the night security guard as he made his way to the parking lot and got into his car. He sighed. *It had been a long and exhausting day. There was still no news of Manish.*

A persistent feeling of dread clouded Rakesh's thoughts. He passed a hand over his eyes as if to wipe the worry away, put the key into the ignition, and fired the engine. Two minutes into his homeward journey, he noticed something unusual. Headlights in the rearview mirror. They'd disappear for a while and then reappear. To determine if he was being stalked, he deliberately turned right off a street, then another right, and another, essentially looping in a circle. The headlights followed. It was the same black Kia.

He had to figure out what this was about. There was a diversion ahead, a turn off onto a little-used road. It was straight and narrow, but more significantly, it was well illuminated. He deliberately took that road. He estimated the distance between his car and his stalker's and pulled to a stop a short distance ahead of a streetlight. As expected, the pursuing vehicle was forced to stop almost below the streetlight. Rakesh saw in his rearview mirror the same two heads within the car that he had spotted from the window facing the street outside his house. For half a minute, he sat at the wheel of his car, gazing at the black vehicle. Then, Rakesh's irritation boiled over and got the better of him at this undue harassment. He got out of his car, slammed the door forcefully, and headed purposefully towards the black vehicle. His long strides ate up the distance quickly: 50 metres, 30 metres—he whipped out his phone from his pocket and took a quick shot of the car head-on—10 metres. Almost there...

'Who the fuck are you?' Rakesh called out angrily as he walked ahead. 'Get out and face me, if you've got the balls!'

Suddenly, the headlights of his pursuers' car turned on full power, nearly blinding him. The driver revved the engine, the car swerved and sped off. Rakesh bolted back to his vehicle, climbed in and gave chase. The road that ended at the main intersection one kilometre away was desolate this time of the night. Rakesh wanted to catch up with the vehicle before it hit the main junction. But luck wasn't on his side that night. By the time he reached the main crossing, his pursuers had melted into the traffic. Rakesh cursed and pulled to the side.

What was happening? Who were these guys? And why were they tailing him?

∽

2025
Abujmarh

Isha started to work on her clandestine project almost immediately. She would enter the restricted network room in the morning and emerge only when the sun had long disappeared below the horizon. She asked Manu to get her meals and place them outside the door. Often, when he brought fresh food, he'd find the plates from before still there, untouched and forgotten. Monitoring the ongoing work and diving into past records was a back-breaking task but she refused to buckle under physical and mental pressure. Slowly, through all the potent data about arms and drug deals, she began to piece together more information about RED.

Manish had already explained rather dramatically how the Russians had perfected the prototype of a high-tech defence system in Siberia, and how it suddenly vanished from there. After a long period of complete silence, intel had started to trickle in that the system was in Chinese territory. The three STF19 colleagues had also learnt that LalTara was somehow involved with the Chinese and RED.

The new information that Isha had unearthed through the data records indicated that the Iraqis were interested in purchasing the technology. The Chinese were expected to first offer their customers an opportunity to test the prototype, before releasing the full version of the finished product. And LalTara—rather, Bishen—was leading this deal between the Chinese and the Iraqis by playing the middleman. Once the Iraqis approved the demo, they were expected to transfer the funds to Bishen's offshore account. Bishen would then pay a portion of the funds to the Chinese and also accept RED's delivery from the China-Nepal border, and hand it over to the Iraqis. It was simple. In essence, LalTara was brokering an illegal defence deal between two countries.

Isha slumped back in her chair. *This was the prototype that was being delivered when she and Team Alpha had attempted to intercept it! That day, LalTara had received the RED prototype and she had captured Sangha.* The Iraqis, she gathered, had been invited to test the prototype here in Abujmarh.

I'll have to be extra vigilant, Isha thought to herself. *The STF needs to be informed as soon as I hear from the buyers.*

With Tej in a coma, Kundanlal despatched to hell, and Rambhakt in her clutches, Isha was able to focus solely on the crucial part of her mission in LalTara to unearth incriminating evidence. However, it also meant that thoughts of her life in Raipur, her home, Baba and Neel, pushed to the back of her mind, started to resurface painfully and frequently. This yearning for 'normalcy' was somewhat assuaged during her chats with Manu. He confided in her about what he wanted out of life: the tea stall he wanted to set up, the school he wanted to return to. However, inevitably the tumult would surge again. She found some comfort in how much she had already achieved. *Now for the final phase. Once she knew where RED was, she could call in the troops. And then...then she would return to Baba and to Neel.*

A few days passed. Then, one night, as she sat at the system, a message beeped: *This Friday we will do Namaaz together.* Isha stood up so fast, her chair toppled and clattered to the floor behind her. She ran out of the network centre and relayed it to Bishen, word for word.

He smiled.

'Prepare,' he said. 'Tell Rambhakt, the Iraqis are coming!'

36

Oblivion

Manish smirked inwardly at the irony: *sweat, malnourished limbs and blood-soaked ropes were loosening the very bonds meant to hold him captive.* It had taken days of quiet, agonizing struggle but at last, he could twist his wrist free. Even then, he waited—patient, calculating—for the perfect moment. Late one night, sensing his chance had come, he stealthily untied the remaining knots and crawled towards the window, every movement laced with caution.

He was on the second floor of the warehouse and a jump could be seriously incapacitating, if not fatal. However, directly below the window was a black car which might just soften the fall. Battered and bloodied, Manish closed his eyes and took a leap of faith.

He went through the window, directing his falling body to land on the bonnet before rolling onto the road below. The moment he hit the ground, a searing pain shot through his leg—it was broken but he was not.

The silence of the night was disturbed first by the deafening sound of the fall and then by the urgent yelling of a few agitated men out to hunt him back.

But nothing made any difference to Manish. He gasped for breath as he hobbled through the dark lanes as fast as he possibly could. He knew he was being chased. *He had to reach Rakesh. He had to phone for help. But his energy was waning.*

His brain, however, was whizzing with thoughts. *What*

if he could not make it out of this situation alive? What if they caught him and...? He had to inform Rakesh sir that he had been here, at this point. In an instant, he took out his STF19 identity card, dirty and blood-stained, from his pocket, traced something on it with his fingers and flung it to the side of the road. *Maybe Rakesh sir would find it and figure everything out.*

He continued running, as fast as his pounding heart and broken leg would allow. Suddenly, in the distance, he noticed the headlights of an approaching car. His hope, almost extinguished, was rekindled. He waved frantically, praying that the car would stop before his pursuers could catch up with him.

The vehicle slowed down as it neared him. Manish did likewise, his chest heaving with exertion, yet alive with optimism. However, when the car was a few feet away, it accelerated and headed directly towards him.

Manish noticed the dented bonnet too late. It was the same car parked outside the warehouse—the very one he had jumped onto. The same vehicle that had broken his fall. And now, here it was, about to despatch him straight to hell.

The last visual of Manish's life was a smiling Isha.

37

The Agony and the Agony

The lights on the road were dim, but the headlights of the police jeep were strong enough to light up for Rakesh what he wished he did not have to see. *The body bag being zipped up on the face of the corpse he had just identified as Manish.*

If the young techie's cracked blue lips could have spoken, Manish would have said, 'I'm sorry, sir! This was all my greed. I found out where the money trail ended. I attempted to blackmail them to free myself from debt, but they locked me up and tortured me. Yet, I didn't share any information about Operation Trojan Horse. I somehow managed to escape, sir, but they got to me in the street. It was not an accident, sir! It was *him*!'

Rakesh's thoughts were interrupted by the sub-inspector. 'Sir, we are sending the body to the morgue.'

'I want to take another look at him,' said Rakesh, needing to check the bruise marks on the body. His sharp eyes had caught the skin discolouration not only at the wrists, but also at the ankles. He gazed at Manish's ID card found a distance away, which the forensic guy was now wrapping into a plastic packet. He noticed random blood marks on it. *Manish's blood. The sheer fact that the card was such a long way off from the body underlined the fact that it was not just a hit-and-run, but a planned killing.*

But wait. He stopped in his tracks. *The blood marks on*

the card were not random, but drawn as the number 8. Eight? What could this clue be? What was Manish trying to tell him? Rakesh's mind stopped working.

The young, dynamic techie had now dived into silence forever. All Rakesh longed for at this moment was the young man to spring up on his feet and start chattering again.

∞

Rakesh, with his face drained of colour and his heart as heavy as lead, stepped through the threshold of his house; his once familiar surroundings seemed to have lost all their warmth.

How could he possibly break the news to Isha, far away in enemy camp, that her confidant and partner-in-mischief was no more? The very thought was painfully unbearable, like treading on fragile glass. He dreaded having to eventually convey to her the crushing truth that her best friend was no more.

In a voice thick with grief, Rakesh recounted the tragic sequence of events to Sangha. Every word felt like a burden, an acknowledgement of a reality that was as cruel as it was unfathomable.

Although Sangha had not known Manish, she had caught, in her brief interaction with him, a whiff of his boyish and endearing demeanour. Strangely, the same heart-wrenching emotions that Rakesh experienced seemed to wash over her and she couldn't help but wonder, *'Am I becoming one of them to feel this way?'*

When Sangha went up to her father and sat down next to him to console the grieving man, his near-stoic façade cracked and tears welled up in his eyes. In that poignant moment, an unspoken bond developed between a grieving father and a long-lost daughter—a shared connection in the face of loss and sorrow.

In the midst of this unstated kinship, the doorbell rang impatiently and within moments, Neel barged into the room. 'Why won't the police let me see his body? Manish wasn't picking up my calls—I should have sensed something was amiss!' Rakesh stood up and reassuringly put his arm around Neel's shoulders to soothe him. Neel, emotionally shattered after losing his best friend, could not help blaming himself.

Sangha got off the chair and approached Neel to offer him a glass of water. In that quiet gesture, Neel felt a flicker of comfort, a glimmer of peace amidst the chaos. Turning to the grief-stricken men, Sangha's voice was gentle yet steady. 'We will find a way through this.'

But Rakesh was motionless. His mind still delving into the circumstances of Manish's mysterious death. *What had Manish discovered that had cost him his life? What was the number 8 that Manish had conveyed to him moments before his death? Could it be connected to the black Kia tailing him?* thought Rakesh. *Were Bishen's associates closer than anticipated?*

An urgent anger surged within Rakesh. As the head of the Special Task Force, he promptly ordered Manish's laptops and computers, from both his house and his office, to be transported to the headquarters. Rakesh was determined to expunge any traces of the Operation Trojan Horse videos from the system before the police inquiry nosed in. No evidence of Isha and Sangha's switch could come to any one's knowledge at any cost. Additionally, he speculated that Manish's system might hold crucial information linked to his untimely death.

The pieces of the puzzle were scattered, and Rakesh was determined to put them together. *Time was of the essence.* And he would have to beat it.

38

Killing Machines

2025
Abujmarh

This Friday we will do Namaaz together. Ever since Isha relayed that cryptic message to Bishen Rao, sleep had eluded her. *This was it!* The reason why she was here as the Trojan Horse, willing to accept danger, and even reconciled to the possibility that she may never see her father or her fiancé again. *Could this be the beginning of the endgame?* Isha didn't know. The only thing she could do was continue to play her part well. Actually, having come so far, she could not afford any slip-ups, now more than ever. It was most important to find out RED's location when the Iraqis came.

Bishen had not been seen around the camp over the past three days. He would leave in his ATV before daybreak and return long after the camp had settled for the night. He hadn't included her in whatever he was doing, and she didn't want to push it. So, she continued with her task of monitoring LalTara's work.

As Thursday arrived, Isha's excitement reached fever pitch. *What would tomorrow bring? Bishen still hadn't disclosed anything.* As she lay on her bed, her thoughts ran on an endless loop.

Today was THE day. Friday. It was not even 5:00 a.m. when a knock on the door awakened her from a fitful bout of sleep. A message was conveyed. Bishen wanted her to be ready in ten minutes. She complied with alacrity, the heaviness of disturbed rest erased by the adrenaline coursing through her veins. As she sat next to Bishen Rao in the speeding ATV, the cool morning air refreshed her further. Bishen's serious face didn't invite any conversation, so it was a silent ride to the denser part of the jungle. Eventually, the vehicle halted.

'Walk!' Bishen said with a grunt. She peered into the dimness and observed a thinning of the forest cover rather than a path. Seeing Bishen's nod, Isha forged ahead in that direction. They walked slowly through sharp shrubs in the grey light, minimally helped by torches. Bishen couldn't risk being seen, even in that dense wilderness. After about ten minutes, they reached a huge clearing, roughly the size of two tennis courts. It contained a massive structure. Although its roof and sides were skilfully camouflaged with vegetation, Isha could make out the man-made lines. On one side, Isha saw four sentries and surmised that it had to be the entrance. The guards straightened their spines and saluted Bishen, who nodded and gestured Isha to follow him. As Isha stepped through the entryway, she gasped.

At the far end of the hall, there were crates arranged in neat rows, while the foreground was populated by rows of rough-hewn tables. On the tables lay arms, ammunition and combat gear. There were a variety of machine guns and rifles, hand grenades, bullets, knives and bayonets, while ammunition was arranged neatly by weapon type. Isha thought she saw some Sako TRG 42s, the latest sniper rifles in use by the Indian Army, but before she could get a closer look, something else attracted her attention. Positioned at a distance from the array of tactical equipment, two machines were placed on a couple of upturned crates. Their smooth cylindrical bodies standing on caterpillar treads—a circular chain belt—were topped by bullet-shaped heads. Four arms sprouted from their matte black trunks, two of which ended in smooth, round barrels, the third limb had a pincer, while the fourth sported a round serrated blade. Robots! She recognized them as robots. And not just any old robot. Military robots! *This was RED!*

'Sangha!' The strident call from Bishen snapped her attention away from the scene in front of her. She looked where he was standing and was surprised to see Rambhakt and Marachhiya beside him. She hadn't even noticed their arrival. As she hurried towards them, a long, piercing whistle from outside transcended the hum of the morning insects.

'Our guests are here,' Bishen announced as she approached the trio. About five minutes later, four men stepped into the hall, their arrival silent and stealthy. Bishen walked towards them, hand raised in greeting.

'Welcome, welcome,' he smiled at the shortest one in the group. 'Finally we meet, Kaled. Welcome to LalTara.'

Isha studied the newcomers. *One was clearly local, the guide perhaps. He had quickly retired to the background. Of the remaining three, the man Bishen had addressed as Kaled seemed to be in charge. He was fair-skinned like his companions, but that's where the similarity ended. Where his colleagues possessed a powerful leanness, Kaled's body had a cheerful rotundness.* Dabbing the sweat from his forehead with a pristine white handkerchief, Kaled returned Bishen's smile and grasped his extended palm with both his strong hands.

'Likewise, Bishen Rao, likewise. No time to lose though. Let's start, shall we?'

Bishen gave him a mock salute, surprising Isha, who wasn't used to such levity from LalTara's commander. *Things must be really going his way,* she thought to herself.

'Give me the control,' Bishen ordered Rambhakt, who scurried forward with a laptop, already running some sort of a programme on its screen.

Bishen pressed some keys, and one machine of the pair fired up. It rolled smoothly on its caterpillar tracks, manoeuvring the rough ground with ease.

'Do you see that tree, the one with the yellow flowers?' Bishen asked the group.

The collective gaze of everyone present, Isha included, turned to the spot where Bishen was pointing. There was a bright, fleeting flash from one arm of the activated robot and with a crash, the target toppled over.

Hearing Bishen's delighted guffaw, Isha turned to look at him. His fingers hovered over the laptop.

'Now, watch this!' he exclaimed, as delighted as a little child with a new toy. He tapped some more commands into the laptop and the other machine moved to life. Both the robots rolled through the tree cover, sawing the thorny shrubs and vegetation that stood in the way. Recalling the machines, Bishen shouted: 'Bring the hares!' Four men shuffled into view with a couple of cages and opened them. Out spewed about two dozen frightened animals, loping hither and tither in the clearing.

'Stand back,' LalTara's supremo warned the group as he fed more commands onto the laptop. The robots trundled forward, their guns ready. Their barrel arms began blazing and one by one, the running animals were picked off, some mid-jump. It was over in seconds.

Bishen rubbed his hands in glee. 'Aren't they beautiful, Kaled?'

'Impressive,' was the Iraqi's monosyllabic response.

Bishen roared with laughter. 'Just imagine what they, an army of these, will do for you! But for now, I think we can return to the camp to complete the deal and celebrate.'

Silently, Isha got into the car with Rambhakt and Marachhiya. No one spoke on their return journey, but Isha could clearly see the delight on Marachhiya's face.

Fuck, Isha thought. *A robotic army with hundreds of these killing machines, if not more! What was Bishen doing? This could cause a global upheaval, and change the way wars are fought. Bishen,* Isha continued musing, *would initiate the first falling domino tile that would start a devastating chain reaction across the world.*

༄

Back in the camp, Rambhakt quickly ushered their Iraqi guests to the network room where the deal was going to be completed. Bishen, Marachhiya and Sangha had returned to camp as well, and gathered in Bishen's quarters.

To maintain the impression that Sangha was pleased with the way things were progressing, Isha said jubilantly: 'Everything went off so well. We've worked damn hard for this.' She smiled.

'Yes. And now for the fruits of our labour...' Bishen responded. 'Let's go to the network room. Kaled is waiting there to complete the money transfer.'

In their excitement, Bishen and Marachhiya strode rapidly towards the room, leaving Isha to follow in their footsteps. She looked at his retreating back, her stomach clenching with anxiety. He stopped and turned to look at her with a frown.

'What's the matter?' he asked.

'No, no, nothing,' she stammered, marching towards him and the network room.

Inside the room, there was a tableau of hushed expectancy: the Iraqis were waiting to conclude the transaction and be on their way; Marachhiya and Rambhakt were elated with the successful conclusion of the deal and whatever monetary benefits it would bring LalTara and them.

Bishen walked to a cupboard and opened it with a set of keys he had extracted from his pocket. He then unlocked a digital safe within the cupboard and removed a small, oblong black device with a smooth black face and a USB port at one end. A USB authentication token, Isha noted automatically. He walked over to the computer and plugged it in. Immediately, the screen switched to an offshore bank interface, a small red dot glowing on one corner.

'You know what to do, Sangha,' he told Isha, pointing to the plugged-in device that was now glowing red. Place your eye close to the screen—it will scan your retina.'

Isha swallowed hard. She felt as though something was lodged in her throat. She hesitated for a moment before leaning in, her slightly tremulous hands gripping the edge of the desk. Nothing. The dot continued to display the red glow.

After a few seconds, she cleared her throat, wiped her damp palms against the side of her pants, and took a deep breath. *God, if I ever need any help from you, it's now*! She sent a silent prayer into the universe. She leaned forward again, aligning her eyes with the scanner. Once more, nothing.

The room seemed to go still. From the corner of her eye, Isha caught a glimpse of Bishen moving closer.

'What the hell,' she heard him growl.

Isha desperately wanted to run away, but she knew her shaking legs wouldn't support her in the flight. Her mind raced furiously, gauging her chances of making it alive from this situation. And then, *ding!* The screen chimed, and the light turned a reassuring green. *Fuck, fuck, fuck,* Isha's mind chanted. *Access granted. Lifeline maintained.* She went limp with relief, her mind replaying the scene at the safe house, when Sangha had revealed Bishen's plan to them.

༄

A few months ago
The Rowghat safe house

Rao is preparing something big, Sangha had told them. 'I know I am a significant part of that plan, and not in a good way. He's got my retinal scan as the access point for the money transfer. I then learnt that he's planning to leave us, and make a run for it with Marachhiya and Lipi. We're just cogs in the machinery, pawns in his game. We don't matter to him.'

She had then turned to Isha and met her gaze directly. 'You're planning to switch with me, that's fine. But what will you do when it's time for the transfer?'

That reality check had dampened their spirits for some time until Manish had returned with a strategy. He planned to replicate retinal patterns onto superfine, nearly invisible lenses that could deceive such systems. It had taken a while, but finally, they had managed to perfect the lenses as evidenced by several trial runs at the facility using a variety of retina access control systems. The lenses had successfully fooled these devices, every single time.

༄

Bishen's whoop of joy brought Isha back from her reverie and into the present. *The Iraqi funds were now in her account.*

Bishen and Kaled patted each other on the back and shook hands.

'Inshallah, we will take the delivery of the robots and the blueprint of RED at the China-Nepal border next Friday.'

Isha joined in on the festivities, but there were too many thoughts running through her head. *She desperately needed to touch base with STF19 headquarters, consult her father, and inform them of the happenings at LalTara so that STF19 could apprehend the delivery of RED. She didn't have much time at her disposal!*

39

The Eye of the Storm

2025
Raipur

Manish's death weighed heavily on Rakesh; his mind was restless, grasping for elusive answers. *Why couldn't he connect the pieces of this puzzle?* He was convinced that the solution lay just within arm's reach. A small shard could complete the entire picture. Yet, that missing fragment remained shrouded in a mist of uncertainty, an enigma slipping through his fingers. Even his attempt to trace the car through the number plate had been unsuccessful. The registration number was fake, which did not really surprise Rakesh.

As Sangha entered the living room, her eyes fell on Rakesh seated in a chair, looking desolate, his countenance etched with exhaustion and grief. The toll of Manish's passing was evident in the lines on his face; it seemed as if he had aged overnight. An unfamiliar warmth, a tenderness that she had recently started to feel towards her father, tugged at Sangha's heart; it was evidence of a connection that seemed to be deepening with time. She approached her father with gentle determination.

'You're not alone in this, you know. We can talk,' she said.

'Trying to make sense of Manish's accident is tormenting me. I keep wondering if there is anything I could have done to help him. Perhaps he could be alive today,' said Rakesh as he looked up at Sangha, a mixture of pain and worry reflected in his eyes.

Sangha moved closer to console her grieving father. There was a noticeable shift in the dynamics between her and Rakesh. *Was the bond of blood finally seeping into her emotions?*

With a deep breath, Rakesh began to open up to Sangha, his voice quivering as he began to speak.

'I feel as if I let him down. I am responsible...' his voice trailed off, heavy with unspoken regret.

'You can't blame yourself for events beyond your control. Manish's fate was shaped by circumstances you couldn't have foreseen,' Sangha remarked sagely.

'I should have,' Rakesh muttered with the composed discipline of a soldier.

'We all have our what-if moments,' said Sangha, trying to push the ghosts of her own past into a far corner. They troubled her far less these days. Being away from Bishen and around Rakesh and Neel had helped her. She had to admit that something was healing within her.

With quiet resolve, Sangha knelt beside her father and gently placed her hand over his. The stoic father wrapped his fingers over hers, drawing them to his forehead. He said nothing, but the silence between them carried the weight of all the words left unsaid. Sangha found herself unable to resist the urge to embrace him.

'Grief has its own way of healing and your memories of Manish will always keep his spirit alive,' Sangha murmured, as she hugged her father.

As Rakesh met Sangha's gaze, a profound connection formed between them. The reserved soldier's composure gave way to regret and remorse. 'I am sorry I gave up looking for you. I should have never stopped. Forgive me, my child,' a distraught father pleaded as they both wept together for the lost years in their lives.

A loss which had created a seemingly unbridgeable gulf between the two was now bringing them together. A father's lacerated heart was mending and the hurt his daughter carried was slowly dissipating.

'I shall never let you down again. Ever,' said the father.

'I won't either,' declared the daughter.

They sat in silence, savouring this new closeness. Then Rakesh spoke up: 'Beta, I need to see Rawat-ji. He knows about Manish, but I will have to update him personally about this development.' Sangha nodded. She realized that adhering to professional protocol was important, but meeting Binod Rawat would also help to lighten Rakesh's grief about losing Manish.

∞

It was evening when Rakesh parked his car and, after clearing security, entered Binod Rawat's house. The weight of Manish's death burdened every step that he took. His legs felt as though they were made of lead. However, a sixth sense—or was it merely wishful thinking—told him that Operation Trojan Horse was almost over and the day when he would reunite with Isha and have both his daughters with him wasn't too distant.

Walking into Rawat's elegantly illuminated, upscale living room, Rakesh was greeted by the man himself, who enveloped him in a warm embrace. 'I'm so sorry, my friend,' Rawat said. 'I know how much you loved that boy. I was so happy to hear about Isha and Neel taking the next step in their relationship. And then this...'

The two men moved apart, and the home minister gestured for his guest to sit down. He then placed a glass of Scotch in Rakesh's hands.

Rakesh was touched by this solicitude, but he kept his gaze fixed on the drink. 'I can't shake off the feeling that I let that kid down,' he finally spoke, the weight of remorse palpable in his voice.

Rawat, perceptive as ever, offered a comforting presence. 'Rakesh, you can't shoulder all the blame. We all have our part to play,' he said, his tone gentle and understanding. 'Manish might have uncovered more information than he ought to have.'

'Like what?' asked Rakesh.

Rawat shrugged. 'Anything that points to the perpetrators, something connected with the money trail maybe? An operation of this nature is bound to involve some financial transactions. Did he ever confide in you?'

Rakesh's gaze shifted, a mix of regret and uncertainty in his eyes. 'He did. But all the evidence, everything he found, it's like it never existed. He wiped out all traces from his computer system.'

Rawat's brows furrowed thoughtfully. 'That's curious,' he mused aloud. 'Why would he erase his own work? Unless... unless he was forced to do so. Threatened perhaps?'

Rakesh's mind swirled with a storm of possibilities, and his thoughts painted a vivid canvas of potential scenarios. Rawat's calm demeanour helped to soothe the turbulent undercurrent of their conversation. He leaned back, letting out a sigh. Yet, something his friend said bothered him.

Seeing Rakesh's preoccupied look, Rawat reached out and patted Rakesh's hand with a warm and understanding smile. 'Sometimes, my friend, closure comes not from knowing every detail, but from accepting that some stories remain incomplete. Manish was bright and resilient. Whatever path he took, he chose it for a reason.'

As the conversation concluded, Rawat's soothing words wrapped around Rakesh like a comforting blanket, but something niggled at him. He just could not pin it down.

Eventually, Rakesh stood up, his eyes reflecting a mixture of lingering doubt and newfound solace. With a final nod, he bid Rawat farewell and left the room, carrying the weight of his thoughts and feelings with him.

Ensconced in his vehicle parked outside Rawat's residence, Rakesh's gaze settled on a disturbing detail in the rearview mirror: the black Kia, a vessel of ominous intrigue cradling two shadowy figures, parked across the road. *Were these the ones who killed Manish?* Rakesh's mind raced, desperate for answers that seemed so close yet just beyond his immediate reach. Without realizing it, Rakesh automatically noted the dent in the bonnet.

Gripping the steering wheel, Rakesh started his car and swiftly executed a U-turn, approaching the Kia head-on and catching its driver off guard. Accelerating with determination, he pressed forward, his heart pounding. *Who were these people? And what were they doing here? While starting for Rawat's residence from his house, he was certain there was no one tailing him. How did they know he was with the home minister?* Rakesh's thoughts raced. The Kia reversed before vanishing around a sharp corner, leaving Rakesh in pursuit, his mind consumed by a mix of curiosity and unease.

The chase meandered through the quiet city streets. He could see the tail lights of the car, now close, sometimes far. Rakesh gritted his teeth and persisted. *He was going to catch those bloody fuckers. He wanted answers.* The chase led him to the outskirts of the city. The roads were lonely here, winding through sleepy villages. For a minute, Rakesh lost the two red pinpricks of light to a turn, but then spied them at a distance as he negotiated the bend. The pursuit continued. Another bend and then darkness! Rakesh pressed on the accelerator and continued speeding in the hope that he would catch up with his pursuers. However, just like before, luck seemed to favour the devils.

Damn! Rakesh cursed in his mind, easing the car to a stop at the edge of a lonely road. His hands were shaking from the adrenaline rush. He rubbed them and flexed his fingers. However, the excitement of the chase had also sharpened Rakesh's mind. Pieces of the puzzle began to click into place, forming a chaotic yet comprehensible picture. 'Manish was onto something big,' he muttered to himself, the urgency of his thoughts matched by the pounding of his heart. The accident had silenced Manish's voice but his quest for truth echoed loudly in Rakesh's mind.

Binod Rawat's mention of the money trail earlier that day stirred something deep within him—a realization that Rawat's knowledge could only have come from one source: Manish.

The Kia parked outside Rawat's residence was another clue. Apart from himself, only two people knew about his unscheduled visit to the home minister: the minister himself and Sangha. While he had told Sangha just moments before leaving his house, Rawat had been expecting him for hours.

Then, another thought struck him.

He recalled the blood-stained ID card found at the scene where Manish had been killed. *The scribbled mark that looked like the number 8 at the time was actually an alphabet.*

It was the letter B.

The hair on the back of Rakesh's neck stood on end as he whispered, 'God save us!' *It's him! Binod Rawat is working hand in glove with LalTara. The home minister is at the epicentre of this web of deception. It was he who had Manish killed!*

Rakesh's mind was racing, replaying every revelation, every missing link that had finally fallen into place. However, he barely had time to enjoy the elation of unravelling the skein of the problems. So consumed was he that he neither heard nor saw the black Kia creeping up behind him, its predatory stillness masked by the distant hum of the city.

Then, without warning, the engine roared—like a beast striking down its prey, the car lunged forward. The brutal impact sent a sickening jolt through Rakesh's vehicle, launching it forward, skidding across the asphalt with merciless precision. The airbag erupted from the steering wheel, but the sheer momentum flung Rakesh forward before it could cushion him. His seatbelt yanked him back, but not before his head slammed into the windscreen. A white-hot explosion of pain ripped through his skull. He felt blood flowing down his face and a sudden light-headedness, as if his blood pressure had plummeted dangerously. His head, hurting agonizingly, felt as if it was on fire, but his body felt cold. He started to shudder uncontrollably. A surreal image flooded his mind—Mitali, fading away, her eyes imploring him, her voice echoing, 'Save our children, Rakesh.'

And then, as his breath wavered and his consciousness ebbed, he struggled to hold the fleeting array of thoughts that danced on the edge of his awareness. *What had Manish discovered? What did they want from him?* But even those questions dissolved into nothingness. The last visual that Rakesh could see in his mind's eye as he was swept into an unending vortex of darkness was that of a laughing young woman cradling two babies.

⚭

The satellite phone in Rakesh's locker at home beeped. It was a text message from a special number assigned to Isha.

Had he been alive to act on the message his daughter had sent, he could have changed the course of events.

⚭

40

The Hero

2025
Abujmarh

Isha sat with unseeing eyes before the monitor in the network room. The system made its usual beeps and clicks, but her mind was far away with Baba. Ever since the demo with the Iraqis, she had been trying to get in touch with him, but to no avail. The deal was set to go down in two days and yet, her encrypted satellite phone remained silent. The tentacles of unease were increasingly tightening their hold on her heart.

'Akka, Akka,' Manu's voice sounded from beyond a thousand layers of cotton wool wrapped around her mind. The boy suddenly burst into the room the entry to which was strictly controlled. *Something serious must have happened for Manu to violate the protocol in this manner,* she thought.

'*Kya hua?*' Isha asked, her voice laced with concern.

'Radu has been found. He is recaptured,' the boy whispered, panting like a beleaguered engine.

Ignoring the nausea that threatened to spill out the contents of her stomach, Isha ran out of her quarters, gesturing to Manu to take her where her colleague was being held prisoner.

The first sight of the rookie engulfed her in a wave of dizziness. He sat on a chair, slumped forward, hands tied behind his back. A powerful stench of decay and urine emanated from him. His clothes were torn and his exposed flesh was slick with blood. His hair hung in sweaty, damp strands around his face, which was probably better, as Isha did not have the courage to look at it.

Bishen had hunkered down in front of the man, like a predator who'd spotted its prey. Two of LalTara's strongmen stood a little apart, like hyenas waiting for a piece of the action.

Isha gulped, consciously steadied her voice, and questioned the room in general, 'Where was he found?'

Rambhakt emerged from the shadows in the room, his eyes glinting with fear and anger as he looked at her. *He had avoided her since the day she had blackmailed him.*

He knew Sangha had framed Kundanlal, making her responsible for Tej's current condition. But he also knew that if he revealed this to Bishen, Sangha would expose the photographs of him stealing the drugs and his role in Kundanlal's death.

Now, with Radu captured, he was certain that the battered man would spill the truth to Bishen—paving Isha's way to hell. 'The villagers brought him to our contact, Sanghakka,' he replied to the question in an even, flat tone. 'They had found him half-dead. They nursed him back to health as much as they could. When word reached our spies that there was a stranger among the locals, our people went to check and got him back.'

Isha desperately fought the urge to catch Manu's eye. 'Did he say who helped him escape?'

This time, Rao replied. 'We tried to find out, but no luck so far. He keeps drifting in and out. I don't think he'll be able to withstand any more of our methods.' He stood up and stretched his back.

Isha swallowed, struggling to hold down her food. 'What's his name? Maybe I could give it a go.'

'I think it's Radu,' Manu piped up from behind her, 'I... I overhead Tej Anna calling him that, one time.'

The hair on the back of Isha's neck stood upright. Hearing Radu and Tej's name together made the horror of the situation sharper, more painful. *Her young colleague had been through hell. In fact, he was still there. How much more of this torture would he be able to endure? What would happen when he reached breaking point?*

Isha strode up to the seated man and squatted down close to him. 'Radu, Radu,' she called out softly. The figure continued to remain slumped, his head hanging down almost to his knees. 'Radu,' she called out again. This time he stirred. Isha stood up and propped the wounded man against the back of the chair, the metallic stench of his blood coating the back of her throat unpleasantly. Ignoring the reek of his wounds, she gently lifted his chin.

The man opened his eyes and looked at Isha, his gaze, initially unfocused, sharpened suddenly. A frisson of energy seemed to pass through his failing body.

'Radu, my name is Sangha. Can you hear me? I'm Sangha. I'm here to help you. Tell me, how did you escape? If you tell me, I'll make the hurt stop now.'

The young man breathed heavily, shuddering in pain with every two dry rasps of air filling his lungs. He steadied his head. 'Water,' he moaned.

'You'll get it, Radu. Just tell me the name of the person who helped you escape,' Isha insisted. Her every nerve end was tingling. She was unsure how this gamble was going to turn out. Behind her, she heard Rao growl.

Radu's head lolled and then somehow it righted itself.

He stared at Isha, and then scanned the room with his bloodshot eyes. He closed them briefly, as though the movement had been too much for his exhausted body, and then opened them again. This time, they locked on Rambhakt. His head moved feebly and his cracked lips shaped two words:

'That one.'

A scream of animal fury erupted from Rambhakt's throat. 'Liar! Liar! He's lying. It's not true!' Everyone looked flabbergasted, but before anyone could react, Rambhakt whipped out a gun from his belt and poured a barrage of bullets into Radu's wasted body.

'Liar, liar, liar, liar,' he continued shouting.

Isha heard Rambhakt's exclamations as if from miles away. She saw the blood pouring from Radu's poor, frail body—so much blood. She wanted to close her eyes but could not. She could not let the horror of this scene sweep across her face. She had to play her part; she had to react to the situation.

Bishen stood rooted to the earth. Then, quickly, he motioned to his strongmen to overpower the frenzied Rambhakt. Through all the pandemonium caused by this totally unforeseen development, his mind continued to work furiously. *Why had Rambhakt killed the man? If Rambhakt was really innocent, why silence the man who was accusing him? There was something more to this.*

Rambhakt brandished the firearm towards the approaching men. 'No, no, I'm innocent. Rao, I'm innocent. I'll tell you all... It's...' and he fell down as if poleaxed.

Isha had quietly stolen behind the screaming man in the midst of this fracas and brought down her gun hard on his skull.

'Get rid of this man,' she said, pointing towards Radu's body, 'and take Rambhakt inside. I'll deal with him.'

Belatedly, Isha realized she had taken the lead in this situation without waiting for Bishen's orders. She turned to LalTara's commander in deference. Bishen gave her a faint smile and nodded.

Isha smiled and saluted Rao, but inwardly she felt lacerated. *Radu had saved the day and in doing that, lost any chance that he might have had of seeing his own wife and child. This sacrifice must not go in vain.*

But first, she had to develop a strategy to deal with Rambhakt.

41
A Killer Plan

Incapacitating Rambhakt was the only option available to Isha in that moment. She could not afford for him to blurt out anything that would implicate her to Bishen. Now, sitting inside a small room, she waited patiently for Rambhakt to regain consciousness. During that time, she thought furiously and frantically about the plan ahead. She had convinced Bishen to entrust her with the interrogation of the 'traitor', promising to notify him as soon as the truth started to emerge, hopefully without too much cajoling. Consequently, only a messenger stood outside the door, vigorously rubbing tobacco in the palm of his hand, while Isha and the prisoner were quite alone.

Isha's thoughts turned to her Baba as she waited. She was puzzled by the deafening silence at his end and did not know what to make of it. What was worse, even Manish seemed to have been swallowed up by that dark, frightening abyss of uncertainty. Their small house in Raipur, her mother's jasmine tree, Vishnu Kaka... Neel! *They all seemed sepia-toned images from a past life. Would she ever see them again?*

A moan from the captive wrenched her mind away from the bout of reminiscing and brought her back to the fraught present. Rambhakt moved his head feebly to an upright position. He opened his eyes and stared, uncomprehendingly, at his surroundings, and then struggled, a bit surprised, against the restraints that chained him to the chair.

'What the...' He tried to shake his head, as if to clear away the cobwebs in his mind, and winced as he felt a jolt of sharp pain pierce his brain. Then, he noticed Isha and obscenities spewed from his mouth, as if a floodgate had been opened.

'You fucking bitch! You will regret this. You will never get away with this. I'll tell them all...'

Isha held up her hand.

'You're right, Rambhakt. I will regret this and I shall never get away with this. But the fun fact is, you won't either. I can't take too much pain. So the moment they start turning the screws on me, I have only one ace up my sleeve and you know what it is. So Rambhakt, my friend, we're both up shit creek and perhaps you and I need to help each other.'

The silence from the other end told Isha that she had the man's attention. She continued, 'This is what we're going to do. You are going to need a pee break and as I refuse to hold your dick for you, I shall have to untie you. Then you are going to overpower me, take my gun and hold me hostage. Rao needs me alive and I'll make sure to cover you. There's an SUV with a key in its ignition. Our getaway vehicle. Our one chance to get out of this. Got it?'

The man nodded.

'Okay. I'm going to call Kancha now to cover me, while I untie you, okay? Once I do that, get into action.'

The man nodded again.

Isha gave Rambhakt the thumbs up, and yelled for the guard at the door. When the pudgy man stepped inside, wiping his tobacco-stained hands on his pants, she ordered: 'Guy wants to take a leak. Cover me with your gun while I untie him. If he tries anything funny, shoot the bastard.'

Kancha, a man of few words, grunted.

Isha stepped close to the chair, with her back to Kancha and her eyes fixed on Rambhakt. A signal passed between them. Kneeling in front of the chair, she loosened the rope around his ankles first and then went around the back, and did the same with his wrists. She pulled the gun out of her waistband and prodded him in the back.

'Get up,' she ordered.

To Kancha, what followed after that seemed like a scene from one of the B-grade films he watched in the run-down theatres in the town nearby, complete with rumbustious fights and luscious women.

Kancha saw Rambhakt turn around suddenly, overpower Sangha madam, wrestle the gun from her hand, and pin her hand behind her back. He placed the gun at her temple and growled at Kancha: 'Don't make a sound or she dies.'

'Don't be a fool, Rambhakt,' Isha hissed. The man ignored her and pushed her forward a little.

Appearing to lose balance, Isha stumbled and ducked before she turned around to deftly extract a kukri from her right boot. She now faced Rambhakt.

'This ends here, Rambhakt.' He realized too late that he'd been had. In a red rage, he pressed the trigger of the gun, only for it to click impotently. Before he could utter another word, Isha was upon him, burying the wicked blade in his chest again and again.

Later, Kancha, his tongue loosened by the scene that had unfolded before him, would describe to a rapt crowd how Sanghakka pounced on the traitor like an avenging fury and bathed in his gore. And how Rambhakt had toppled back, his shirt slick with blood and a growing dampness staining the crotch of his pants. The poor man had at least had his last pee.

42

The Forever Plan

2025
Raipur

Rakesh's demise was a devastating blow for Sangha, leaving a hollow ache within her. Despite their limited time together, his absence made her heart feel heavy. *Is it because he was my father or because of those moments we shared?* She pondered. Sangha fought to contain her emotions, but her stoicism intermittently dissolved into tears. The funeral was a harsh reminder that she was now an orphan and this realization offered no solace. It was a stark indication of loss and finality.

With unspoken gentleness, Neel supported her and was a source of strength for Sangha. Rawat also came to the funeral and later hugged her. He was somewhat surprised to see no recognition of him in her eyes. She stood with her hands folded, with silent, genuine tears streaming uncontrollably from her eyes.

Once Sangha returned home, the empty house with a broken Vishnu Kaka haunted her even more. That night, Neel chose to stay home with her, offering his presence as a comforting embrace in her time of need.

In his arms, Sangha found refuge from her grief, a place to release the torrents of sorrow that engulfed her. She questioned the intensity of her tears, likening them to the anguish she had felt with Suryamani's passing. The enigma of Bishen's involvement swirled in her thoughts. *Could he be the one responsible for Rakesh and Manish's deaths? And if so, what would he do next?*

Doubts surfaced regarding her own safety. *How long could Isha keep up the act? The charade she maintained would eventually unravel. Then, will Bishen hunt me down and kill me like he killed Suryamma?*

There was also the looming shadow of Neel's eventual discovery of the truth about her and Isha. *What will happen when he learns the truth? No, no, no...stop it,* she thought. *Not tonight. She could not think about any of that tonight. She would just soak in the comfort of Neel's presence.*

As the night deepened, Neel's lips met hers, a shared intimacy that held her completely. *This moment feels so right, so real,* thought Sangha. The journey from fear to reciprocation, from love to surrender, was etched in every touch, every sigh, prolonging their emotional bond. Their hearts merged in a tender dance of compassion and vulnerability. His lips met hers in a soft, understanding kiss. In that fleeting moment, the world seemed to fade, leaving only the warmth of their shared connection.

Sangha's fingers found solace in the strands of Neel's hair, a gentle touch that conveyed his reassuring presence. 'You're here with me now,' he said, and she felt a calming sense of comfort that she hadn't experienced in a long time. His hands traced soothing patterns on her skin, each stroke a silent promise of support and solidarity.

Time seemed to stand still as they explored the contours of each other's vulnerabilities, igniting desires and awakening dormant feelings. Their bodies moved in harmony, a delicate balance of giving and receiving, of trust and surrender. As

Neel entered her and moved within her, she could feel the power of the union. She surrendered to him fully and completely, engulfed by a surge of passion she had never felt before. Her breath quickened and she could feel her body shudder with pleasure as he explored every inch of her. Sangha rode a wave of ecstasy that touched her soul. Her entire life before that moment felt like a blur and this union was the only truth. In the quiet aftermath, their breaths mingled, a testament to the intimacy they had shared.

This isn't just a fleeting moment; it is the culmination of a connection we share, thought Sangha. *A bond of compassion and empathy that linked him to her.* As they lay together, a profound sense of oneness enveloped Sangha.

Neel was surprised with her reciprocation, her need to cling to him. He read it as a consequence of the turmoil she had been through, and understood her pain. He said to himself with resolve, 'I have to help to rebuild Isha, to mend the frayed pieces of her soul.'

In this moment of quiet introspection, Sangha resolved to reshape her fate, to cast aside the spectres of fear and uncertainty that held her captive.

With Rakesh and Manish gone, no one other than Isha knew of Sangha's secret. What if Bishen never discovered Isha's truth? Would Isha be confined to Abujmarh? Then she could have Neel to herself forever!

43

Stuck in Hell

2025
Abujmarh

Isha's anxiety about both her father and Manish being unreachable reached fever pitch. Like a woman on the brink of losing her mind, she screamed out her frustration, and talked to them, albeit in her head.

Manish, where the fuck are you? Is something wrong with your tech devices? Baba, are you okay? Why haven't you moved heaven and earth to establish contact with me? The deal is going to close soon, Baba. I need you to bring in the troops. What am I going to do without intervention? What would you do if you were in my place?

Isha's thoughts raced around in her head like a trapped animal, probing around for a way out, searching for an escape route—yet no chink of light rent that thick veil of darkness. If there was no assistance coming her way, she needed to know Bishen's wily plans. *But how?* A profound sense of helplessness stole over her.

She could see that things were heating up in LalTara. Every time she saw Bishen Rao, she could sense the excitement in his body. It was as if he pulsed and throbbed with energy. She could almost see the sparks of jubilation arcing between him and Marachhiya. The furtive smiles and the little touches between the two sickened her.

And then, something sparked her memory. *Bishen is a big talker after lovemaking,* Sangha's words rang in her ears. *That's how I discovered he was going to sell us all out and disappear with that bitch and his darling daughter.*

Could this be worth a try? Perhaps being so close to victory was acting as an aphrodisiac for Bishen and Marachhiya. Given Sangha's experience, maybe the man would divulge something in a satiated post-coital state. Isha had a mission now.

She stepped out. It was late and much of the camp had settled in for the night. She sauntered towards Rao's quarters. She scanned her surroundings. Guards, yes. But no one paid her much attention. She withdrew into the shadows of a building and waited. A dim light glowed through the curtained windows of Bishen and Marachhiya's room. Isha started inching towards the illuminated square of the window. Sticking close to the wall of the room, she poured all her energy into her ears. At first, she heard nothing. Then a faint tinkle of bangles.

'Get me a glass of water,' she heard Bishen's deep voice. A sound of movement, followed by liquid being poured in a container, reached her ears.

'Bishen,' she heard Marachhiya say. 'Kundan gone, now Rambhakt. I don't get a good feeling. Something's not right.'

'It happens, Mara, when organizations become big and people running them become ambitious. Anyway, we shall be out of here soon. The Chinese will deliver the package at the Lhasa border tomorrow, the Iraqis will take charge of it, and we will get our cash to freedom. After that it's you, me, Lipi, and a life of normalcy. So just a little more patience, Mara; it won't be long now. The delivery will happen tomorrow evening.'

The delivery will happen tomorrow evening. The words

Stuck in Hell » 287

continued to echo in Isha's ears as she stood outside Bishen's room. Bishen had advanced the hand-over schedule to take everybody by surprise! It was less than twenty-four hours till the delivery of RED, and here she was, completely alone in enemy territory, and without any assistance coming from either Baba or Manish.

Isha retraced her steps and headed back to her room, her mind churning furiously. How could she put a spoke in Bishen's wheel? *What was the one thing that could stop the transaction?* Abruptly, she halted. There was a way. Yes! There was a way—perhaps the only way—to fuck things up for Bishen, and she would probably die doing it!

44

The Day After

2025
Raipur

The morning sun was still a shy visitor as Neel awoke, his gaze drawn to Isha's peaceful form beside him. She slept soundly, exuding a tranquillity he hadn't witnessed in her for a while. *When was the last time I saw her so at ease like this?* he wondered, his thoughts a mix of concern and tenderness.

While stepping out for a walk, he spoke to the distraught Vishnu Kaka and realized the profound shock that had gripped the home after Rakesh's passing. The weight of his loss lingered, touching every corner of their lives. *What must Isha be feeling?* he thought, and resolved to provide her all the support he could.

Upon returning, he settled into the study, a cup of warm water in hand. The practicalities of the day beckoned; emails to be sent, responsibilities to be fulfilled. In search of Isha's laptop, Neel opened her drawer and found the device covered in dust. *How long has it been since she used this?* he wondered idly. His fingers hovered over the keyboard as he contemplated the password. His mind travelled back to their first vacation together as a couple, where Isha had laughingly reset his computer password as her name. *The things one does for love!* He laughed silently, typing out a password on Isha's machine now. It bleeped to life. *Gotcha, Isha, you romantic softie*, he grinned. *She'd used his name as her password.*

As he gained access to the machine, messages from Isha's Google Drive flashed on the laptop's screen, catching his attention. Amidst the notifications, one name stood out—Manish! *First, he had gone missing, and then died under mysterious circumstances. What was his message still doing on Isha's computer? Why had Isha not accessed her laptop for so long? What had Manish wanted to convey?* A million questions raced through his mind. A sense of unease crept in as Neel delved deeper. On reading the notification, it seemed Manish had taken deliberate steps to upload a folder onto Isha's Gmail account. By doing so, he had circumvented his own system, thereby relying on her account to safeguard his secrets.

Why would he do that? Neel questioned, intrigue flickering in his eyes as he clicked on the message. A folder with an enigmatic title, Trojan Horse, appeared on the screen. Propelled by curiosity, when he clicked on it, the screen unfurled to reveal the secrets Manish had entrusted to Isha's care.

Neel stared at the screen, first confused, and then absolutely stupefied. His world came crashing down as he felt a catch in his stomach and his breath tightened in his chest.

'What the fuck? What the fuck!' he exclaimed, gazing at the laptop in disbelief.

The unease that had been gnawing at him hardened into certainty. It all fell into place—Rakesh's reluctance to let him meet 'Isha', her lukewarm responses to his proposal, her quick cover-up for the scene with Prisha, her picking Salman Khan over Shah Rukh Khan as her favourite actor, and—of all things—the way she casually ate the mushrooms that were supposedly off-limits to her.

The signs had been there all along. And now, staring at the screen, he couldn't unsee them.

45

Red for Danger

2025
Abujmarh

The jungle was alive with the promise of a new day. The sky was gradually brightening over the treetops, the light pouring dimension and colour into the dark silhouettes. Isha watched this shift with unseeing, gritty eyes.

Today was the day RED was meant to change hands, but there was no assistance for Isha forthcoming from the STF. *She was alone, and whatever had to be done, she would have to do by herself.* In the distance, she caught sight of Bishen pacing up and down, satellite phone glued to his ear. He noticed her and gave her a thumbs-up. Isha gulped. That meant all was going well. The LalTara contingent was at the border, overseeing the delivery of RED from the Chinese to the Iraqis. Bishen turned away, still talking on the phone and then punched the air in a celebratory gesture. Isha felt sick to the stomach, but could not pull her eyes away from the jubilant figure.

Bishen spun around once more and waved to Isha to follow him to his quarters. She walked into the room in a daze, not quite sure how she got there. Everything had taken on a blurry, hazy appearance. She saw Bishen as a spectral figure who offered her the USB authentication token. This was the tipping point.

As if in a dream, she took the device from her uncle's hand and plugged it into the laptop, which had already been set up for this purpose. The screen flickered to life, and a tiny red dot blinked ominously in one corner. Heart pounding, she leaned in, aligning her face with the scanner. The dot remained red—red for danger.

'These devices,' Bishen growled. 'These fucking devices work like this country. Stop and go, stop and go. Try again, Sangha.'

Mechanically, and with a mounting sense of dread, Isha yanked the USB token from the port, blew on it, and shoved it back in. The screen refreshed, but the dot still blinked red. She tried again. Still red.

Her pulse quickened. The air in the room felt heavy, charged.

Bishen screamed, 'What the fuck's wrong with this thing, Sangha?'

'How will it work?' A voice hissed from the door. Phoolma walked in. 'How will it work, Rao,' she repeated, 'when this is not Sangha?'

Bishen staggered back as if hit in the jaw by a particularly powerful uppercut. 'What?' was all he managed to say.

'Tej has woken up,' Phoolma exclaimed as she glared at Isha. Her son's awakening and this incendiary news had rejuvenated her sinking spirits. Her eyes were shining; she was raring to return into the thick of things.

Isha hadn't anticipated this turn of events but she was prepared for the consequences of her retina scan not going through. While Bishen was taking in perhaps the most shocking news he had received in recent years, she had whipped out her gun and lunged towards LalTara's commander. Her gun was now trained on his forehead.

'No. I'm not Sangha,' she said, surprised at how steady her voice sounded. 'I'm her twin Isha. I'm the one whose mother you killed, you bastard. I was wearing lenses imprinted with Sangha's retina structure. And now I've destroyed them. Fuck you, Bishen Rao.'

46

Unmasked!

2025
Raipur

Sangha's eyes fluttered open in the fading darkness that still shrouded the room. The curtains were drawn but she could see that Neel was not by her side. Neel's touch and the memory of their intimate connection still lingered, entwined with the present moment. She smiled as she thought about it. She sighed as she stretched out, arching her back. After the night with Neel, she felt that the chaos that had defined her journey through life so far was finally appearing to settle into a semblance of order. She emerged from her room, greeted by the stillness of the early hour. She went downstairs where she noticed Vishnu Kaka, still looking distraught. Giving her a cup of tea, he said, 'I was just coming up to your room, beta.' Vishnu Kaka's grief-ravaged face had a sobering effect on her. *How the faithful retainer had adored her father!* A feeling of empathy for the old house help flooded her and she gave him a hug. 'May the good lord be with you, *bitia*,' the old man sighed wearily as he blessed her.

Sangha smiled as she stepped back. 'Kaka, where is Neel?'

He pointed her to the study room and began walking in its direction with the tea tray.

Sangha stopped him with a smile and said, 'Let me take

it, Kaka.' Vishnu gave her a knowing nod and returned to the kitchen.

In the study, Neel sat still like a statue, his gaze fixed on the entrance. As Sangha stepped in, their eyes met. His eyes were as dark as coal, a kind of gaze that falls like a shroud to block out everything else.

He rose from the chair and walked up to her, unsmiling, his inscrutable expression giving away nothing. He firmly held her arm above the elbow and led her to the table, pulled out a chair and guided her into the seat. Sangha placed the tea tray on the table, somewhat taken aback with this gesture. This was not the response she had anticipated after last night.

With a press of a key, the laptop stirred from its slumber and the screen flickered to life. That is when reality hit her. A mosaic of windows unveiled a familiar world, of which Neel had no clue until he had fired up Isha's laptop. There were videos of her and Isha, dental scans, training clips, and intricate details of LalTara's scheme. The secrets of the Sangha-Isha switch were revealed before her, along with the labyrinthine money trail that had once been shrouded in shadows. Everything was exposed, as though the walls of deception had crumbled.

Sangha's hands trembled; her breath caught in her throat. The weight of her actions, her choices, and the tangled web she had spun seemed to crush her from all sides. The enormity of the revelation threatened to engulf her and a sense of doom cast its shadow over her.

Aware of the sensitivity of the data, Manish had meticulously safeguarded every piece of it, discreetly funnelling it onto Isha's Google Drive. His intention was clear; he wanted to keep the information safe, away from his computer system in case he was compromised. And the safest haven was Isha's computer!

Neel's voice, soft as a whisper, reached Sangha's ears. When she gazed at him, his eyes were laden with pain and guilt, from the memories of the previous night. He leaned closer, his words grazing her ear like a chilling breeze. 'Will you connect me to Isha, or should I call in the authorities?'

The gravity of the decision lay heavy in the air. Neel's words were a reminder that the world she had carefully constructed over the past few weeks had crumbled and she stood at a crossroad, the path ahead fraught with uncertainty.

Sangha knew then, in that moment, that it was over with Neel. *She had only one choice. To tell him the truth. The entire truth.*

47

The Unravelling

2025
Abujmarh

The room seemed to go into a state of suspended animation, as a stunned Bishen stared at Isha pointing a gun at him.

Nobody moved. And suddenly, Manu staggered onto the scene and stumbled onto the floor. Marachhiya walked in after him and placed her foot on his chest, with a gun trained on his face. 'Look what I found—a snitch. Guess who helped this two-faced bitch? Tej regained consciousness at the right time. You, whatever your name is,' she looked at Isha balefully, 'put your gun down, or he dies.'

Isha turned to look at Manu, at his heaving chest, the bruises on his face and his tearful eyes. Suddenly Radu's face floated into her thoughts. *No! Not another murder, not another death, not on her account.* She hadn't quite finished lowering her gun when she felt Bishen's fist slam like a sledgehammer on the side of her face, making her lose her balance and fall to the floor.

'Bitch!' he screamed. 'Bitch! Bitch! Bitch!' Each time he uttered the expletive, he hit her: in the stomach, in the ribs, on her face, igniting a fire as different parts of Isha's body erupted with pain. She squeezed her body into a small ball, offering as little space as possible for Bishen's target practice. Something roared in her ears and then the ringing started. Isha first thought the strident ringing had something to do with her damaged ears, but then she realized that the thrashing had ceased. She peered out from beneath her arms. It was Bishen's satellite phone that was ringing and demanded his attention.

'Damn, it's Kaled,' he said, looking at its screen. 'Yes, brother,' he spoke into the phone.

Squawking sounds erupted from the device—vexed noises that were audible even five feet away. Isha understood what was being spoken at the other end. As Bishen could no longer transfer money to the Chinese, they must have returned without delivering RED to the Iraqis.

'No, no, bhai. Everything is under control,' Bishen's placatory tones interrupted the agitated flow. 'It's just some technical glitch. You saw how it was the other day. We're sorting things out. Don't worry. Everything will soon be on track. And if not, I shall return the money to you!'

Bishen lowered the satellite phone and approached Isha. He hunkered down next to her. 'My dear niece. You have twenty-four hours to get Sangha here. Twenty-four hours. Otherwise Manu dies. And so do you!'

48

The Beginning of the End

2025
Raipur

The weight of Sangha's detailed confession hung heavy in the air. A deafening silence reverberated in the stillness of the room, even as a tempest rose within Neel, who was horrified at what had transpired and Isha's uncertain fate. His first response, an instinctual urge to react violently, was held at bay by sheer self-control.

Before them lay the satellite phone, a stark reminder of the intricate web in which they were entangled. 'This was the connection between Rakesh and Isha, but it was hidden from everyone,' Sangha revealed. 'Only Manish knew about it as he had set up the device. I knew about it, but I have never touched it,' she concluded her statement, faltering, remembering how she had been tempted to eliminate this connection with Isha last night. But thankfully, she had refrained from acting on her initial impulse.

It was clear to her. *The truth, however painful, was that Neel was solely Isha's. The brief yet beautiful connection between her and Neel was a by-product of an extended deception. She was a fool to have even dreamt of a future with him.* Sangha's heart constricted as Neel's fiery gaze shifted from her face to the messages on the screen, where each word from Isha—from information about LalTara to her last desperate cries for help—was etched in digital permanence. The gravity of the situation dawned on him, a chilling realization that the threads connecting their lives were rapidly unravelling. The guilt of his own actions with Sangha gnawed at him and weighed him down.

His trembling hands reached for the phone, his thoughts a whirlwind of uncertainty. Just then, the device vibrated unexpectedly, shattering the tense atmosphere. Isha's call came through, a lifeline connecting him to her. Without thinking, Neel quickly picked up the phone and spoke her name, his voice trembling. He heard Isha's voice at the other end, a mix of desperation and confusion. 'Neel! What...? What are you doing there? How do you have this phone? Where's Baba? *And Manish*?' Her questions hung heavy in the air.

Neel swallowed the lump in this throat. The dam that held his emotions in check threatened to burst as he felt torn between relief that Isha was alive, and dread about the news he had to break to her. However, before Neel could respond, he heard the phone being snatched away and another voice reached his ears.

'*Where is that traitor?*' Bishen Rao's words burst through the satellite phone with such intensity that even Sangha could hear them. His venom and lust for vengeance came through clearly and sent a shiver down her spine. Her darkest fears were manifesting before her eyes.

'Neel, Neel...' He could hear Isha's desperate cries followed by Bishen's roar. 'Shut up, you bitch!' Neel then clearly heard the sound of flesh striking flesh and Isha's voice being cut off abruptly. The sounds of assault continued and Isha began to scream.

Helpless and cornered, Neel's desperation reached its

peak. 'Please, please don't hurt her. I'll do whatever you ask of me,' he yelled into the phone, his voice shaking with a mix of fear and determination.

With a sinister whisper bearing the powerful weight of peril, Bishen's voice slithered back, 'Whoever you are, if you want to save this bitch, get me mine.'

The words hung in the air like a dark omen, sealing their fates and leaving them with a choice they couldn't escape.

Operation Trojan Horse was officially dead!

PART FOUR

Endgame

49

The Prep

2025
Raipur

Neel sat cradling his head in his hands. Isha's screams still reverberated in his ears. He squeezed his eyes shut tight as if to block out the nightmarish reality, but his mind conjured up terrifying scenes of Isha's torture, as the realization struck hard—*Isha was in grave jeopardy and he couldn't stand by idly.*

He straightened his posture and said decisively, 'Manish will be our lifeline.' Neel's words carried both conviction and urgency. Sangha's surprise was palpable. She began to doubt Neel's coherence, thinking he might be in a state of shock. 'How can Manish help?' Sangha asked disbelievingly. 'He's no longer with us. He is dead and gone, Neel.' Her voice was laced with tenderness.

Neel's response held a touch of melancholic certainty. 'Physically gone, yes. But Manish, my dear friend and tech enthusiast, has left a digital trail to guide us through this crisis.' He stood up, and with a new sense of purpose animating his stride, picked up his mobile phone and walked towards the window. His voice was strong and confident as he conversed with someone.

Seeing his determined profile, a wave of desolation washed over Sangha. *She never had this...this protection—*

someone looking out for her. Although Amma had been there for her as an emotional salve of sorts, she had been taken away far too soon. And now the dream of keeping Neel to herself was burnt to ashes.

As the subject of her thoughts concluded his conversation and returned, a veneer of stability masked his contemplative state. 'Let's move,' he directed Sangha without meeting her eyes. Sangha fell into step with him, a silent observer to Neel's unyielding determination.

∞

In a comfortably lit office, the chief minister's gaze was fixed on Isha's laptop, the gravity of the situation etched onto his face. 'Are you sure about this, Neel?' he asked, his voice inflected with concern.

Neel's reply resonated with quiet confidence. 'I've located the files, sir. Everything we need to expose the truth is right here with you. We need to get Binod Rawat first. He is deeply linked with LalTara's Bishen Rao. We need to take firm action, sir. Manish, my friend,' his voice caught, choked by emotion, '...died for this. And I am certain Rakesh Srivastava's death is also connected with Rawat. The man has blood on his hands.' Sangha could sense the grief in Neel's voice.

A heavy silence enveloped the room as the chief minister absorbed the weight of Neel's words. His response blended urgency and caution. 'You understand the implications, Neel? The stakes are higher than ever.' Unyielding, Neel's resolve shone through. 'I do, sir. And that's why we have to bring this to light. For justice.'

The chief minister's gaze shifted to Sangha. The similarity between her and Isha was unmistakable. She was living proof that Operation Trojan Horse was real. The truth that Neel had presented was undeniable. With a nod, the chief minister picked up his phone and summoned his secretary. He needed to ensure that various institutions worked together seamlessly to combine their strength and support the operation with their unified might.

Neel and Sangha stood aside as the two busy men orchestrated a series of phone calls to top law-enforcement authorities in the state, reaching out to high-ranking officials in the state police, the CBI and the CRPF, the internal security agency, to assist in a sensitive joint operation. The wheels of action were set in motion and the stage was assembled for a daring plan.

As preparations started for the Sangha-Isha exchange, Sangha's thoughts churned with a whirlwind of emotions. This endeavour transcended their personal stakes; it was about safeguarding Isha and dismantling Bishen's LalTara.

The profound, unbreakable bond between Neel and Isha continued to tug at Sangha's heart. She could do nothing but live with this awareness. *It also meant she had no place in Neel's heart.*

Sangha's betrayal haunted Neel's thoughts. Her deliberate deception, her conscious choice to impersonate Isha even during their intimate moments gnawed at his mind. He had to keep clearing his thoughts in order to focus on the need of the moment.

Neel's actions set in motion a web of events.

The path was paved for Sangha's return to the treacherous realm of LalTara and the malevolent Bishen. As uncertainty loomed, she steeled herself for the trials ahead, a silent acknowledgement that the journey she was embarking upon was fated.

She was going to do it for Neel. She was risking going back to Rao so that Isha could live, so that Isha and Neel could be together, just the way he wanted.

Sangha drew in a deep breath as these thoughts played out in her mind. *She prepared for her doom.*

∞

50

Breaking Point

2025
Abujmarh

It was time for the exchange. As the sun descended, painting the sky in a brilliant tapestry of fiery scarlet hues, Sangha and Neel embarked on their journey in a bulletproof SUV, driven by a skilled retired military officer.

Accompanied by a cadre of armed guards in two more vehicles, they proceeded towards the exchange coordinates provided by Bishen.

At first glance, the proposed swap seemed straightforward: Isha would be handed over to Neel, and Sangha to Bishen. While both parties held a person valuable to the other, it was Bishen who was dictating the plan, and that left Sangha with a growing sense of unease. The familiar fear inculcated in her by her upbringing lingered within her. This feeling of dread prevented her and Neel from taking charge of the situation.

Rao had fixed the location of the exchange but she knew better than to underestimate Bishen's cunningness. *He was bound to have some sinister plan or the other up his sleeve.* All they could do was wait and watch.

The car moved steadily along the winding road to the pre-determined coordinates. Outside, the darkness had devoured the landscape, making the path seem like a tunnel-like passage flanked by sentinel trees. The only sound in the car was the low hum of the engine. To Sangha, the situation seemed surreal. On the one hand, this was familiar territory, while on the other, there was an unsettling feeling that they were entering a realm of uncertainty.

As they arrived at the designated location, the absence of Bishen and his men added to the suspense, heightening the anticipation and the veil of tension in the car. Sangha's mind whirled with possibilities for what might unfold in the next few moments. The tranquillity of the deserted scene belied the roiling anxiety in her heart. In an attempt to reassure herself, Sangha focused on the commandos strategically positioned in the surrounding landscape. Their presence was a source of comfort, a reminder that they were not alone in this tense venture. Yet, despite the preparations, the air remained charged with uncertainty.

From the SUV's window, Neel's gaze caught a fleeting glimpse of a small, fluttering flag, its edge barely visible above the ground.

'That would be a message from Bishen,' Sangha responded to the inquisitiveness in Neel's eyes. She knew the way Rao operated. He never stuck to plan.

The driver exited the vehicle, retrieved a small package from beside the flag and passed it to Sangha. Opening the carton, Sangha recognized Isha's satellite phone as she handed it to Neel.

'This is a warning,' Sangha said. 'Rao wants us to know how completely compromised Isha is. We're being cautioned to cooperate.'

'But where are they?' Neel asked, his eyes scanning the surroundings. Just then, the phone in his hands sprang to life, vibrating ominously. A message beeped and Neel's gaze snapped to the screen, his heart racing.

'New coordinates,' Sangha replied, looking at its screen.

The timing of the text made it abundantly clear that they were being watched.

'Damn!' Neel swore. But that's all he could do. Rao was calling the shots.

Neel instructed the driver about the change of location and the SUV headed out towards another unknown destination. There was an uncomfortable silence in the car. Sangha's heart pounded in sync with her frantic thoughts, each beat amplifying her dread. *Rao had scored this round and stripped them of their strategic extra cover. They were now driving straight into his den with just their armed escort in the two cars; the commandos who were waiting camouflaged near the previous exchange points could not protect them now.*

They drove through the scrub and bushes into the underbelly of the forest, until they reached a crudely constructed hand-made wooden suspension bridge with rope railings. It seemed to be suspended over the blackness of a gorge. The sound of flowing water betrayed the presence of a stream running beneath it.

'We're very close to LalTara,' Sangha murmured. Suddenly, bright lights—seemingly from the headlights of a couple of cars across the gorge—lit up the area, illuminating the sway bridge. *The LalTara faction was already there!* Sangha could feel the air crackle with expectation, a blend of resolve, anxiety and uncertainty gripping everyone present. Neel and Sangha disembarked from their vehicle and waited, facing the suspension bridge. The two sisters on opposite sides.

Across the bridge, Isha, with her hands tied in front

of her and her battered face streaked with blood, strained to make out Sangha's distant figure. The blood that had run down her forehead had dried into crimson stains that resembled the warpaint of the warrior goddess Durga,[34] and seemed like the female divinity's third eye. Like the goddess, Isha was now poised to battle the demon Bishen.

But a flicker of surprise crossed Isha's face as her gaze fell upon a familiar figure standing beside Sangha. *It couldn't be! But there he was—Neel.* Her heart raced as the realization struck her like a bolt of lightning. *Neel knew. He knew the truth, he understood the stakes and he was here.*

Questions spun through her mind like a whirlwind. *How did Neel find out? And more importantly, why was he here?* Her thoughts raced to her father, her Baba. *Where was he? Manish not being here was understandable. He was always at the back end devising some strategy, some ingenious plan to turn the tide of the battle in her favour.* But Rakesh's absence puzzled her. Where was the man who had always been her guiding light, her pillar of strength?

As the seconds ticked by, a cascade of emotions swirled within Isha—surprise, confusion, anticipation, anxiety. Her heart yearned for answers, for reassurance and for the sight of her father's familiar face.

Bishen caught the query in Isha's eyes.

'Looking for your father?' Bishen's voice cut through the silence. Isha looked at him, and noting the sneer on his face and the menace in his eyes, her stomach dropped. Bishen leaned in, his proximity intensifying the tension. The whisper that followed was like a venomous serpent, injecting

---

[34]Durga (दुर्गा): A Sanskrit word, literally meaning 'invincible', 'impassable', or 'unassailable'

its poison directly into Isha's heart. 'Dead and gone! Like all of Bishen's enemies. Rakesh has been eliminated.' The words struck her like a physical blow and for a moment, the world seemed to dissolve around her, crushing her completely.

Blood rushed to Isha's head and her vision blurred with a mix of rage and despair. The revelation sent shockwaves throughout her being and struck her with a force that shattered her. Isha raged impotently like a tigress in iron shackles, the rope chafing the soft skin of her wrists. In that moment, Isha grappled not only with the grief of losing her Baba, but also with the overwhelming urge to kill the man who had orchestrated her father's death. Bishen slapped her hard across the face as he hissed into her ears, 'My snipers have their target locked on that lover boy of yours. So behave and obey.'

Isha knew that he would not pause for a second before ordering Neel's execution. She ceased her struggles and screamed; it was the only way she could vent her frustration and grief. Bishen smiled, savouring her helplessness. Then, peering at the other side of the bridge, Bishen bellowed, 'Make the exchange!'

The switch began under the sharp eyes of the observers—the mercenaries of LalTara, who had their guns trained on the few CRPF commandos standing beside Neel. Destinies entwined with each other and precariously hung in balance, as if by a fragile thread, as the two sisters—Isha prodded in the back with a gun by Marachhiya, and Sangha accompanied by Neel—started to walk towards each other, creating a tense atmosphere that was brittle to the point of shattering.

Isha carefully trod over the rough-hewn planks, her mind probing all possibilities of somehow gaining an upper hand in this grim situation. With four people walking over it, the bridge swayed, not alarmingly, but enough to make someone who was not paying attention lose their balance. Recovering her equilibrium, Isha looked up, first at Neel, and then, wrenching her gaze away from him with great difficulty, at Sangha.

As she locked eyes with her twin, Sangha felt a small jolt as if her sister was trying to convey something to her. She could feel the call of blood, the connection twins share, from starting their lives in the same womb. Sangha focused on trying to fathom the thoughts those eyes—burning with anger and brimming with tears—were trying to convey. Sangha felt another jolt—*she knew, just knew, that Isha knew Rakesh was dead and she had decided to avenge his death.*

Standing at one end of the bridge, Bishen's eyes were fixed on the twins—the back of one and the face of the other—both looked so much like their mother Mitali, his sister and betrayer. Fanned by these memories, the embers of his rage smouldered and spluttered. 'Should have finished both of them off that day,' he muttered under his breath, consumed by regret. He could not see Isha's face, but he didn't need to. Notwithstanding the wobbly bridge, her defiance and arrogance were evident in her straight back. A worm of unease wriggled in his gut.

Bishen should have trusted his instincts.

Towards the centre of the bridge, as she closed the distance, Isha locked eyes with Sangha, an imperceptible nod passing between them. There was no need for words—both knew this was their moment to strike.

And then, in a matter of seconds, it was over.

With a sudden burst of motion, Isha dropped into a half-squat and drove her elbow backward with all her might, aiming for Marachhiya's midriff. At the same time, Sangha sprang into action, lunging low and grabbing Marachhiya's wrist before she could react.

The dual attack caught Marachhiya off guard. Isha felt the sharp give of flesh beneath her elbow, heard the choked gasp as air was forced from Marachhiya's lungs. The impact made Marachhiya's grip on the gun falter, and before she could tighten her hold, Sangha twisted her arm sharply. The weapon slipped from her fingers, clattered onto the wooden planks, and vanished through the gap between them.

Isha spun, bent at the waist, and rammed her shoulder into Marachhiya's chest, shoving her backward against the rope railing.

'Now!' Isha barked.

Sangha didn't hesitate. She latched onto Marachhiya's legs with an unrelenting grip, pinning her in place as Isha used the power of her shoulders to tip their struggling opponent over the edge.

Marachhiya screamed, thrashed, but it was too late.

With one final heave, the sisters sent her over the railing.

It had all happened so fast—too fast for anyone on the sidelines to react.

The shriek echoed through the jungle—and then, just as suddenly, it was gone.

Aghast, Bishen watched the horror unfolding in front of his eyes. In his terror, he believed he heard Marachhiya's skull split open on the sharply pointed rocks, her blood and brains mingling with the water below. Reflexively, he almost made a start to run towards where Marachhiya had stood. But then he noticed Isha, Sangha and Neel running towards him. Self-preservation trumped grief.

'Tarzans activate!' ordered Bishen.

This was the cue for Bishen's men, hiding in the dense foliage atop the trees, to descend upon the surprised CRPF commandos.

Meanwhile, the trio on the bridge continued to advance towards Bishen, but this time, Sangha led the charge and provided cover for Isha. Behind her, still running, Neel removed his knife and worked on sawing off the rope that bound Isha's hands while fervently praying that he didn't hurt her.

'Hold your fire,' Bishen screamed, seeing Sangha shielding the other two with her body. He wanted Sangha alive—her retinal scan held the key to the biggest transaction of his life. Bishen was ready to embrace strategy over revenge for Marachhiya. His three adversaries had reached the end of the bridge and were already on firm ground. He prepared himself for the inevitable encounter that loomed like a storm in the sky.

He had one more ace up his sleeve. 'Blow her up,' he bellowed. *Boom*! Within seconds, the end of the bridge, where Sangha and Neel had stood moments earlier, went up in flames. This meant that the commandos accompanying Sangha and Neel would not be able to cross over. The sisters and the young man were now under Bishen's control.

They could hear the gunfire that continued to erupt from across the gorge, in the fight between the CRPF commandos and Rao's 'Tarzans', even as an uneasy stillness prevailed at their end. With guns out of the equation lest a stray bullet hit Sangha, the battle became a hand-to-hand combat.

Isha lunged at Bishen with the full force of her anger, landing a powerful blow to his jaw. The next blow swiftly followed as her right foot struck with full force at his left temple, sending a surge of pain through Bishen's skull.

Each blow was fuelled by a visceral demand for justice, for the death of her father and the murder of a mother she'd never known. The relentless assault continued as a torrent of punches, each strike on Bishen carrying the weight of a daughter's fierce determination to avenge her loved ones. Bishen attempted to fight back but found himself overwhelmed as Isha unleashed her pent-up rage.

Meanwhile, Sangha and Neel were successfully holding LalTara's cadre from defending their commander. Sangha was like an enraged tigress—her reputation as a formidable fighter won half her battle with Bishen's gang. Neel, too, shone with his body combat and martial art moves, and decimated his enemies. His dedication and love for Isha, coupled with his prowess, transformed this journalist into a daunting force on the battlefield. For a while, the trio had the upper hand and everything seemed to be going well, until it didn't.

Panting and sweating, Isha kicked Bishen to the ground. The fallen man coughed and wheezed; his head sunk between his shoulder blades. Isha stopped, trying to catch her breath. Just then, Bishen gathered all his energy, shot a kick at her ankle and toppled Isha, grabbing a gun that lay nearby. He then stood up and slammed Isha in her stomach, aiming the gun at her forehead. The course of the battle had shifted! As Isha tried to move again, he kicked her hard, again and again. As she started retching, Bishen fired the gun in the air, bringing the frenzied fight around him to a standstill.

'Stop, you motherfuckers, or I will shoot the bitch,' he thundered.

Sangha and Neel froze. They were horrified to see Isha fallen on the ground, writhing in pain, with blood trickling down the side of her mouth. Bishen's men wasted no time in asserting their dominance over the situation. Swiftly, they bound Sangha and Neel, rendering them completely immobile.

Anger dripped from Bishen's eyes as he relished the sight of the sisters and Neel, now vulnerable and helplessly bound before him. The tables had turned and the once-defiant trio now faced the harsh reality of their predicament. The air was thick with the tension of impending consequences as Bishen savoured his moment of triumph.

'Let's get this done. First Sangha. Let's get your eye scanned for the money transfer and then you can watch your sister and her friend go to hell. You, I will preserve till all the monies in your account are transferred to me and then you can join them,' he growled.

Isha glared at Bishen, making his move towards Sangha. She knew that this time the retinal identification would go through and that would be the triumph of Bishen Rao. *All the sacrifices they'd made to catch this predator would be wasted.*

Sangha remained calm as she looked up at the sky and drew in a deep breath. 'Pray to whoever you want,' Bishen sniggered triumphantly. Just then, as if in answer to Sangha's prayers, a low thrumming sound filled the air and Bishen's gloating quickly gave way to wonderment. Everyone looked up at the sky as the sound gradually increased until it seemed to fill the whole sky. The landscape pulsated with an invisible energy. Even the treetops rustled faintly. In an unexpected turn of events, the sky itself had become an ally.

Predator drones of the Indian Army, requested by the CRPF, descended from above, their lethal payload targeting Bishen's faction. It was as if the heavens had unleashed their wrath, the cacophony of bullets raining down on Bishen's men scattered them like leaves by the force of a typhoon.

Isha looked up at the skies and smiled. She was certain this was Manish's choreography. Little did she know then that he was truly beyond the skies and gone from this world.

The confrontation did not end here. The air was heavy with the stench of gunpowder as Bishen ran to seek cover, frantically ducking from the bullets. To his horror, he heard the deafening sound of a blast and then the forest behind him erupted with the sound of a ferocious cackling fire.

Bishen's Lanka had been targeted; LalTara—a few kilometres away—was being bombed!

Bullets, like ravenous predators, tore through the air, finding their targets with deadly precision. The ground bore witness to this dance of death as blood spilled forth. It was a brutal ballet of conflict, an agonizing struggle for dominance that etched its memory into the very earth of the Abujmarh forest.

The gunfire and the frenzy of bullets that grew wilder and appeared like a volley of fireworks in the darkness of the night eventually brought Bishen's empire on its knees.

∽

Later, when the army would go through the remains of LalTara, they would find Tej and Phoolma's lifeless bodies. Tej, still sitting in his wheelchair, and Phoolma slumped on one of the wheels, her sari tangled in the spokes, a twisted recreation of the umbilical cord that once united them. She had died protecting her son during the bombing.

∽

51

Two Sisters

Bishen's world was exploding in a mad show of violence. *LalTara was gone. Marachhiya was dead and most likely, so was Lipi.* He had never, in his wildest nightmares, imagined that the end would be so gruesome. He drew comfort from the fact that he was still alive and was determined to remain so. He had to save himself if he wanted to live to fight another day. Taking advantage of the chaos and the carnage erupting around him, Bishen fled. He was aware of a shortcut through the denser part of the jungle to a village. If he could just reach there, he would still have a chance to survive.

Putting the idea into action, Bishen hurried through the thickest portion of the forest, dodging the trees and hacking through the shrubs. His gun was gone but he still had his trusted kukri. His heart was pounding so hard, it felt as if someone was beating a drum inside his chest. With his senses on high alert, he became aware of a sound. *What was that sound? Was someone following him?* Ducking behind a tree, he took a quick peep and saw two figures. *Damn! The bitches were on his tail.* And then his mind, rendered numb by the events that had just unfolded, started to function again at full power. Back there, he didn't have a chance. But here in the forest, on his home ground, where he knew every stick and every stone, he could still wrest command of the situation.

Like Bishen, Isha, Sangha and Neel had taken cover while the bullets rained from the heavens. Isha lay face down, covering her head with her hands. As the onslaught eased a little, she looked up, her eyes searching for Bishen. The scene was strewn with bodies, some still, others moving painfully—but no Bishen. Then she sensed a movement in the corner of her eye. Turning her head in that direction, she saw the LalTara commander running low towards the thicker part of the jungle. Forgetting her pain, she quickly sprang to her feet and ran in his direction, calling for Sangha to follow her.

Neel, some distance away, was having trouble with his eyes. A bullet had exploded near him and spat dirt in them. By the time he got them reasonably cleaned, he saw Sangha's back disappearing beyond the line of trees. He swore softly, whipped out his phone and dialled a number.

∽

Sangha pounded furiously after Isha, catching up with her within a couple of minutes.

'There's a village some way off from the clearing by the camp,' she panted, running alongside her twin. 'I'm sure he's going there.'

'I think I know what you're talking about. What's the plan?' her sister came straight to the point.

'I'll try and outflank him. You continue in this direction. So you'll be on his tail and I'll circle around him and face him. Keep the stream to your right.'

'Copy that,' Isha responded, giving Sangha a thumbs-up but she had already sprinted ahead.

∽

Ahead of the sisters, Bishen's mind was in overdrive, matching the speed of his pumping feet. He had grasped the futility of escaping this pursuit. *Sangha knows all my escape routes and the other bitch has also mapped the terrain*, he thought to himself. *There was no alternative; he would have to engage in a direct confrontation.* He reasoned that his best shot was to catch them unprepared with a surprise attack. He would kill Isha and try to take Sangha captive. He needed her retinal scan. He still had a chance to complete this deal. His eyes frantically darted everywhere, trying to find a place to hide. His aim was to reach the village.

∽

Sangha eased her breathing, making it slow and deep. In and out. In and out. She had to conserve her strength. Occasionally, she paused to listen intently. Her ears picked up sounds of movement. At first from ahead, and then parallel to her. *She seemed to be outrunning Bishen.* She slowed down until she could sense the faint rustle of his movements and an occasional snap of twigs behind her. Then she stopped and took cover behind a shrub. *Yes, she had outflanked Rao. She could now hunt the hunter.* Focusing all of her senses in her ears, she inched forward. Silence. The sound of distant gunfire, which had accompanied her so far, had also ceased. *Nothing.* The hair on her neck stood on end. The silence seemed evil, menacing, predatory. *Where was Rao?* To sharpen her focus, Sangha closed her eyes to block out all distractions, and delved into the depths of her instincts.

∽

Perched atop a towering tree, Bishen's gaze was fixed on a moving figure below. Sangha! Good. He could ambush her, neutralize her, and drag her deep into the forest with him. He caressed his kukri, drawing strength from the cold steel of its blade. Shifting his grip to a leafy branch, he readied himself to make the leap.

That instant, Sangha heard a faint rustling. She inhaled sharply and opened her eyes to look up, only to see Bishen's agile form hurtling toward her, a glinting kukri gripped menacingly in his hand.

Reacting with lightning reflexes, Sangha evaded him, causing Bishen to land on the ground near her with the grace of a predatory cat. Swiftly, lashing with his feet, he tripped her, thwarting her attempt to draw her firearm. The gun jumped from her hands and disappeared into the darkness of the jungle. Sangha readied herself for hand-to-hand combat.

It was a clash of youth and agility, against experience and tactics. Sangha's sprightliness was pitted against Bishen's seasoned technique. Smeared with sweat and soil, the two combatants engaged in a gruelling battle. It was a pivotal moment when uncle and niece charged at each other. Sangha surged forward, aiming to use her momentum to crash into Rao's heart and halt it forever. But Bishen had anticipated her move. He sprang into the air to execute his counterattack. His powerful foot connected with Sangha's temple, striking her out of consciousness. She crumpled to the ground incapacitated.

Just as Bishen towered over her, with his foot on Sangha's stomach to pin her down and his arm raised, ready to thrust the kukri into her thigh, his vision blurred as perspiration from his forehead dripped into his eyes, its saltiness causing an annoying sting. Reflexively, he wiped away the discomfort with the sleeve of his other arm. As his vision cleared, he was taken aback by the sight that confronted him: Isha stood with her gun pointed at him, eyes locked on her target with a determination that sent chills down his spine.

Bishen made a split-second decision. He hurled his kukri at Isha, who reacted with astonishing agility. She contorted her body into a yogic pose, her back arched with her head nearly grazing the ground behind her, a stance that allowed the weapon to sail harmlessly over her. As the kukri clattered away, she steadied herself to regain her balance and turned her attention to the fleeing man. She whipped out her gun and fired a round but it didn't find its mark. *Damn!*

Sangha watched Isha take off after Bishen through fuzzy, pain-blurred eyes. She groaned, forcing herself up. There was no way she'd let Isha face the demon alone.

She stumbled forward, unsure of her path, but her instincts didn't fail her. Soon, the sounds of grunting and a scuffle reached her ears. As she neared, horror gripped her—Bishen had overpowered Isha, wrested the gun from her, and aimed it at her twin.

Sangha didn't hesitate. She hurled herself in front of Isha, shielding her from the threat.

At that moment, Bishen's gun fired, sending the bullet tearing through Sangha, propelling her backward before she crashed to the ground.

Sangha lay still for what seemed like an eternity. Her breaths were shallow and laboured, but her eyes held a determination that transcended her physical frailty. She was aware that Bishen had escaped.

As her gaze met Isha's, a faint smile touched her lips. In a voice Isha could barely hear, she whispered: 'Go, Isha. Finish that demon, for us, for Ma and Baba.'

Her eyes brimming with tears, Isha clutched Sangha's

hand. 'I can't leave you here like this,' she said, her voice quivering with raw emotion.

As she tried to speak, Sangha coughed and a trickle of blood spilled from the corner of her mouth. 'You have to... go... Neel...' As her life force ebbed, Sangha caught sight of Neel approaching them with an armed search party in tow. Her heart filled with relief and a bittersweet joy. *Now she could relax and finally let go of the breath she was holding on to so fiercely. She had nothing to tell him. She had played her part in his eternal happiness; she had saved his Isha.* Her vision blurred and her eyes closed. She felt someone take her hand. That touch! It could only be him! The memories of her union with Neel took over as she slipped into an eternal stillness.

Isha sat next to Sangha's body, her chest heaving with sobs. Neel had tried to hug her, but she pushed him away roughly. Baba gone, now her sister. Her eyes settled on a trail of blood on the muddy forest floor and followed it through the trees, where she could still glimpse Bishen fleeing deeper into the forest. A fire suddenly flared up in her being and filled her with an uncontainable rage. Grasping Bishen's kukri which was still wedged in her waistband, she ran after him. Neel called out to her, asking her to stop, but the roar in her ears had drowned out all other sounds.

She could see her target ahead, limping, falling down, picking himself up. She caught up and was upon him like a storm unleashed. She took Bishen by his hair and yanked his head back. All she had to do now was swipe that blade—that very knife which had claimed her mother's life—across the bastard's throat. But just as the knife touched Bishen's skin, Neel's voice rang out, a plea rooted in reason and restraint.

'Don't stain your hands with his blood, Isha. Let him face his own torment.'

As she paused, Bishen freed himself from her fury with mocking laughter that cut through the night air and his eyes ablaze with defiance. 'You think you've won, Isha? Nah! Never!' His exclamation burnt into Isha's ears. 'It's only a matter of time,' he spat out. 'I got your mother and I shall get you too,' he warned.

Isha's hands trembled with anger and the effort of resisting the temptation to slit his throat. *Neel was right. It was better to let Bishen live and rot in his personal hell.* Isha's eyes bore into Bishen's, her voice laced with unyielding determination, 'Your reign of terror ends here, Bishen. You may have created chaos, but we will rebuild everything from the ashes.'

Bishen was soon subdued and taken into custody, but his taunts seemed to rend the air. They had won the battle, but it was a victory paid for with pain, sacrifice, loss and unwavering resolve. The scars were etched deep in all their souls.

Isha then ran back to where Sangha lay. She cradled Sangha's lifeless head on her lap and turned to Neel, 'Inform Manish immediately. He will arrange to get her airlifted. He knows the drill.' Neel walked up to her, firmly placed his hands on her shoulders, and stood still, his head hanging low, 'Isha...'

With a feeling of dread, Isha asked him, 'What are you not telling me, Neel?'

This time, she did not resist Neel's embrace. In the protective fold of his arms, she learnt of Manish's death. She went still as the realization hit her hard. *Her entire family was gone, as was her friend and colleague.*

Neel was surprised that she did not cry. She just slumped into silence. With her stone-like face and her emotions steeled, Isha said, 'Let's go back to Raipur. I have unfinished business.'

52

Despatching the Demon

In a dimly lit corner of the custody area of Raipur Jail, Isha stood face to face with Bishen again, a man who had once held her life in his hands. Binod Rawat was also confined in the same area, his eyes shifting uneasily between the two. As Isha's gaze locked onto Bishen's, she could sense his desperation and defiance.

Meanwhile, Rawat couldn't resist speaking up. His voice trembled as he tried to break through the tense atmosphere, 'Isha, you have to listen to me. I'm not guilty. I've been set up, framed!'

Isha's eyes narrowed but did not leave Bishen. Her lips barely moved as she responded calmly, her voice echoing a feigned conviction, 'I am sure justice will be done.'

Bishen's frustration boiled over but he remained stoic and calm. He wanted Isha to make the first move. *What does she want from me? Why has she come here to see me?* These questions darted through his mind.

Isha faced him, her eyes reflecting a calm patience that seemed detached from the current situation. She pulled out a mobile phone. Bishen's astonishment was clear as he saw his bank's name appear on the screen. Then, as Isha looked at it, the account details opened up with a welcoming beep. The phone had acknowledged her presence and was ready to serve her.

Bishen went slack-jawed. *Sangha was dead, so how did the scan work? Was Sangha dead? Or was this Sangha?* Isha looked at his incredulous face. 'Manish always made things in pairs,' she said laconically. Bishen's eyes widened. *The bastards! They had one more set of contact lenses that mirrored Sangha's retinal scan. This meant all was not lost. The deal could technically still be concluded!* He only needed to persuade her. 'We can still make this happen, Isha. You'll be set up for life. You won't have to do this thankless sarkari job. You can live like a queen anywhere in the world with that boyfriend of yours,' Bishen gibbered.

Isha stared at him wordlessly.

'All you have to do is transfer the funds to the Chinese,' he wheedled. 'I will give you the coordinates and then you can deliver the consignment to the Iraqis.'

Isha's expression didn't change.

Bishen continued, a note of desperation creeping into his voice. 'You can only let me go once the deal is concluded. I will wait here for you, so you have no doubts about my intention. Only after the deal, you can go your way, and I will go mine. I promise never to interfere in your life, ever.'

'Tell me the Chinese account details,' she said, breaking her silence.

As soon as Bishen divulged the information, the monies were transferred within moments. Bishen's elation knew no bounds. He began to explain their plan to deliver the consignment to the Iraqis, only for Isha to interrupt him with cold certainty: 'The Chinese will make the delivery now, but not to the Iraqis. To us.'

'Fool,' Bishen snarled in a fit of rage. 'Brainless idiot! Just like your mother.' Isha clenched her jaw. With her fists clenched, she turned and left the room, leaving a screaming Bishen in the depths of hell.

A fortnight later

It was a routine day at the Raipur Jail. The police van arrived to escort Bishen to his scheduled court hearing. Accompanied by two armed policemen, Bishen was bundled into the back of the van, with his hands cuffed and legs shackled. The vehicle exited the jail premises and turned onto the main road.

Bishen watched, through the reinforced windows, the ordered chaos of a typical town, aware of the unwavering, inscrutable gaze of the sentries. The journey continued for another fifteen minutes that stretched into another half an hour. They were now on a less frequented path, in the depths of a forested area.

'Where the fuck are they taking me?' Bishen questioned one guard. He did not receive any response.

Bishen's heart raced when the van stopped abruptly, and the guards, like dark figures of authority, moved towards him. They quickly blindfolded him with a piece of rough cloth, throwing him into a state of panic and confusion. He stumbled as they pulled him out of the van—his feet still shackled—onto the ground that felt unsteady beneath him.

'No! Stop!' he grunted, agitation flooding his voice. But with his hands cuffed behind him and his feet restrained, he couldn't fight back, although his resistance persisted. He croaked and protested but it was useless.

Like a puppet tied to strings, he was thrown onto the rough terrain, the cold outside making him shiver. The door of the van slammed shut as the engine roared to life, drowning out his last cries. As the van drove off, it left Bishen—blindfolded and restrained—in the silence of the dense forest.

As the unpredictability of the situation started seeping in, Bishen started yelling, but the roar of a new engine drowned out his voice. He struggled to free himself, but it seemed impossible. He sensed a vehicle stop close by. This time, it sounded like a smaller van.

Bishen heard voices again, too muffled to decipher.

'What the hell is going on?' he screamed, kicking the air and repeating the statement like a looping video.

Just then, someone yanked off his blindfold; the sudden light almost blinded him for a moment.

Fair, rotund and cheerful. It was Kaled! 'Hello friend!' his voice boomed into Bishen's ears.

Bishen was left speechless. *The Iraqis were here to get him!* They had paid him but hadn't received the product. The reality of Iraqi torture and revenge was well known to him. He knew the cruel price of betrayal and the lengths to which they could go to settle a score. He had done it himself. Now he was at the receiving end.

He had been outplayed by that Srivastava girl. Isha had made the perfect move, a masterstroke that turned the game against him. With a twist of fate, she had handed him the bitter end he had long deserved.

The once fearless warrior froze. Only his horror-stricken eyes moved to Kaled's smiling visage. And then his mouth opened. 'Please...please, have mercy...' But Kaled's men had already thrown him into the van. As it started moving, the violence had already begun inside the four-wheeler.

Bishen's pleas for mercy turned to wails and grew fainter as the van sped far away.

Isha and Neel, far away in the jungle, well hidden within the dense foliage of the Abujmarh, watched the happenings with their binoculars.

Unruffled and unsmiling, Isha pulled in a deep breath. *Bishen was now a lamb on his way to slaughter.*

She had accomplished her mission—the end of Bishen Rao. This was for her mother, her father, Manish and Sangha, whose sacrifices had paved the way for her own survival. She had paid a high price with many loved ones lost, too many memories to deal with, but she had finally shoved Bishen, the demon, into the depths of an infernal hellhole, the one that he deserved to be in. She yearned for her Baba's approval in that moment. She had never got to say goodbye. Her stoic stance dissolved as she squeezed her eyes shut, hoping to hold back her tears, but they still streamed down her cheeks.

She opened her eyes, only to meet Neel's gentle, sombre gaze. He had been right by her side throughout the operation of handing Bishen to the Iraqis. In his eyes, she found an ocean of love and unwavering strength. He reached out and gently patted her on her back. 'You did well, my soldier.'

Isha, her eyes swollen and her nose a little snotty, smiled a thin, watery smile. The midday sun gently touched her face, its warmth reminiscent of her father's unwavering strength flowing into her. It infused her with the courage she held deep within and empowered her to confront the world with her innate valour. She believed that she had finally closed the chapter of a haunting past. It was now time to reclaim her present and her future. 'I am okay, Baba,' she whispered softly.

And then, just like Rakesh when he used to suppress the truth, she scratched her nose.

Epilogue

Sangha was given a martyr's funeral, even as Isha consigned the last of her bloodline to the flames. This was a sister she never knew she had. A sister who had died saving her. Isha felt an emptiness within her, a painful void. Baba gone, now Sangha. She had known Sangha only briefly; they hadn't grown up together. *Perhaps that was a joy for another life.*

Isha held Neel's hand as they watched the flames flicker and dance. She knew it then that Sangha's sacrifice had not been in vain. The Chinese had finally delivered RED. With a resolve to prevent any international misuse of RED, Isha had first orchestrated its handover to India's Defence Research and Development Organisation (DRDO), and then to the United Nations, so that unlawful terrorism would be off limits. With utmost care, the weapons were transported to an undisclosed location identified by the UN, where RED was sealed and safely locked away.

Given the success of Operation Trojan Horse, Isha was feted and promoted to helm STF19. Every day was a tribute to her father, to Manish and to her sister—the people who had made the ultimate sacrifice for a safer world. Their sacrifices had propelled her forward to accomplish her mission.

Both Isha and Neel had also taken Manu—who thankfully escaped the gunfire and the destruction of LalTara—under their wing. They brought him to Baba's house, and tried to provide him with a stable and secure environment. Neel had made it his mission to track down Manu's parents, in which he eventually succeeded. He had gently broken the news of their son's survival to the incredulous couple and they had readily agreed to come to Raipur to take him back.

The scene of the reunion was heart-wrenching. The father, racked by the guilt of having sold his son to LalTara for money, had slumped to the floor of Isha's living room and covered his face with his hands, tears dripping down his arms. His mother had rushed to her child and fiercely folded him in her arms, weeping as if she'd never stop. Later, both had fallen at Isha's feet to thank and bless her.

Isha had insisted that they stay with her for a couple of days, to allow the new surroundings to help heal their wounds. They had accepted her suggestion, in deep gratitude for the return of their son. Two days later, when the emotional upheaval had quietened somewhat, the parents timidly approached Isha and told her what they had observed: her tenderness and love for their child, and Manu's reciprocation of this affection. Also, a realization that they had no future to give their son. So, would she consider giving him one? Although Isha was touched by their trust, she insisted that Manu should get to make that decision. He had once been forced into a situation he did not want; she would not repeat that same mistake. When they called Manu to tell him what they had been considering, the joy on his face left no doubt about what he wanted.

Isha could not dwell on her own future, although her present seemed promising. They'd finally bought the house Neel had shown her months ago, when all Isha had to worry about was his mother's approval—fortunately, all was well on that front. On the other hand, Neel's vision for their future seemed to be taking shape. He'd wanted a house full of children and dogs. They hadn't planned children of their own yet—perhaps they never would. They had Lipi,

Bishen's daughter, who had been extracted from under her bed, cowering with terror and fiercely hugging her dog, Bullet. They had officially adopted the girl and her canine companion. The child was slowly coming out of her shell. Even now, she romped in the courtyard of her house, chasing Manu and Bullet, who was fabulously living up to his name.

Isha would often muse on how strange it was that the universe had chosen to bring these people, all of whom needed a little help to get on, together as a family. Little Lipi, who had seen horrors a child should never have to see; Manu, who had faced terrible hardships through his young life; and she herself, who carried in her heart the weight of her family history every single day.

Isha felt a hand on her shoulder. *Neel! Her rock! Her one solid constant amidst all the uncertainty.* She rested her head against his chest and together, they watched the two children and the dog living in the moment, joyful and excited.

'Neel, when Lipi learns that I was the reason for her parents' death, will she ever forgive me?' she asked her husband for the umpteenth time.

Neel's arm pulled her closer in a comforting warmth. She looked up. His eyes met hers, reassuring and tender.

'We'll raise her with the same values your father instilled in you. The rest, my love, is beyond our control. *Que sera, sera*...whatever will be, will be.'